## Praise for **Starship: Mutiny**

"Just the kind of easygoing and unabashedly old-school space opera romp for which we've come to know and love [Mike Resnick] . . . whip-smart, fast-paced pure entertainment . . . simply pure escapism, impossible to resist by anyone who still remembers that good old-fashioned sense of wonder."

—*SF Reviews*

"Resnick's writing is effortless, full of snappy dialogue and a fast-moving plot. . . . This is high-quality work. . . . There's a veneer of quality and above all believability that makes this heads above many space operas. . . . It's damn good fun."

—*SFCrowsnest*

## Praise for **Starship: Pirate**

"A memorable ride with a handful of Resnick's trademark oddball characters, a shipload of faster-than-light buccaneers, and a pirate queen to die for, all lightly seasoned by Charles Dickens. A rollicking good time."

—Jack McDevitt
Award-winning author
of *Odyssey* and *Outbound*

"Mike Resnick is one of the finest writers the science fiction field has ever produced, and *Starship: Pirate* is one of his very best works. A wonderful book."

—Robert J. Sawyer
Hugo Award–winning
author of *Hominids*

# STARSHIP:
# MERCENARY

## ALSO AVAILABLE BY MIKE RESNICK

IVORY

NEW DREAMS FOR OLD

### STARSHIP: MUTINY
BOOK ONE

### STARSHIP: PIRATE
BOOK TWO

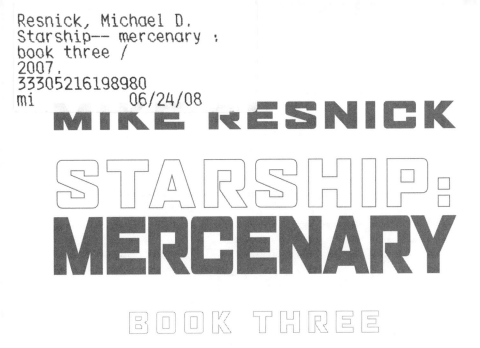

# MIKE RESNICK

# STARSHIP:
# MERCENARY

## BOOK THREE

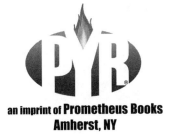

an imprint of **Prometheus Books**
**Amherst, NY**

Published 2007 by Pyr®, an imprint of Prometheus Books

Inquiries should be addressed to
Pyr
59 John Glenn Drive
Amherst, New York 14228–2119
VOICE: 716–691–0133, ext. 210
FAX: 716–691–0137
WWW.PYRSF.COM

11 10 09 08 07     5 4 3 2 1

Library of Congress Cataloging-in-Publication Data

Resnick, Michael D.
    Starship—mercenary : book three / by Mike Resnick.
        p. cm.
    ISBN: 978–1–59102–599–3
    1. Space ships—Fiction. 2. Mercenary—Fiction. I. Title.

Printed in the United States on acid-free paper

*To Carol, as always*

And to absent friends:

Bob Bloch
Jacques Chambon
Jack Chalker
Hal Clement
George Alec Effinger
Kelly Freas
Jack C. Haldeman
Virginia Kidd
George Laskowski
Bea Mahaffey
Mary Martin
Bruce Pelz
E. Hoffman Price
Hank Reinhardt
Darrell C. Richardson
John F. Roy
Julius Schwartz
Bob Sheckley
Charles Sheffield
Ross H. Spencer
Lou Tabakow
Bob Tucker
James White
Jack Williamson
Ed Wood

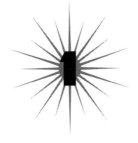

"David," said the disembodied voice on the *Theodore Roosevelt*'s communication system, "I don't know where the hell you're hiding, but we have to talk. You show up in my office in five minutes or the next thing this ship fires on is going to be *you*."

"Five'll get you ten the Captain has to go hunting for him," said a crew member.

"I'll take that bet, ten credits to five," said the tall, redheaded Third Officer. "If there's one person aboard this ship that you don't want mad at you—besides me, that is—it's the Captain." Suddenly she looked amused. "Besides," she added, "how the hell many places can you hide on this ship?"

"More than you think, or the Captain wouldn't have threatened him."

"The Captain's in a bad mood," said the Third Officer. "Wouldn't you be?"

Suddenly a bulkhead panel slid open, and an odd-looking creature of vaguely human proportions, but dressed like a Victorian dandy, stepped out into the corridor. His eyes were set at the sides of his elongated head, his large triangular ears were capable of independent movement, his mouth was absolutely circular and had no lips at all, and his neck was long and incredibly flexible. His torso was broad and half again as long as a man's, and his short, stubby legs had an extra joint in them. His skin may have possessed a greenish tint, but his bearing and manner were properly upper-class British at all times.

"I wish you wouldn't talk about me as if I wasn't here," he said.

"Right," said the Third Officer with a laugh. "You just *wish* you weren't here."

"My dear Olivia . . ." he began in hurt tones.

"Call me Val," she replied.

"A mere convenience for the crew," he said with a shrug. "To me you will always be Olivia Twist."

"I hate that name," she said ominously. "You'd do well to fall in love with some other human author."

"Other than the immortal Charles?" he said with almost-genuine horror. "There *are* no other authors. Just scribblers and dabblers."

"David," said the voice on the intercom. "You have three minutes to find out whether I'm kidding or not." Pause. Then, ominously: "You want a hint?"

"I really must go," said the alien apologetically.

As he scuttled away, Val held out her hand to the crewman. "Pay up. It serves you right for betting against the Captain."

The elegantly dressed alien made his way to an airlift, ascended two levels, got off, and finally reached the Captain's office.

"My dear Steerforth!" he said with false enthusiasm. "That was beautifully handled! Just beautifully! I can't tell you how proud I am of you!"

"Shut up," said Wilson Cole. "And stop calling me Steerforth."

"But that's your name!" protested the alien. "I am David Copperfield and you are my old school chum, Steerforth."

"You can call me Captain, Wilson, or Cole once we're on speaking terms again. I'll continue calling you David, since you haven't seen fit to give me your real name." Cole stared at the alien. "I don't think you can possibly imagine how mad I am at you."

"But we won!" said David Copperfield. "There were five ships and you destroyed them all!"

"There were supposed to be two class-H ships!" snapped Cole. "We had to fight off four class-Ks and a class-M!"

"For which we were well paid," the alien pointed out.

"What we were paid will barely replace the shuttle we lost and repair the damages we sustained," said Cole. "David, I explained it to you after the last debacle: there's more to this business than getting the biggest contract."

"That's *your* end of the business," said Copperfield defensively. "*My* job is handling the financial arrangements. I get the contracts, you fight the battles."

"And if they offered you ten times as much to take on a dreadnought, or face Admiral Garcia's flagship, would you take it?"

"Certainly not," said Copperfield. "The *Teddy R* can't beat a dreadnought."

"The *Teddy R* was goddamned lucky to come out of this morning's skirmish in one piece," said Cole.

"My dear Steerforth, if you want to be a mercenary, you must expect to fight in some pitched battles. It goes with the job."

"I don't think I'm getting through to you at all," said Cole. "You're our business agent. You are supposed to get us assignments we can handle. We're lucky any of us are alive right now."

"But you *are* alive," protested Copperfield. "So clearly it was a good bargain. Two million Maria Theresa dollars for guarding Barios II against potential attack during the Jewelers' Exhibition."

"Damn it, David, there was nothing *potential* about that attack!" growled Cole. "They knew we were there, they knew what armaments we had, they knew what we were and weren't capable of doing. If Val and Four Eyes hadn't done things nobody's supposed to do with our shuttlecrafts, we'd be orbiting the goddamned planet in a billion pieces right now."

"I *could* get you an assignment protecting small schoolchildren from playground bullies," offered the dapper alien, "but it wouldn't pay your expenses."

"Shut up," said Cole.

David Copperfield fell silent.

"We're going to have to make a few changes in how we operate," continued Cole.

"You mean the ship?"

"I mean you and me. I can't let you keep endangering us the way you've been doing."

"But you have been victorious!" protested Copperfield. "So I am not endangering you."

"We're operating with half the crew this ship needs, we can't go into the Republic for repairs or supplies, we still don't have a doctor on board . . ."

"And you have overcome every one of those obstacles," noted Copperfield. "I don't understand why you are so upset."

"Then why were you hiding inside a bulkhead?" demanded Cole.

Copperfield paused, considering his answer. "It was cozy?"

A burst of feminine laughter echoed through the small office, and a moment later the holographic image of Sharon Blacksmith appeared, hovering over Cole's desk.

"That's a good one, David!" she said, still laughing. "I hope you don't mind if I play it for the entire crew. If you ever get tired of being . . . well, whatever it is you're being, you can always get work as a comedian."

"You were listening?" asked Copperfield.

"I'm the Chief of Security," answered Sharon. "Of course I was listening. There is an excellent chance that our glorious leader is going to strangle you before you leave his office, and such an action really requires a witness."

"Strangle me?" scoffed Copperfield. "We've been friends since we were in boarding school together."

"David, I really think you're losing it," said Sharon. "The two of you never met until last year. You are not old school chums. You are not even a human being, and your real name isn't David Copperfield. You are—or at least you were—the biggest fence on the Inner Frontier. Now, I know that's unpleasant, but those are the facts."

"Facts are the enemy of truth!" snapped Copperfield. "Do you think I'd have shown Steerforth how to avoid a lifetime of piracy if we hadn't been lifelong friends? Do you think I'd have enticed the Hammerhead Shark to my world if I weren't doing a favor for a classmate? Do you think I'd have turned my back on everything I'd been and come away with you if we didn't share a special bond?"

Cole and Sharon exchanged looks. "I'll take it from here," he said, and her image vanished. "David, you enticed the Shark to Riverwind because you didn't have any choice, and you came away with me because half a dozen different pirates were all out for your head."

"Well, that too," admitted Copperfield.

"Do you want me to return you to Riverwind?"

"No, certainly not. They might still be looking for me there."

"Would you like me to set you down on the next colony world we come to?"

"No."

"Fine. But if you're staying aboard the *Teddy R*, we're going to need some new ground rules."

"Surely you don't want to go back to piracy," said Copperfield.

"No," replied Cole. "We're a military ship and a military crew. We were uniquely unfit to be pirates. I'm surprised we lasted almost a whole year at it." He paused. "We can't go back to the Republic. There's still a price on my head, and a huge reward for the capture or destruction of the *Teddy R*, so we'll practice our military trade here on the Frontier, as mercenaries."

"Which is precisely what I suggested to you two months ago," said Copperfield.

"I know, and it was a good suggestion—but we'd like to live long enough to enjoy what we earn. Twice in a row now you've chosen the best price without considering what we had to do to earn it. The *Teddy R* is not a dreadnought. It's a century-old ship that should have been decommissioned seventy-five years ago, except that the Republic kept getting into one war after another. There probably aren't a thousand ships in the Republic's fleet of almost two million that can't outrun and outgun us. One-on-one we can probably take just about any independent ship on the Inner Frontier—but you keep putting us in situations that *aren't* one-on-one. We've been lucky, but we can't *stay* lucky. So from now on, you bring every offer to me, and I will decide whether or not we accept it."

"But that hurts my credibility, to say nothing of my bargaining position."

"It doesn't hurt it as much as a laser blast, or a pulse ray, or slow torture, all of which almost certainly await you if you keep putting us into these situations."

"How did you get to be the most decorated officer in the fleet with that attitude?" said Copperfield bitterly.

"He is the most decorated officer *out* of the fleet," said Sharon's disembodied voice, "to say nothing of its most-wanted criminal. We're all proud of him, even if he's the reason none of us can ever go home again."

"You shut up too," said Cole. He turned back to Copperfield. "That's it, David. You will bring every offer to me for my approval—and I have to know more than what they're paying; I have to know everything that might happen, starting with why someone is paying enough for us to consider accepting the job in the first place. If you can't get the information I need, then either I or one of my officers will speak directly to the supplicant to determine the full range of possible dangers we might face."

"That emasculates my position," protested Copperfield.

"Oh, I like that word," said Sharon.

"It makes me little more than an errand boy," continued the alien.

"We tried it your way, and we're luckier to be alive than I think you'll ever realize," said Cole. "Now we do it my way."

"I don't know if I can."

"It's your decision. We can always use another gunnery sergeant."

"But I'll give it a try," said Copperfield hastily.

"All right," said Cole. "You'll still be our point man, you'll still make the contacts. The Republic's still got huge rewards posted for me, Four Eyes, and Sharon, and there's a couple of dozen worlds that want Val dead or alive—and those two men and the alien we picked up on Cyrano all have prices on their heads. You're about the only one who can leave the ship with a reasonable chance of returning unapprehended. So tell Christine or whoever's working the bridge where you want to go next, and we'll take you there—but you no longer have the authority to commit us to a mission. Is that clear?"

"Yes, Steerforth." Pause. "I mean, yes, Wilson."

"All right. We're done. You can leave." The alien turned and walked to the door. "And David?"

"Yes, Steerforth?"

"The next time you try hiding from me inside a bulkhead, I'm going to have the panel fused into place."

"You knew?" asked Copperfield, surprised.

"The man has spies everywhere," said Sharon's voice. "It's positively fiendish."

Copperfield left without another word.

"So, you want to meet me in the mess hall for coffee?" asked Sharon, her image appearing again.

"Not yet," said Cole. "Send Four Eyes to me. I need a damage report."

"What about Christine and Val?" asked Sharon. "After all, they *are* your Second and Third Officers."

"First Four Eyes, then coffee, then a nap, then the rest of the damages. We're still functioning, we still have air, we still have gravity, and we sure as hell know our weapons work. Everything else can wait."

"Including your love life?" she asked with a smile.

"Take a tranquilizer," he replied. "I've got captainly things to do."

"I don't *want* a tranquilizer."

"Fine. Pay a visit to David. He'll explain to you that we're old school chums and we share everything."

"Seven thousand, one hundred and forty-five," said Sharon.

"What's that supposed to be?"

"The number of nights you're sleeping alone for that remark."

Forrice, the burly, three-legged Molarian First Officer, spun down the corridor with surprising grace, waited for the Spy-Eye above the door to Cole's office to identify him, and entered.

"That was nice work you did today, Four Eyes," said Cole.

"I thought so too," replied Forrice. "Shuttles weren't made for those kinds of maneuvers." He paused. "I see we lost the *Alice*."

"Yeah," said Cole. "Teddy Roosevelt would never forgive us. We've lost three of his kids—*Quentin*, *Archie*, and *Alice*. The only original shuttle we have left is the *Kermit*."

"The two new ones—the *Edith* and the *Junior*—did pretty well," said the Molarian. "The Valkyrie put the *Edith* through maneuvers that should have broken it in half."

"I know. But she was lucky. So were you."

"I'd rather be lucky than good."

"I'd rather be safe than either," said Cole. "What's the injury list like?"

"Some burns, some breaks, everyone's alive. I wish we had a medic."

"We're supposed to have two—one for humans, one for non-humans," said Cole. "Problem is, we've been so busy getting shot at that we haven't had time to hunt up anyone who can patch us up." He paused. "How about the ship? What kind of damage did it sustain?"

"Well, it's still running," said Forrice. "I've got Slick out there now, walking the exterior, checking it out."

"I don't know what we'd do without him," said Cole, referring to the ship's sole Tolobite, a unique alien that, protected by its symbiotic

Gorib, which acted as a protective second skin, was able to function in the airless cold of space for hours at a time.

"Every ship ought to have a Tolobite," agreed the Molarian. "Have you killed David yet?" he added pleasantly.

"The thought has crossed my mind."

"Where the hell did those five ships come from?" continued Forrice. "I thought we were preparing for a couple of class-H vessels—an easy day's work."

"It's as much my fault as his," said Cole. "There are close to two thousand mining worlds on the Inner Frontier. You have to figure a jewelers' convention will draw every fucking thief for five hundred light-years. I should have figured they were sugar-coating the threat for David so he wouldn't ask a higher price."

"He's a fence, not a military man," agreed Forrice. "If you trust him again, it'll happen again."

"I know. From this moment on, all he is is a conduit. He brings offers to me, and I say yes or no."

"I can live with that," said Forrice. "Longer, if not richer."

"The convention's over tomorrow," said Cole. "We're obligated to stay on call until then, though I don't imagine there'll be another attack. Tomorrow, when the planet's rotated enough so that the convention's on the nightside, take Bull Pampas and a couple of other formidable-looking crewmen and collect our money."

"Val's the most formidable of all," noted the Molarian. "There's not a man or alien on board she can't whip without working up a sweat—including Bull."

"Yeah, I know," said Cole. "But if they're reluctant to come up with the money, you'll threaten to shoot 'em all and eventually they'll pay what they owe. If I send *her* down and they're slow to produce the money, she'll kill them all."

"She would at that," agreed Forrice. "I suppose that's the benefit of a nonmilitary education." He emitted a few hoots of alien laughter at his own observation. "Still, she probably saved the ship today."

"It wasn't the first time, it won't be the last," said Cole. "That's why she's here."

"She's the only one who looks fresh and ready to fight again," observed Forrice. "If she was a Molarian, I'd stick around for years until she came into season."

"Spare me your sexual obsessions," said Cole. "It's been a long day."

Suddenly the ship shuddered.

"And about to get longer," muttered Forrice. "I'm off to the bridge."

"No," said Cole. "Get down to Gunnery and make sure everything's working. I'll go to the bridge."

They left the office together, and a moment later Cole entered the bridge.

"What's going on?" he demanded of Christine Mboya, who was the ranking officer there.

"One of the class-K ships we killed today just exploded," she replied. "A big chunk of the hull hit one of our shuttle bays."

"Is Slick still out there?"

"I don't know, sir," she said. "I'll check." She scanned her computer screens. "Yes, sir."

"Put it on audio," ordered Cole. "Slick, can you hear me?"

"Yes, sir," said the Tolobite.

"Are you okay?"

"I'm fine, not sure, but my Gorib has suffered some superficial injuries. I'm going to have to come inside very soon."

"Have you got time to check and make sure that the ship's physical integrity hasn't been compromised?"

"Yes, sir, I'm sure I have."

"Good. Get right on it, and then come back inside." Cole signaled Christine to break the connection. "Is Mustapha Odom awake?" he asked, referring to the ship's master engineer.

"I think everyone is, sir."

"So much for three shifts," he muttered. "All right, tell him to inspect the shuttle bay from the inside and make sure there are no leaks, that it's totally intact. Then, if he says it is, have him check for weak spots that we may have to reinforce in the near future."

"Yes, sir," said Christine.

"Pilot?"

"Yes?" said Wxakgini, the sleepless alien pilot whose brain was literally tied in to the ship's navigational computer.

"Take us out half a light-year," said Cole. "We can't stay lucky forever. If anything else blows up, I want plenty of warning before any part of it can reach us. Mr. Briggs?"

"Sir?" said the young lieutenant at the sensor module.

"Track the other four ships, and let me know if they do anything besides float there dead in space."

"It's a pity you killed them all," said a familiar voice, and Cole turned to face Val, his six-foot-eight-inch Third Officer.

"You'd have preferred to play bumper tag with them?" he asked sardonically.

"I need a ship," she replied. "I could have used one of those."

"I thought you'd joined us permanently," said Cole.

"I have. But two ships can take on bigger, better-paying jobs than just the *Teddy R*," she said. "The bigger a fleet we can put together, the more money we can make."

"And the more bad guys we'll attract."

She smiled. "Attract and capture enough of them and someday we can even go to war with the Republic."

"Yeah, we're only ten or twelve million ships short," he said sardonically.

"You have to start somewhere."

"I sent David to bed without his supper," said Cole. "That's enough of a start for one day."

"Want me to be your negotiator?" offered Val.

He shook his head. "How far would you get? You're wanted on almost as many worlds as I am."

"But they're different worlds," she said.

"Thanks, but no thanks," said Cole. "You're most valuable doing just what you do."

She shrugged. "You're the captain." Then: "But I wish you'd saved one of those ships for me."

"Think about it," said Cole. "Do you *want* a ship that can't beat the *Teddy R* with four sister ships on your side?"

"*I* could beat it," said Val.

He considered the statement for a few seconds. "Probably you could," he admitted.

"So next time, don't kill every last ship."

"They were all shooting at us, and they'd damned near englobed us."

"You can't englobe with less than six ships, and twelve is optimum," put in Malcolm Briggs helpfully.

"I said 'damned near,'" said Cole irritably.

"Next time let me take a shuttle and approach the enemy under a flag of truce," she said. "Slick can hide on the outside of it until we've docked at the ship I want."

"Under a flag of truce?" repeated Cole.

"I promise there won't be any survivors to file a complaint after Slick and I get done with 'em," said Val.

"We'll see," said Cole.

"Okay, but remember what I told you: two ships can get more lucrative assignments."

"I'll remember."

"Sir," said Slick's voice. "The damage is superficial. I see no reason to address it until the next time we put into port."

"The *Teddy R* doesn't put into ports, Slick," said Cole. "It has an aversion to atmospheres."

"I mean, the next time we dock at an orbiting station."

"I'll take it under advisement," said Cole. "Now get back inside the ship. Do you need anyone to help you tend to your Gorib?"

"No, thank you, sir," said Slick. "We can manage by ourselves."

*Too bad*, thought Cole. *I've been on this ship for more than two years, and I still don't know what you look like without your second skin.*

"We've moved out half a light-year," announced Wxakgini, who seemed to have decided never to add a "sir" until Cole learned how to pronounce his name and stopped calling him "Pilot."

"Thanks, Pilot," said Cole. He turned back to Christine. "Tell Four Eyes he can leave the Gunnery section. It'd probably be a good idea if he went to bed. *Someone* on this ship ought to be wide awake ten or twelve hours from now." He looked around, couldn't find anything else requiring his attention, and decided to go down to the mess hall, where he sat at his usual table in the corner and ordered a sandwich and a beer.

"You look terrible," said Sharon Blacksmith, entering the mess hall and sitting down opposite him.

"Flattery will get you nowhere," said Cole. "There are a couple of twenty-two-year-old ensigns on this ship who happen to think that I look great."

"That's because they're young and inexperienced," said Sharon. "Seriously, when's the last time you had any sleep?"

"Let me see. The attack came right at the end of blue shift, and I'd been up for a few hours. Then we fought through red shift, and now it's about six hours into white shift. So I've been up, I don't know, maybe twenty-two or twenty-three hours."

"When you're through feeding your face, go to bed."

"Not 'come to bed'?"

"You'd fall asleep in the middle of it," said Sharon. "My vanity couldn't stand that."

"Well, if you think you're *that* uninteresting . . ."

"Of course, you don't have to drink all that beer. I could just throw it in your face."

"You know," said Cole after a moment, "given what we've been through the past couple of weeks, I think maybe the whole crew needs a rest. Nobody signed on to face the kind of odds David has been putting us up against."

"Well, when you get right down to it," she said thoughtfully, "we haven't had shore leave since we were still a respected member of the Navy. That's got to be a year and a half or so, cooped up in this damned ship."

"Then I guess that's our next order of business."

"Aren't you supposed to consult with your fellow officers, now that we're a military vessel again—or at least a pseudo-military one."

"Not necessary," said Cole. "I already know what their responses will be."

"Oh?"

He nodded. "Four Eyes won't be interested unless I can find a world with lady Molarians in season. Christine will say she's happy with whatever the rest of us decide, and then when we get there she won't want to leave the ship anyway. And Val—Val will go anywhere they've got good drinkin' stuff and she can get into a couple of bar fights before the locals realize what they're up against."

"So where are we going?"

He shrugged. "Wherever the crew can blow off some steam while we're patching up the damages and making sure the shuttle bay's not about to collapse. Wherever it is, it'd be nice if we could pick up a doctor or two there."

"Well, there's a pleasure planet called Calliope . . ." she began.

"No," said Cole. "I know that world. It's only a few light-years from the Republic. When we're deep in the Frontier, being the notorious Wilson Cole and the *Teddy R* works to our advantage; everyone out there hates the Republic and loves its enemies. But when we're only eight or ten light-years from the border, it's too easy for someone to report our presence to the Navy—and when we're that close, the Navy will come after us and claim hot pursuit."

"There's always Serengeti," she suggested, referring to the zoo world. Then she shook her head. "No, that's in the Republic too."

"I suppose we ought to go to the source," said Cole.

"Val?"

"She spent a dozen years as a successful pirate on the Inner Frontier. She'll know where the action is."

He touched the communicator on his wrist and uttered Val's personal code.

"What is it?" said Val as her image suddenly appeared, hovering above the table.

"Time for some R-and-R," said Cole. "We don't have any paychecks, but let's get the money David collected for us and pay the crew."

"Past time," she responded.

"Where's the best place to go, preferably a world that's more than a thousand light-years from the Republic? Something the crew will like, with the facilities to patch up the ship."

"There's only one place," answered Val, her face lighting up. "But it's not a world."

"What is it?"

"Have you ever heard of Singapore Station?"

"Maybe once or twice, in passing," said Cole. "I figured it was just a space station."

"Sure," said Val. "And the Crab Nebula is just a little flickering light in the sky."

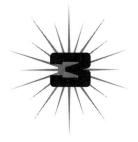

It had taken literally a millennium for Singapore Station to attain its current form. Parts of it were almost fifteen centuries old. Parts were still being built. And parts had not yet even been conceived, let alone built.

It began almost eleven hundred years earlier, in the 883rd year of the Galactic Era. Two small space stations, built midway between the Genoa and the Kalatina systems, were splitting all the business in the sector and fast going broke. So, in desperation, their owners decided to form a partnership. The two stations were moved to a midpoint by space tugs, workmen and robots labored for a month joining them physically, and when they reopened they found that business was booming.

Word went out from that time and place that profits increased with size, and independent stations all over the Inner Frontier began joining like lost lovers. By the fourteenth century G.E. there were dozens of such super-stations across the Frontier, and they kept combining and growing. By the sixteenth century almost two hundred such stations had combined into one enormous station—Singapore Station—that was as heavily populated as any colony world, and measured some seven miles in diameter (though "diameter" is a misleading term, since the station was not circular). It consisted of nine levels, and docking facilities that could handle almost ten thousand ships, from huge military and passenger vessels to the little one- and two-man jobs that were commonplace on the Frontier.

They tried a few other names, but because the super-station catered to all races, they eventually went back to Singapore Station, since men were still the dominant race on the Frontier and Singapore had been a fabled international city back on old Earth.

Singapore Station was halfway between the Republic and the huge black hole at the galactic core, and eventually it occurred to warring parties—there were *always* wars going on in the galaxy—that they needed a Switzerland, a neutral territory where all sides could meet in safety and secrecy, where currencies could be exchanged, where men and aliens could come and go regardless of their political and military affiliation. (In fact, there was some sentiment for renaming it Zurich Station, but the original name was already too well known to change.)

The station's neutrality had, for the most part, been respected. Now and then a soldier, a sailor, or a diplomat was killed or kidnapped, but despite the total lack of law enforcement (or, for that matter, laws) on the station such incidents occurred much less often than on any populated world.

Singapore Station was known as a wide-open venue. Whorehouses catering to all sexes and species abounded. So did bars, drug dens, casinos, huge open black markets (because by definition no item was illegal or contraband on Singapore Station). There were elegant hotels, comparable to the finest on Deluros VIII, and because of the nature of the business that was sometimes done behind their closed doors, the security was outstanding. There were gourmet restaurants, side by side with slop houses, as well as alien restaurants catering to more than one hundred non-human species.

There was no weapon that one couldn't buy at Singapore Station, no vessel short of a military ship that wasn't for sale. There were assay offices that evaluated what independent miners from other worlds had dug up. There were legitimate medical facilities, and there were quacks of last resort for those who couldn't be cured by the former. There were legal robots and illegal androids (and at least two brothels that specialized in providing androids of both sexes).

Four of the levels had what had come to be known as Standard gravity and atmosphere, though no one ever knew if that was Earth Standard or Deluros Standard—and since they were almost identical, no one really cared. There was a level for chlorine breathers, one for methane breathers, another for ammonia breathers, and one small level with no atmosphere at all, where space-suited men and spacesuited aliens could meet as uncomfortable equals. A middle level provided automatic transport for all.

"That's the biggest damned thing I ever saw!" said Vladimir Sokolov, staring at a viewscreen as Wxakgini maneuvered the ship on its final approach to the enormous docking facility, which provided visitors with a monorail taking them the final miles to the station itself.

"There have *got* to be some friendly Molarian females in a place that big!" said Forrice. "As soon as we land, Lieutenant Braxite and I are going looking for them."

"I'm glad to see you've got your priorities in order," said Cole sardonically.

"You don't understand, Wilson," said Forrice.

"Enlighten me."

"You say that our two races are so similar, because we're the only two species that can laugh and have a sense of humor. But there is one major difference."

"Which I hear about every day."

"If Sharon Blacksmith was glad to see you for only three days every eight months, you'd know a little something about our priorities."

"Someday I really must give you a book on Zen Buddhism and self-denial as the spiritual road to enlightenment," said Cole.

But Forrice and Braxite were too busy studying maps of the station to pay him any further attention.

As Cole had predicted, Christine volunteered to stay on the ship, and he selected four more to remain with her for two Standard days, at which point five crew members would return to the ship and Christine and the other four would be free to visit the various attractions of Singapore Station. Christine offered to stay on the ship the whole time it was docked and being repaired, but Cole insisted that she take her turn in the station, even if she did nothing but rent a room and take a fiction cube along.

The ship docked, Cole had Mustapha Odom show the mechanics exactly what needed repairing or reinforcing, and then shore leave commenced. Cole remained on board until everyone but his senior officers had left.

"I can't imagine anything will go wrong," he said to Christine, "but don't hesitate to contact me if there's any problem, no matter how slight."

"I won't, sir," she replied. "Have a good time, sir."

"I plan to," said Cole. "And the first thing I'm going to do is eat a steak made of real meat, instead of these goddamned soya imitations I've been forcing down for the past few years."

"We're off," said Forrice as he and Braxite walked to the airlift. "Wish us luck."

"I think I'll wish it to any lady Molarians who can't duck fast enough," said Cole.

Both Molarians responded with hoots of alien laughter as they descended to the exit hatch.

"Well, there's just you and me left, Val," he said to the tall redhead. "What do you plan to do there, or don't I want to know?"

"I plan to drink up a storm," was her reply. "Then I plan to hunt up the grubbiest, dirtiest bar on the station and fight up a storm. And finally, if anyone's left standing, I plan to fuck up a storm."

"Well, I like a sweet, innocent, refined young lady who knows her own mind," said Cole. "Have fun."

"You're coming with me," said Val.

"It's thoughtful of you to ask, but I'm meeting Sharon for dinner."

"It'll wait."

"I don't know how to break this to you gently," said Cole, "but drinking and fighting are not my idea of a good time."

"What about fucking?"

"I'm very fond of it, but it sounds kind of indiscriminate the way you describe it."

"Of course it's indiscriminate," she replied. "I'm never going to see any of them again."

"Good luck to you and good luck to them, but I'm off to dinner."

She reached out and closed her hand over his biceps. "You really want to come with me."

"Why?"

"Because you want to meet the man who runs Singapore Station."

"And you know him?"

"Of course I do," she replied. "I rode the Inner Frontier spaceways as a pirate for thirteen years, remember?" She paused. "Think about it. This is the guy who knows every deal that's going down here."

"I'm sure that's useful to a pirate," began Cole without much enthusiasm. "But . . ."

"*Think*, Wilson!" she said forcefully. "He'll know everyone who needs protection, or soon will need it. He'll know everyone who needs a little muscle to get a job done. He'll know who will pay and who won't, who you can trust and who you can't turn your back on."

"And he'll tell it all to a friend of the redheaded Pirate Queen?" suggested Cole.

"You got it."

"I guess I'm coming with you," said Cole.

"Let's go." She led him to the airlift.

"As soon as I let Sharon know I'll be late," said Cole. He left her a quick message, then joined Val as they stepped onto the cushion of air and began descending. "By the way," he asked, "what's the name of this pillar of the community?"

"The Platinum Duke."

"What's he got—a bunch of platinum rings on his fingers?"

Val smiled in amusement. "You'll see soon enough," she promised him.

"It's a world of its own," said Cole as they wandered down the metal corridor that was as broad as any street, passing scores of metal-and-glass storefronts. "How do they light it?"

"The metal on the ceiling has been chemically treated. It generates its own light."

"You mean it's phosphorescent?"

Val shook her head. "That just reflects light. This generates it." She smiled. "It's a twenty-four-hour-a-day city—or however many hours you're used to in a day. It never sleeps, it never gets dark, it never slows down."

"How many permanent residents are there?" asked Cole.

She shrugged. "Maybe sixty thousand, maybe more. If they're permanent, they either work here or they're hiding from the law, the Navy, or from someone on the Inner Frontier who's after them. I'm told that on any given day there are about half a million Men and aliens here who *aren't* permanent residents."

"I had no idea it was this big."

"No reason why you should have. You were fighting a war against the Teroni Federation, and they tell me you were stationed to hell and gone on the Rim. But your Fleet Admiral Susan Garcia knows it's here."

"She's been here?" said Cole, surprised.

"Twice," answered Val. "Both times to arrange prisoner exchanges with the Teronis."

"Is that hearsay, or did you actually see her here?"

"I saw her once. Did you ever meet her?"

"Yeah, we've met," said Cole with an ironic smile. "We don't get along very well."

"She's the one who demoted you?"

"Twice," said Cole. "On the other hand, she also gave me three of my Medals of Courage. Begrudgingly."

"Too bad she won't be here today," said Val. "You could settle some old scores."

"She's not the enemy," said Cole. "She's probably better qualified to run this war than anyone else. We just don't see eye-to-eye on certain things." He paused. "If you ever hear of a Polonoi officer named Podok coming here, *that's* something I'd like to know about."

"Podok?" repeated Val. "I've heard the crew mention that name. Wasn't he the captain when you mutinied?"

"Yes . . . and Podok is a she."

"Everyone says she deserved it."

"She did," replied Cole. "She was about to kill five million Men and destroy a planet rather than let the Teroni Fleet raid their fuel dump."

"That's what I heard," agreed Val. "She must have been a real piece of work."

"She was. But she's still serving in the Navy, and I can never go back to the Republic."

Val smiled. "Did anyone ever tell you life was fair?"

"Not lately," he answered without smiling.

They continued walking, passing all sorts of bars and restaurants.

"Something's wrong over there," said Cole, indicating a somewhat narrower corridor that went off to their left.

"No, it's fine."

"Whatever they treated the ceiling with is wearing off," he noted. "The lighting is half what it is here."

"That's for atmosphere," said Val. "The two biggest whorehouses on the station are down that corridor."

Cole peered into the dim light. "It sure doesn't look like there's anything that big down there."

"Trust me, they're there."

"You're a patron?"

"Once in a while."

"You're a gorgeous and exotic-looking woman," said Cole. "I'm surprised you feel a need to pay for it."

"Oh, I'd never pay a *man*," she said. "The house on the left has nothing but androids." She grinned. "I like their staying power."

"Whatever makes you happy," said Cole. Suddenly he tensed. "I think we're being followed."

"Figures," she said. "There's just two of us, and if we're in this section of the station we've obviously got money to spend."

Without warning she stopped and turned, and Cole followed suit. Three beings—one man and two Mollutei—were approaching them slowly, each armed with a dagger.

"Watch this," whispered Val. "Good evening, gentlebeings," she said aloud. "If you'll drop your weapons and hand over your money, no one will get hurt."

The man laughed instantly. It took a few seconds for the Mollutei's T-packs to translate what she'd said, but then they croaked in amusement.

"Well," said Val, stepping forward, "you can't say you weren't warned."

It took Cole about five seconds to decide whether to step forward with her or draw his burner—and by then it was a moot point, because all three of their stalkers lay broken and moaning on the floor of the broad corridor, twitching in agony.

"Should we take their money?" asked Val. "After all, they were going to take ours."

"No, we're not thieves, at least not any longer. Let's just tell the local police to round them up. I'll fill out a statement later."

"I told you—there *aren't* any police on Singapore Station."

"Then if we pass a hospital, we'll tell them to come by and collect them."

"And if we don't?"

He shrugged. "That's the risk you take when you become a thief."

She laughed aloud, and the two of them began walking again without another backward glance.

"Let's hope none of them shoots us in the back," commented Cole.

"If they'd had any burners or screechers, they'd have shown them," said Val with certainty. "You're a lot more likely to give your money to someone who can kill you from ten yards away than someone who has to get close enough to stab you." She nodded, as if to herself. "I think I'll come back this way to do my serious drinking."

They walked another fifty yards, then turned in to a small side corridor and came to a garish casino named Duke's Place. Small furry aliens of a species that Cole had never seen before carried drink trays to the players, human and non-human alike, who crowded the tables.

"They never learn," said Val, shaking her head. "Look at that table."

"What's the game?" asked Cole. "I don't recognize it."

"*Jabob*," she replied. "I think it originated on Lodin XI, or maybe Moritat. Huge break for the house. Your money'll last longer if you burn it to keep warm, but aliens just love that game."

"I see a man at the table, too."

"He's just running the game for the house."

"Fine," said Cole. "I assume you didn't take me here to gamble."

"No," she said, signaling to one of the small alien servers. "Tell the Duke that Joan of Arc is here."

"Joan of Arc?" repeated Cole as the alien scurried off.

"I had a lot of names before you gave me this one," answered Val.

The alien returned a moment later. "He will see you now," it said through its T-pack.

"Let's go," said Val, starting off across the casino. Cole fell into step behind her, and they soon reached a sparkling curtain of almost solid light. When she was within three feet of it she stopped so suddenly that he almost bumped into her.

"What's the problem?" he asked.

She picked up an empty glass from a nearby table and tossed it through the curtain. It was instantly atomized.

"Security system," she explained.

They waited about half a minute, and then a voice said, "Enter, Joan of Arc. Commander Cole—or is it Captain again?—may enter too."

Val stepped forward, and when she didn't disappear Cole followed her into a large, lavishly furnished office. Colorful alien songbirds shared a golden cage that seemed to float in the air with no visible support. There were a pair of three-dimensional holographic scenes of distant worlds that were static until Cole turned to look at them, at which point the scenes became a flurry of motion, only to become static again when he looked elsewhere. The lush carpet yielded to their footsteps, then re-formed as they moved forward. Leather chairs that molded themselves to their occupants hovered a few inches above the floor, and there was a well-stocked bar along one wall. Two robots, even taller than Val, flanked a shining metal desk—but the most unusual thing in the room was the man who sat behind the desk.

At first Cole thought he was a robot too, but upon closer observation he wasn't so sure. Most of him—arms, legs, torso, hands, feet, skull—was a sleek, shining metal, probably platinum. But the mouth and lips were definitely human, and there was a totally incongruous handlebar mustache swirling down from his upper lip. The left eye glowed an unholy blue, but the right eye possessed both iris and pupil. He was wearing a pair of sleek black shorts, with a tuxedo stripe down each leg.

"You didn't prepare him, Joan," said the man.

"It's more fun to watch them when they first meet you," replied Val. "And my name's Val this week."

"Cleopatra, Nefertiti, Joan of Arc . . . you just never tire of changing names. Who was Val?"

"It's short for Valkyrie," she replied.

"In that case I approve." He turned to Cole. "And you are the man that the Republic is offering ten million credits for?"

Cole stared at him and said nothing.

"Do not worry, Wilson Cole," he said. "I have no intention of selling you to the Republic. Singapore Station couldn't stay in business if people stopped trusting our discretion. Allow me to properly introduce myself: I am the Platinum Duke."

"So I see," said Cole.

"Ah, but you only see the end result. There was a time, many years ago, when I was just like you. In fact, I served in the Navy. My captain was Susan Garcia, who has gone on to far greater things."

"What happened?" asked Cole, curious in spite of himself.

"I lost my left leg in the Battle of Barbosa," answered the Duke. "They gave me a prosthetic leg made, I believe, of a titanium alloy. The interesting thing is that it worked better than the original had: it never tired, it never felt pain, it could withstand extremes of cold and gravity." He paused. "I was back on active duty four months later, just in time for the Battle of Tybor IV."

"I've heard about that one," said Cole. "I think we took eighty percent casualties."

"Eighty-two percent," said the Duke. "I was one of them. Lost both my arms and my left eye. They kept me alive long enough to transport me to a field hospital, where I was fitted out with prosthetic arms and an eye—and, as before, they functioned better than the originals. I was mustered out of the service shortly thereafter—I guess they felt that three limbs and an eye were enough to give to the Republic— and I came to the Inner Frontier, and eventually to Singapore Station. Along the way I'd made my fortune, we needn't discuss how, and I decided that platinum was more in keeping with my new status than titanium. I also decided that while I was undergoing these . . . *improvements*, I might as well go the whole route: another leg, eardrums, epidermis, all but a small handful of things. All that remains of the original me, Captain Cole, is my mouth and taste buds—I couldn't live without the ability to taste my favorite foods and drink—and I kept my lips, because I am a vain man (if I weren't why would I have converted to platinum?) and I was always proud of my mustache. My right eye remains for a practical reason: though my left eye sees farther and more clearly, and can even see into the infrared and ultraviolet spectrums, it does not adjust to changes in illumination as quickly as my real pupil does. All else—heart, lungs, you name it—is artificial." Suddenly he smiled. "With one exception. I was assured that I could experience sexual pleasure with an artificial organ, but I was unwilling to trust them. I mean, if they were wrong, I couldn't go back . . . so I have retained my own organ. That is why I am wearing these ridiculous shorts—out of consideration for poor innocents like Val here."

"That explains the Platinum," said Cole. "What about the Duke?"

"Simple. I run Singapore Station. It is my fiefdom; I am its duke."

"It's a lot for one man to run," commented Cole.

"So is a starship," responded the Duke. "We each have the power of life and death over our serfs."

"I don't have any serfs."

"Then by all means let us call them honored subordinates," said the Duke. "I shall be meeting one of them in another two hours."

"Let me guess," said Cole. "David Copperfield?"

"How did you know?"

"He's the only member of my ship besides Val who's ever been here before," answered Cole. "At least, I assumed he'd been here. I know none of the others have."

"Remarkable creature, isn't he?" said the Platinum Duke. "And how he cherishes that Dickens collection of his!"

"His appearance doesn't bother you?" asked Cole. "I mean, a very strange-looking alien dressed up exactly like Pickwick or Sydney Carlton?"

"What would you think of me if I criticized the way someone *else* looked?" said the Duke with a smile that displayed his platinum teeth. "By the way, have you any idea what he wants to see me about?"

"To put himself right with me," said Cole.

"I beg your pardon?"

"It's a long story," said Cole. "Suffice it to say that the *Theodore Roosevelt* is now in the mercenary business. I've been told, as I'm sure David has, that you are the best source for determining who might need our services, what they are willing to pay, and whether they can be counted on to give us accurate information and to honor their financial commitments."

"Easily done," said the Duke. "Ordinarily I would charge ten percent for my services, but because you are in the company of the remarkable Valkyrie, and especially because you are in the bad graces of Susan Garcia, who kept ordering me into harm's way and saw to it that there are pieces of me all across the Teroni Federation, I will charge you only five percent. How does that strike you?"

"It seems fair," said Cole. "But there's one more thing."

"Isn't there always?" said the Duke. "Shall I guess?"

"If it makes you happy."

"You don't want to get in a situation where you're overmatched," suggested the Duke. "After all, you haven't mentioned any support ships, any backup capabilities of any kind whatsoever."

"True," agreed Cole. "But that's a given. What I had in mind were some ethical considerations."

"Ethical considerations in a mercenary?" said the Duke, laughing. "Now, *that's* a novel concept!"

"I'm glad you're so easily amused," said Cole dryly. "We won't provide military support for anyone dealing in drugs. We won't supply military support for any action that will serve the purposes of the Teroni Federation. And we won't provide military support for any action that will be detrimental to the Republic or its Navy. We may be on the run from them, but we spent our lives serving their cause and we won't go to war with them."

"You'd feel differently if you were wearing some artificial limbs," said the Duke.

"Perhaps, but I'm not."

"All right," said the Duke. "In point of fact, your ethical considerations probably don't eliminate more than three or four percent of the people, planets, and interests that would be interested in your services."

"Fine," said Cole. "Lay the best of them out for David when he shows up, and understand that he is not empowered to commit the *Theodore Roosevelt* to any action. Only I can do that. He'll bring your various proposals to me, and I'll make my decision. I'll probably get back to you with some questions first."

"That is satisfactory," said the Duke. "When David shows up tonight I will send him away and tell him to come back in another day or two. I know who are the likeliest to require your services, but I cannot possibly contact them all before David arrives."

"Fair enough," said Cole. "I'm sure we'll meet again. Val can stay if she wants, but I'm late for a dinner appointment."

"Oh? Where?"

"Some place called the Fatted Calf."

"When you get there, a table in a private room will be waiting for you," said the Duke. "There will be no bill for you or any member of your party."

"You own it?" asked Cole.

"No."

"Then . . . ?"

"I am not without friends on Singapore Station," said the Platinum Duke with a modest smile. "I trust you are about to become one of them."

He extended his hand, and Cole took it. "Sounds good to me. I have a feeling we're going to need all the friends we can get."

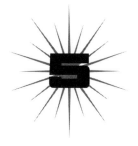

The ship was repaired in five days.

As his crew staggered in, Cole had a feeling that it would take more than five days to repair *them*.

Forrice never said a word. He simply returned to the *Teddy R* with a big alien grin on his face, went off to his cabin, and slept for thirty hours. Braxite looked almost as happy and slept almost as long. Jacillios, the third Molarian on the ship, had clearly gone to the wrong place: he came back in a foul mood and didn't sleep at all.

Vladimir Sokolov, Bull Pampas, Malcolm Briggs, Luthor Chadwick, and the two newest human members of the team, James Nichols and Dan Moyer, hit every bar they could find, then hit them all again.

Cole had no idea what Jaxtaboxl, the ship's only Mollutei, did for fun, and he didn't even want to think about how Lieutenant Domak, a warrior-caste Polonoi, blew off steam. He knew that Rachel Marcos, Idena Mueller, and some of the other human women had gone to see some plays—there was even an all-Shakespeare theater on the station —and had put together a list of restaurants and safe nightclubs based on the Duke's recommendations. Bujandi, the ship's only Pepon, was always talking about the savannahs and vistas on his home planet. He returned sullen and morose, and Cole had a feeling he'd gone looking for something green on Singapore Station and wasn't exactly thrilled with the scenery he'd found.

Val was one of the last to return. She was nursing a black eye, a split lip, heavily bandaged knuckles, a hangover, and a very contented smile.

That left only Christine Mboya. He was surprised that she wasn't in the vanguard of those returning to the ship, and began getting worried as more crew members returned and he'd had no word from her. He was about to send out a search party when she showed up, looking exactly as she'd looked when she left—well groomed, well manicured, totally poised. She explained that her hotel's computer had crashed, and she'd spent the last two days helping them get it up and running again. Cole was about to voice his sympathy when he decided that fixing the computer was probably the most fun she could have had while on the station.

As for Cole himself, he'd eaten his steak dinner and spent a romantic night in a suite with Sharon, but he simply wasn't interested in gambling, drinking, black-market goods, and brothels, and he returned to the ship within two days, not to leave again. Sharon had beaten him back by almost half a day.

He was idly wondering just how much rest and recuperation time the crew would need to get over their R-and-R on Singapore Station when David Copperfield's image appeared.

"I hope I'm not intruding, Steerforth," said the alien. "But I've had two conferences with the Platinum Duke, and I think it's time you and I discussed our options."

"*Our* options?" said Cole, arching an eyebrow.

"Of course I meant *your* options," said Copperfield hastily. "When would be a convenient time for you?"

"You, Christine, and I are the only three people capable of carrying on a cogent conversation at this moment, and she's busy running the ship, so now's as good a time as any."

"Your office?"

"Yeah, I think so," said Cole. "I'd love to do it over lunch, but there's no sense letting anyone overhear us until I've made up my mind."

"I'll be there in five minutes," said Copperfield. "I just have to gather my notes."

He broke the connection, and Sharon's holographic image immediately popped into the office.

"So I'm not fit to carry on a cogent conversation?" she said.

"Your job is snooping on them, not participating in them," said Cole. "Or you could spy on everyone else and tell me how many crew members are puking our their guts."

"You have such a delicate way of expressing yourself," said Sharon.

"One of us was not into delicate expressions a couple of nights ago, or need I remind you?" said Cole.

"That's it. Good-bye forever."

"Then you won't mind if I take back those flowers I bought you and give them to Rachel Marcos."

"I strongly advise you to reach for the flowers with your left hand. That way, after I cut it off you'll still have your right hand to salute with."

"How thoughtful," said Cole. "I think what I like best about you is that you're always looking out for me."

"Especially when you're sneaking up behind me," said Sharon. "Dinner at 1800 hours?"

"It's a date."

"I'd better sign off. Here comes your schoolmate."

Her image vanished just as the door irised to let David Copperfield through.

"How did you enjoy your shore leave, Steerforth?" asked Copperfield pleasantly.

"Are you *ever* going to address me by my real name?"

"Probably not," replied the alien. "What difference does it make? We both know who I mean."

"We'd both know who I meant if I started calling you Hamlet, or maybe Raskolnikov."

"But you wouldn't," said Copperfield. "You're too considerate of other people's feelings."

"That could be viewed as a serious flaw in a starship captain," noted Cole.

"I really don't know. The immortal Charles never dealt with starship captains."

"One of life's tragedies," said Cole. "Are we going to talk like this much more, or can we get down to business?"

"Business, to be sure," said Copperfield. "Do you mind if I sit down?"

"Pull up a chair," said Cole. "But I don't think you'll find it very comfortable. I could send for one that will suit you better."

"Nonsense," said Copperfield, sitting awkwardly on a chair and shifting his weight uncomfortably. "This is precisely the kind of chair we had in school."

"So what have you got for me?"

"Even I would reject the two that pay the most," said the alien. "Shall I even describe them for you?"

"Don't bother," said Cole. "If *you* think they're too dangerous, that's good enough for me. I've experienced what you *didn't* think was too dangerous."

Copperfield spent the next ten minutes going over the six other offers that the Platinum Duke had solicited. Cole rejected two of them because there was too much likelihood that the forces he would be up against could draw upon additional support from allies. A third put them too close to the Republic, and while he'd changed the ship's registration papers and external insignia, it was still very clearly a Republic warship, and the Navy knew that there was only one Republic warship on the Inner Frontier. Theoretically the Navy couldn't come after him as long as he stayed on the Frontier, but "hot pursuit" could be a very elastic term, and he decided not to chance it.

That left two proposals. One required him to take back a city that had fallen under a local warlord's rule, and that meant fighting on the ground, house to house, with a force of thirty. It was estimated there were some two hundred of the warlord's soldiers there, and while he was sure his crew would have superior weapons and tactics, he couldn't be certain that the warlord might not deploy even more men rather than lose the city.

So it came down, rather easily, to Djamara II, an oxygen planet with considerable gold and silver deposits. There was no sentient native population. An independent mining company had laid claim to the mineral rights, and had begun mining the world some six years earlier. Eventually a regional warlord got wind of what they were digging out of the ground, and made a grab for it. The company was no newcomer to this sort of banditry. They'd hired a small militia, which had twice repelled the warlord's attacks. But they took heavy losses during the second attack, and the company had decided that they would achieve victory more easily by hiring a starship than by fighting on the ground.

"Why didn't the warlord just poison the air and kill them all?" asked Cole. "It's easy enough to do."

"This isn't a war, Steerforth," answered Copperfield. "His army has no more interest in mining gold and silver than the *Teddy R*'s crew does. He wants to steal what they have, or make some kind of deal whereby they'll pay him a tribute to leave them alone. He does *not* want to put his elite warriors to work digging for minerals."

"Okay, that makes sense," said Cole. "This is unfamiliar territory to us. We'll learn, just as we learned piracy." He paused. "What's the bottom line here?"

"They'll pay four million credits, or two million Maria Theresa dollars, or fifteen percent of their annual production for two years if we'll take this warlord and his army out once and for all."

Cole shook his head. "That's *your* bottom line, David. Mine is: What's the opposition. Who are we up against, how many ships has he got, and what kind of firepower has he got?"

"Now we're depending on the Platinum Duke's sources," answered David. "I told him you'd like this one the best, so he's been finding out everything he can. As near as he has been able to tell, the Rock of Ages has six ships—"

"Hold on a minute," interrupted Cole. "The Rock of Ages?"

"That's right."

"And the Platinum Duke, and Cleopatra, and Joan of Arc, and the Hammerhead Shark. Doesn't *anybody* use a real name around here?"

"Welcome to the Inner Frontier," said David Copperfield with a smile. "Since there are no laws, we're free to be whatever we want to be—and that means we're free to call ourselves whatever we want to call ourselves. Most people change names out here as often as you'd change ships or dwellings back in the Republic. I think it's colorful."

"I think it's ridiculous," said Cole. He grimaced. "Okay, go on."

"The Rock had six ships four months ago. He might have added a seventh since then; nobody seems to know."

"That's a lot of ships to go up against," said Cole, frowning.

"You won't have to," said Copperfield. "He's keeping four worlds under his thumb. He doesn't dare take ships away from them, or they might have some unpleasant surprises waiting for him when he comes back."

"So the most we're likely to face is two ships . . ." mused Cole.

"Three, if he's added another."

"Can the Duke find out before I accept the job?"

The alien shrugged. "I don't know. He's been trying for three days, and he hasn't found out yet."

"That means two ships," said Cole decisively. "If they've got a new one and the Platinum Duke, with all his sources, can't find out, that means it's in use somewhere, and isn't likely to come to Djamara II until it gets a distress signal, at which point we've put one or both of the other ships out of commission."

"So you're interested?" said Copperfield.

"Yes, I'm interested," replied Cole. "It'll only be two-on-one, neither of them should be as powerful or well armed as the *Teddy R*, especially since we added the weaponry from Val's old ship, and we'll have the element of surprise on our side." He paused. "And it's nice to know we're preventing a warlord from plundering a planet."

"Does that really matter to you?" asked Copperfield curiously.

"It's what we trained for, David," answered Cole. "It's the reason a lot of us joined the military."

"I thought it was because you were drafted."

"That's another reason," said Cole wryly. He paused thoughtfully, then spoke again. "Once we blow this bastard's first two ships out of the sky, maybe we'll pay a visit to each of the other four worlds he's holding captive. One ship apiece, it should be child's play."

"You'd do that just because it's the moral thing?"

"Well, if each world we freed felt it incumbent upon themselves to pay us a thank-you fee, I wouldn't try to discourage them."

"By God, Steerforth," said David Copperfield enthusiastically, "*now* you're thinking like a mercenary!"

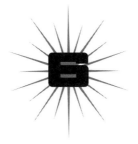

It had been six days since Cole signed the papers that committed the *Teddy R* to the defense of Djamara II. The ship was not in orbit around the planet—he saw no sense advertising its presence—but was stationed out among the dozen moons of Djamara V. Christine, Briggs, and Domak, the three best hands at using both the computers and sensors, worked the red, white, and blue shifts, eight hours apiece, scanning the system, looking for signs of the Rock of Ages' ships.

Cole spent most of his time in his office and his cabin. There just wasn't anything for him to do until the enemy's ships showed up—and even once they did, anything that was happening on the bridge could be transmitted to him wherever he was.

It was on the seventh day that a coded message came through from Singapore Station. Cole had it piped into his cabin.

There was a moment of static, and then the Platinum Duke's image appeared.

"Hi," said Cole. "No sign of him yet."

"Just as well," said the Duke. "It gives you some time to plan."

"I don't like the sound of this," said Cole warily. "What's up?"

"Evidently there's at least one turncoat on Djamara II," said the Duke. "It's hardly surprising, given the numbers, and given the plunder that's at stake."

"You're telling me that the Rock of Ages knows we're here," said Cole.

"That's right."

"Well, he was going to know it sooner or later. We've lost the element of surprise, but I'll still put the *Teddy R* up against whatever he's got. The Navy scraps its warships, it doesn't sell them to third parties. We'll still have the edge in firepower."

"I know it, you know it, and the Rock of Ages knows it. He'll be there tomorrow."

"He knows it and he's still coming?" said Cole, frowning. "What am I missing here?"

"My sources tell me that he's decided if he can't have the mineral wealth of the planet, no one can. He's got some exceptionally dirty bombs—I don't know how many—and he's issued an ultimatum: if the mining company doesn't send you away by the time he gets there, he'll fire the bombs at the planet. You may stop one or two, but I gather he's pretty confident you can't stop them all. It's what in a less sophisticated age they used to call a punishment party."

"Thanks for the information," said Cole.

"What are you going to do?"

"I'm not sure," said Cole. "This is going to require some thought."

"I'm sorry it's turning out this way," said the Duke. "I didn't mean to give you such a problem, certainly not on our very first collaboration."

"It's not your fault," said Cole. "I suppose we could meet him in deep space and have it out there."

The Duke made a face, which Cole hadn't thought possible given the amount of platinum that composed it. "If there are informers in the mining company and on the planet, the Rock has to know he's got some in his organization. I'm sure he won't make a direct approach."

"We're only one ship. We can't patrol everywhere."

"We *could* tell the company that we're canceling out," offered the Duke.

Cole shook his head. "Word would get out tomorrow, and no one would ever hire us again."

"We could suggest that they evacuate Djamara."

"Same problem. They're paying us to keep it open and free. If we can't do it, who'll do business with us in the future?"

"It's a conundrum," agreed the Duke. "If there is anything I can do from this end . . ."

"We'll let you know," said Cole, breaking the connection.

He called an immediate meeting of his senior officers. His office was too small for them to sit comfortably, so he assembled them in the mess hall and made it off-limits to everyone else until the meeting broke up.

Once they'd gathered there, he laid out the situation to them.

"Now," he said when he'd finished filling them in, "what are the odds that we can spot him entering the system?"

"Djamara II is a third of a way around the sun," said Christine. "If we stay here and he approaches from the far side of the sun, we'll never spot him in time."

"Okay, then," said Cole, "what if we take up an orbit around Djamara II?"

Christine shook her head again. "We'd spot him, of course. But unless we managed to destroy him before he saw us—and he knows we're here—he could still fire enough dirty bombs so that one of them would almost certainly get through."

"Does everyone concur with that?" asked Cole.

Forrice, Val, and Sharon all nodded their agreement.

"So we're caught between a rock and a hard place," said Cole. "If we station ourselves where we're sure to spot him, he can still shoot a lot of bombs past us and make the planet uninhabitable before we can destroy him—and if we stay out here where we're harder to spot, we can blow him apart if he approaches from this direction, but the odds are that he'll take any of a dozen other routes, all of which will get him past us."

"Hobson's choice," muttered Val.

"Hobson was an asshole," said Cole harshly.

"I don't understand . . ." said Val.

"It's a big universe, filled to overflowing with choices. We don't like the two most obvious ones. That doesn't mean there aren't any others."

"But if we can't stop the Rock from delivering a dirty bomb . . ." began Forrice.

"If we can't stop him," said Cole, "then we don't even try."

"Cut and run?" said Forrice. "That's not like you—and no one will ever contract for a hired gun who turned and ran."

"That's a hired gun who turns and runs *away*," said Cole. "Let's see if we can think of something that's worth running *toward*."

"You've lost me," said Sharon. "If you have an idea, why not just spell it out?"

"Because it's not fully formed yet," said Cole. "I'm working on it. The one thing I know is that we can't stay in the Djamara system. Now, if we can't stay here, the Rock has no reason to drop his bombs, right?"

"That presupposes he *knows* that we're leaving," said Christine.

"Then we'll have to let him know, won't we?" replied Cole.

"Just contact him by subspace radio and say we changed our minds?" said Val. "He'll never buy it."

"Okay," said Cole. "He won't believe you, and he won't believe me, and he won't even believe the Duke. Who *will* he believe?"

They were silent for a long moment. Then Sharon grinned.

"Oh, shit!" she said. "Of course! They'll believe the mining company. *We're* not going to die if they drop the bombs, but the company stands to lose a few hundred men, and all the planet's mineral resources."

"But how will they know that the mining company isn't lying?" persisted Christine.

"That's easy enough," said Val. "They can say they've rethought their position, they made a mistake, and they're willing to pay for it. They're offering us fifteen percent for two years? What if they offer the Rock of Ages twenty-five percent forever?"

"He'll probably demand a third," said Forrice.

"And they'll agree," said Cole. "They're scared to death, and they'll agree to anything. Of course, he'll still fly here to make sure we're gone, and once he sees that we are, the planet is safe."

"Okay, that's Step One," said Forrice. "We've saved the planet. What next?"

"We contact the Platinum Duke and have him tell us which is the weakest of the four ships that are patrolling the Rock's little empire, we wait until we know the Rock is in the Djamara system, and we capture it."

"Capture it, not kill it?" said Val.

"Right."

"It's a lousy trade," said Val.

"It's not a trade," said Cole. "It's Step Two."

"All right," said Forrice, emitting a hoot of alien laughter. "Now it all makes sense! You're one sly bastard!"

"Stop showing off all the Terran words you've learned and tell me what the hell you're talking about," said Val irritably.

"Step Three is we find out who's the Rock's biggest rival in this section of the Frontier," said Forrice.

"I see," said Christine. "And for Step Four, we program the captured ship, which is still showing the Rock's insignia, to strike at the rival's home world."

"Can it get through their defenses on autopilot?" asked Sharon.

Suddenly Val was smiling too. "It doesn't matter. You think the rival's going to forgive him because an attack didn't succeed?"

"Ah!" said Sharon. "So for Step Five, we sit back and let the two warlords fight it out, then mop up whoever's left."

"We're very short on time," announced Cole. "I'm going to give you four half an hour to find something wrong with that, or to come up with a better plan." He got to his feet. "In the meantime, I need to contact the Duke and find out which of the Rock's ships is the weakest, and which of his rivals is the strongest."

When he returned, no one had come up with a viable alternative.

"All right," said Cole. "Now we come to the hardest part of the exercise."

"What's that?" asked Forrice.

"I've got to take the *Kermit* down to Djamara II and convince them we're not hanging them out to dry."

It took Cole six hours to convince the leader of the small mining colony that he wasn't deserting Djamara II, that indeed he was doing the only possible thing he could to save it. The leader contacted the Platinum Duke twice for assurances, then asked Cole to leave one of his officers on the planet as a gesture of good faith.

"Not a chance," he replied. "My ship is understaffed as it is."

"You are afraid the officer will die with us," said the leader stubbornly.

"You're making this very difficult on both of us," said Cole. "You've got a mole in your organization, and I'm not going to leave any of my people here until you acknowledge that and get rid of him. I was hired to destroy the Rock of Ages' ships, and to make sure he never bothers or harasses Djamara again, and I fully intend to do so. If we do it my way, you'll be embarrassed and humiliated for a few days, and have to make some financial promises that I guarantee you won't be forced to keep. If we do it *your* way, I'll still destroy his ship, and Djamara will never be harassed again—but it'll never be harassed because nothing will or can live here. That's your choice, and we're running out of time."

And because that *was* his choice, he finally consented.

By the time Cole took the *Kermit* back to the *Teddy R*, David Copperfield had been in touch with the Platinum Duke and learned that the least formidable of the Rock's ships was the one orbiting the agricultural colony world of Sandburg, which was not sandy and did not have a burg, or even a small town, on it, but was named for some forgotten poet from the days when Man was still Earthbound.

It took the *Teddy R* four hours, traversing the Myerling Wormhole, to get to the outskirts of the Zamecka system, of which Sandburg was the fourth and only habitable planet.

"Have you located the ship yet?" asked Cole from his office.

"Yes, sir," said Christine.

"What kind of weaponry does she carry?"

"Mr. Sokolov is at the sensors, sir," she replied. "He should know in just another minute or two."

There was a brief silence.

"Sir?" said Sokolov's image. "It's even better than we'd hoped. One front-mounted laser cannon, two side-mounted laser cannons, no torpedo bays, and as far as I can tell its defensive shields can't stand up to our pulse cannons."

"It's in orbit, above the stratosphere," said Cole. "How long will it take to reach light speeds with no friction to slow it down?"

"Let me see," said Christine, as a row of specs appeared on her holoscreen. "It's a late model class-HH, sir. It should take from forty to fifty seconds."

"So we have time to disable it if we have to?"

"Yes, sir."

"All right. Who's in Gunnery right now?"

"Jacillios, sir."

He shook his head. "Get Bull Pampas down there. I want someone I trust."

"Yes, sir."

"And if Four Eyes isn't otherwise occupied, have him go to Gunnery too."

He waited until everyone was where he wanted them to be.

"All right," he said. "Now raise our defenses and approach to within firing range."

The *Teddy R* advanced upon the Rock's ship.

"They're hailing us, sir," said Christine.

"Warning us off, I'll bet," said Val with a contemptuous laugh.

"That's exactly what they're doing," confirmed Christine.

"Don't respond, keep on course, don't speed up, don't slow down," said Cole. "Let's see how close they'll let us get."

There were two more warnings, spaced a minute apart. Then, at just under ninety thousand miles, the Rock's ship fired its laser cannon.

"Missed us, sir," announced Christine.

"Missed or deflected?"

"Missed."

"Okay," said Cole. "That was a warning shot across our bow. Keep going."

At seventy thousand miles the Rock's ship fired again.

"Deflected, sir," said Christine.

"Thank you," said Cole. "Bull, fire the pulse cannon. Make it a clear miss, but a close one."

"Done, sir," reported Bull Pampas a moment later.

"Christine, can you get me a ship-to-ship video transmission?"

"Yes, sir," she replied. "I'm sending it out on more than two million frequencies. They should be able to pick it up on . . . ah! There it is."

"Greetings and felicitations," said Cole, looking into the lens of his transmitter. "I am Wilson Cole, Captain of the *Theodore Roosevelt*. I hope you agree from our mutual demonstrations of firepower that your ship is no match for ours. Nonetheless, we have no desire to destroy you." He paused long enough for what he had said to sink in. "It should be clear to you that you have no adequate defense against our pulse cannon, and equally clear that your laser weapons cannot damage my ship. I have no intention of firing our weapons again unless you fire upon us first, or attempt to escape." Another pause. "There is no humiliation or dishonor in surrendering to a greater power, and that is precisely what we want you to do. If you surrender, no member of your crew will be harmed. You will be allowed to keep all your belongings, including your hand weapons, and you will be set down on the nearest neutral world. Your ship will remain in my custody. There is only one alternative. I don't wish to consider it, and I'm sure you do not either. I will give you five minutes to come to a decision. To repeat: I will fire on you only if you fire first or attempt to escape."

He broke the transmission.

"Did you mean it, sir?" asked Pampas.

"Absolutely, Bull," said Cole. "If they make a run for it, hit 'em full-force. Same thing if they fire on us. Let's hope they're not that stupid."

"They've just sent a transmission to the Djamara system, sir," announced Domak. "I've blocked it."

"Good. Now let's give them a little while to consider their position."

They were contacted three minutes later. The image of a portly, gray-haired man appeared in front of every transmitter on the *Teddy R.*

"I am Forian Bellisarius, Captain of the *Carnivore*," said the man. "I have no choice but to accept your terms."

"A wise decision, Captain," said Cole. "How many crew do you carry?"

"Twenty-four."

"Can they all fit about your shuttlecraft?"

Bellisarius nodded. "Twelve and twelve."

"Do your shuttlecraft possess sufficient fuel to reach the Manitoba system, four light-years from here?"

"Yes."

"All right," said Cole. "Two of my shuttles will make their way to you in the next few minutes. As soon as they reach the *Carnivore*, you are free to go."

"And we can take our sidearms with us?"

"You have my word, Captain."

Cole ended the connection. "Bull, choose a boarding party of six and take the *Edith* over to the *Carnivore*. Val, do the same with the *Junior*. Lieutenant Domak, go with one party or the other."

The two shuttlecraft left the *Teddy R* within five minutes, and reached the *Carnivore* in another five. They boarded the ship and stood at attention while Captain Bellisarius shepherded his crew into their own shuttlecraft and departed.

"They're gone," reported Val.

"Let's make sure," said Cole. "I want you and Bull to split the ship up any way you want, and to search it for anyone they might have left behind, and for any presents they may have left us."

"Presents, sir?" said Pampas.

"Like a bomb," explained Cole. "Lieutenant Domak, while they're making sure the ship is secure, I want you to see if you can rig their navigational and weapons computers so that we can operate them from the *Teddy R*."

"Yes, sir," replied Domak, saluting.

Val and Pampas reported ten minutes later that the ship was secure, and there were no unpleasant surprises in the offing. Domak, operating in concert with Christine and Briggs, had switched control of the *Carnivore* to the *Teddy R*'s bridge within half an hour.

"Well done," said Cole. "I want you all to return to the ship now." A moment later he was in contact with David Copperfield. "Well?" he said. "Did you get what we needed from the Duke?"

"Yes, Steerforth," said the alien. "The Rock's most powerful rival is the Blue Devil, whose home world—well, headquarters world, anyway—is Meritonia III."

"The Blue Devil!" snorted Cole. "Where the hell do they get these names?"

"I wouldn't be too quick to belittle that particular name, my dear Steerforth," said Copperfield. "He controls seven worlds with an iron hand. Or claw. Or whatever. I have no idea if he belongs to your race or some other."

"Makes no difference," said Cole. "All we needed was the name of that world." He cut the connection, then contacted the bridge. "Christine, is Meritonia III in our navigational log, or are we going to have to hunt up its official name?"

"Let me check," she said, scanning her data. "Here it is, sir—Meritonia III."

"How far are we from it?"

"Approximately thirty-two light-years, sir."

"Fine. Send the *Carnivore* there by the most circuitous route, which is to say, don't let it pass within two light-years of any other star system. Or better still, check with Pilot, who seems to know more about wormholes than the computer does, and see if there's one near here that can take it to Meritonia in a hurry."

"I'll ask him, sir." There was a full minute of silence, and then Christine's image appeared again. "He says the Blaindor Hole could get it there in less than five hours, sir—if I can find a way to enter it."

"Do your best, Christine," said Cole. "And let me know when it's on its way."

He cut the connection and suddenly found himself looking at Sharon's face. It took him a few seconds to realize that it was the Security Chief in the flesh and not her holographic image.

"I brought you some beer," she announced, entering his office. "Then I decided you'd think it was rude to drink alone, so I brought some for me, too."

"Thanks," said Cole. "I could use some."

"You really think this is going to work?" she asked.

"It ought to," said Cole. "We'll know in less than six hours."

"I'd love to see the look on the Rock's face when he finds out that he's just attacked the Blue Devil in underwhelming numbers," said Sharon with a chuckle. "What do you think he'll do—run or fight?"

"He's got to join the battle," said Cole with absolute conviction. "If he runs, he's lost his empire, such as it is, and he's not getting it back."

"Do we care who wins?"

"Not really. I suppose we'd prefer the Rock to lose, just to relieve the minds of the miners on Djamara, but it makes no difference. If he loses, we've fulfilled our contract, and if he wins, he'll be pretty banged up and we'll be waiting for him when he returns to Djamara."

It happened exactly as Cole had predicted. The *Carnivore* was blown apart before it could reach Meritonia III's atmosphere. The Blue Devil immediately declared war on the Rock of Ages, who raced to Meritonia to join his remaining ships in an all-out battle against the Blue Devil's more powerful fleet.

The war lasted twenty-one minutes. When it was over the Rock of Ages and all five of his ships had been blown into history, and the Blue Devil's fleet had been reduced from eleven to three.

Cole contacted the miners and told them that the crisis was over and that the *Theodore Roosevelt* had accomplished its mission, then got in touch with the Platinum Duke to apprise him of the situation and remind him to start auditing the company's books.

"That's absolutely remarkable!" said the Duke. "And the amazing thing is that you did it without firing a shot!"

"We fired one shot," Cole corrected him. "We didn't hit anything, or even try to, but it served its purpose."

"You know what I meant," said the Duke. "It's just remarkable! Why do you act so calm, like it was a daily occurrence?"

"It's not a daily occurrence," replied Cole. "But it's nothing to get excited about. There are a zillion species, sentient and otherwise, in the universe. God gave every last one of them teeth and claws. Only a handful of us got brains. It seems to me it'd be criminal not to use them."

"No wonder the Republic wants you dead," said the Duke admiringly. "You make too much sense."

It was two days later, and Cole, Sharon, Val, and David Copperfield were sharing a table, and a round of drinks, with the Platinum Duke at his casino on Singapore Station. Forrice had accompanied them as far as the only Molarian brothel in the sector and had then taken his leave of them, promising to rejoin them later.

"Remarkable!" the Duke was saying. "Just remarkable!"

"Perhaps we should have charged them more," suggested David Copperfield, only half joking.

"It wasn't *that* remarkable," said the Duke with a smile. "But it was a nice few days' work."

"And now you and I should sit down and discuss the next commission," said David.

"We *are* sitting down," noted the Duke dryly.

"You don't really want to discuss such things in public," suggested David.

"If *I* tell people not to get close enough to listen, they'll keep their distance."

"It must be nice to own a world," said Sharon. "Even an artificial all-metal world like this one."

"It has its compensations," replied the Duke.

"I've noticed," said Cole.

"It also has its liabilities," continued the Duke. "For example, this is my casino. I own the profits, but I also have to cover the losses."

"You've been losing?"

"I'm being cheated, I know that. But I don't know how—and the gentleman who has been cheating me six nights in a row is . . . well . . . formidable."

"Where is he?" asked Cole.

"Over there at the card tables," said the Duke. "He's a head or two taller than anyone else."

"I know him," said Val, studying the man in question. He stood close to seven feet tall, was well dressed and well muscled, and was carrying two hand weapons that were visible and probably more that weren't.

"You do?" asked David.

"Well, I know *of* him, anyway," she said. "He's Skullcracker Morrison."

"I remember him!" said Sharon. "Didn't he used to be the freehand heavyweight champion of the Antares Sector?"

"Yes, until he got a little excited in the ring one night and killed his opponent, the referee, and three policemen who tried to arrest him."

"He's obviously not fighting anymore," said Sharon. "I wonder what he's doing for a living?"

"Oh, he's still cracking skulls," said Val. "He's just not doing it in the ring."

"Muscle for hire?" asked Cole.

"Right."

"Almost everyone here is carrying some kind of weapon," noted Cole. "I don't know what good all his strength and skill can do him."

"He doesn't ply his trade here," said the Duke. "He spends his money here—except that he's winning *my* money instead."

"How do you know he's cheating?"

"Every game in this casino gives the house a five to ten percent edge—and that one, *Khalimesh*, gives us twelve percent. I don't care how good you are or how lucky you are, if you come to the tables six nights in a row, you've *got* to have a losing night."

"Looks complicated," observed Cole.

"Seventy-two cards, eight suits, no numbers, all face cards, a dealer and four to six players," replied the Duke. "I think the Canphorites invented it, but it's become very popular out here on the Frontier, even with Men." He paused. "I just wish I knew how he was doing it."

"Bar him from the casino," suggested Sharon.

"I value my few remaining human parts too highly," replied the Duke.

Val stared at the Platinum Duke for a long minute. "If I prove he's cheating, prove it in front of witnesses, will you give us half of what we recover from him?"

"Absolutely!" said the Duke promptly.

"'Us'?" said Cole. "If you can spot what he's doing and make it stick, the money's yours."

"I'm probably going to need a little help," she explained. "If it's a *Teddy R* operation, then the spoils should go into the *Teddy R*'s coffers."

"Do you know how he's cheating?" asked David Copperfield.

"Not yet," answered Val. "But I've been hanging out in joints like this since I arrived on the Frontier fifteen years ago. If he's cheating, I'll spot it, all right." She turned to the Duke. "Give me a couple of hundred Maria Theresa dollars or Far London pounds." He looked sur-prised—as much as his metal face could display *any* reaction. "I can't see what he's doing from here," continued Val. "You can deduct it from what you owe me when I'm done."

"And if you can't spot it, the money is forfeit," said the Duke, handing her the money.

She pushed it back across the table to him. "If you're going to be that cheap, get someone else to show you how he's robbing you."

The Duke sighed and pushed the money across the table again. "When you put it that way . . ."

"All right," she said, picking up the money and getting to her feet.

She walked over to the card table where Morrison was playing, purchased some chips, and bought into the game. The dealer shuffled the deck, dealt out the hands quickly and efficiently, and then called out the various cards and bets.

Val won two tiny pots and lost five larger ones, four of them to Morrison, then returned to the Duke's table.

"Here," she said, handing him some chips. "Remember to subtract them from the two hundred dollars."

"You spotted it already?" asked the Duke.

"There's only one way they can be working it," said Val.

"They?" repeated the Duke.

"The dealer's in on it," she said. "Morrison can't be doing it alone."

"How are they working it?"

"The dealer's got to be using a shiner," said Val.

"Impossible!" said the Duke. "I've got holo cameras zooming in on the dealers' hands. If he was using one, we'd have spotted it."

"What's a shiner?" asked Sharon.

"A tiny mirror," explain Val. "He keeps it below the deck, and as he deals, Morrison will get a quick look at the face of each card as it comes off the deck."

"I know what a shiner is," said the Duke, "and I'm telling you that no one's using one. You want to check the holos?"

"Why bother?" said Val. "You've checked them."

"Then you agree they can't be using a shiner and you've wasted close to two hundred Maria Theresa dollars," said the Duke.

"I didn't say I agreed," replied Val. "I said I didn't see any reason to check the holos."

"You insist that the dealer's using a shiner?"

"That's what I said."

"If we search him and don't find it, will that satisfy you?"

"I wouldn't think it will satisfy *you*," said Val. "I thought you wanted your money back. Well, half of it, anyway."

The Duke threw up his hands in exasperation. "I am totally confused!" he said. "Captain Cole, she works for you. Do you understand her?"

"I *serve* with Cole," said Val. "I work for *me*."

"But to answer your question," replied Cole, "I find that she isn't wrong very often. If she says she knows how they're cheating, I'd be inclined to believe her."

"Then what's your next step?" asked Duke. "Do you want to search the dealer?"

"That's up to Val," said Cole.

"Not much sense searching him," she replied. "I watched him for seven hands. He never went to his pockets, or even his mouth or ears, and he'd never chance trying to palm it while he was shuffling the cards. If it falls onto the table, he's dead meat five seconds later."

"Then I don't understand . . ." began the Duke.

"I know you don't," said Val with a smile. "That's why he's robbing you blind."

"So what do we do now?" asked Cole.

"Now we study the Skullcracker for a few more minutes."

"I thought it was the dealer we were going to expose."

"The dealer has a confederate," said Val. "And it's clearly the Skullcracker. I want to see his tendencies."

"Tendencies?" asked David Copperfield.

"See if he's right-handed or left-handed, see how he holds his head, see what I can learn about him." She smiled. "Cole's got the easy part;

all he has to do is expose the dealer. I've got to get the money back from Skullcracker Morrison."

"It might be easier to just shoot him," suggested the Duke. "I'm all the law there is on Singapore Station. I pardon you in advance."

Val, still smiling, shook her head. "I always thought I was good enough to be the freehand champion if I'd stayed in the Republic. Tonight I'll find out if I was right."

"And if you're not?" asked the Duke.

"Then I don't give a damn what you do to him."

"Before or after he kills your captain?"

"If I'm dead, what do I care?" shot back Val.

"I can't tell you how touched I am by your concern," said Cole wryly. "Are we about ready to get this show on the road?"

"Another minute or two," said Val, studying Morrison intently. "He's right-handed. If he pulls a knife or some other weapon I can't see, it'll be with his right hand."

"Does it matter which hand he pulls a weapon with?" asked David.

"Of course," answered Val. "The first arm I break will be his right one."

"Break his arm?" said David incredulously. "He's as big as a mountain!"

"Just stand clear when he falls," said Val. She studied Morrison for another minute, then nodded. "All right. Let's go earn our money."

Cole handed his burner to Sharon. "Just in case we both need avenging," he said, then turned to follow Val to the table. "It'd be nice if you'd tell me exactly what I'm supposed to do," he said softly.

"Just stand next to Morrison while I'm showing everyone how they're being cheated," she said.

"I hope you don't think I'm going to fight him?"

"No. But he's the one with the money, so we don't want him getting away. Just stick a burner or a pulse gun in his back until I finish with the dealer. I'll take over from there—though if you'd like to disarm him, I'd consider that a personal favor."

"I'll disarm him," said Cole. "What do you know about the dealer that the holo cameras don't show?"

"I know he's cheating. I know it's not a marked deck, because there's never been a marked deck I couldn't read, so I know he's got to be using a shiner.

"But the cameras can't spot it, and I'm sure they search every dealer when they come on the floor and when they quit for the night or even take a break."

"I'm sure, too."

"Then, to repeat: what do you think you know?"

"You're a smart man," she said. "You'll figure it out."

"I can only think of one thing," said Cole. "And if you're wrong, you're going to maim him."

"See?" said Val with another smile. "I told you you'd figure it out."

"Oh, shit!" muttered Cole. "You'd damned well better be right."

Then they were at the table.

"Back for more?" asked the dealer pleasantly, as Cole edged around the table and took up a position directly behind where Morrison was seated.

"No," said Val. "I don't like to be cheated more than once a night."

"There's no reason to be a bad loser, ma'am," said the dealer.

"There was no reason to be a loser at all," she replied. "You've been cheating all week, you and your partner."

"Ma'am, if you become difficult, I'm going to have to call Security."

"Call them," said Val. "It'll save me the trouble. After all, we're going to have to lock you up."

"That's enough!" snapped Morrison.

Cole pressed the end of his pulse gun against Morrison's back.

"Just relax," he said softly. "Don't turn around, and keep your hands on the table."

"Is this a robbery?" asked Morrison, looking straight ahead.

"No, this is the end of a robbery," answered Cole, removing the huge man's burner and screecher.

"Nobody's robbing anyone," said the dealer.

"You've got that right," agreed Val. "How long did you think you could get away with it?"

"I'm not getting away with anything!" said the dealer heatedly.

"Not anymore," agreed Val. "But I have to admit it's the best-hidden shiner I've ever experienced."

The dealer held his hands out, palms up. "Do you see a shiner?" he demanded. He looked around at the crowd that was gathering. "Does anyone see a mirror? Do you want me to roll my sleeves up?"

"Why bother?" said Val. "It's not in your sleeves."

"Then where do *you* think it is?" he snapped.

"I'm looking at it," said Val.

"What are you talking about?"

"This!" she said, grabbing his left wrist with a powerful hand.

"You're hurting me!" yelped the dealer.

"Don't worry," said Val. "What I do next won't hurt a bit."

Suddenly there was a knife in her other hand, and before anyone quite realized what she was doing, she held the dealer's left hand against the table and severed the thumb with a knife.

"Anyone see any blood?" she said triumphantly.

There wasn't any.

"Take a look," she said, holding the prosthetic thumb up for everyone to see. She released her grip on the dealer's hand, and rolled down the skin on the underside of the thumb, revealing a tiny mirror. Then she picked a card up from the table and rubbed the artificial skin back in place with the edge of the pasteboard.

"Neat trick, isn't it?" she said. "Some of you hold him while I have a little chat with his partner." She walked over and stood next to Morrison. "Pay back everything you've won since you got to Singapore Station and you can walk away. No one will stop you."

"No one's going to stop me now," he growled ominously.

"I was hoping you'd say that," said Val, landing a roundhouse blow that knocked the huge man off his chair and onto the floor. "Stand back, Cole," she said. "I'll take it from here."

Cole backed away as Morrison got to his feet.

"Say a short prayer to your God," he told Val. "Because you're not going to live long enough to say a long one."

He took a swing at her, one that might well have decapitated her had it landed. She ducked, stepped in, feinted for his groin, and as he bent over to protect himself she jabbed a thumb in his eye. He howled with pain, raised a hand to cover the eye, and as he did so she landed a heavy kick to his left knee. He bellowed again, caught her on the shoulder with a glancing blow, got a broken nose for his trouble, and as he took a step toward her and reached out with both hands to grab her, she landed a powerful kick full in his groin.

He dropped to his knees, and took four more quick blows to the head. A chop across his throat had him gagging and gasping for air. Another blow demolished what was left of his nose, and he collapsed face-down on the floor.

Val rolled him over, went through his pockets, pulled out a large wad of bills, rolled him back on his stomach, and removed a miniature burner he had bonded to the small of his back. Finally she stood up.

"He let himself get out of shape," she said contemptuously. "Hell, Bull Pampas could have taken him just as easily."

She turned and began walking back to the Duke's table as the crowded parted before her, looking at her with a mixture of awe and fear.

Cole turned to the assembled gamblers. "They're all yours," he said. "But I think we've had enough violence on the premises."

Some of them dragged the unconscious Morrison to an exit, while others prodded the terrified dealer with their weapons until he, too, went to the exit.

"They're going to kill both of them," said Sharon when Cole and Val had reached the table.

"Probably," agreed the Duke. "After all, this *is* the Frontier. There will be no fast-talking lawyers getting them off on technicalities."

"That's very much like justice," said David Copperfield. "Certainly Skullcracker Morrison would have killed the Valkyrie if he could have."

"He never had a chance," said Cole.

"You weren't worried?"

"I've seen her in action."

"Enough chatter," said Val. "Let's get down to business."

She put the bills on the table and began dividing them. When they were done she handed her half over to Cole. "A little over six hundred thousand," she announced. "That's not bad for a one-minute workout."

"You are an exceptional woman!" enthused the Duke. "They could have kept that scam going for weeks, and certainly *I* wasn't about to challenge Skullcracker Morrison. How can I ever thank you?"

"Seriously?" said Val.

"Absolutely," answered the Duke. "I'm too old and have too many artificial parts to give you a courtly bow of sincerity, but try to imagine it."

"Fine," said Val. "Get me my own ship."

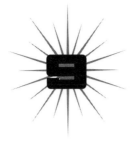

"It's simple enough," explained David Copperfield when the senior officers met aboard the *Teddy R.* "It should take a week, two at the most, and we'll have a million Far London pounds."

"How much is that in real money?" asked Forrice.

"About two million Republic credits, or just under half a million Maria Theresa dollars, give or take," said Copperfield. "And, if Olivia Twist works it right, there's every possibility that she'll wind up with her own ship."

"Why not humor me and call me Val?" she said.

"My dear woman, you've had eleven different names just in the time I've known you," answered Copperfield. "Why don't *you* humor an old man and let me call you the name that pleases me the most?"

"Save it, David," said Val. "You're probably not old, you're certainly not a man, and that name was used just once, by Cole not by me, solely to gain entrance to your office."

"Details, details," replied Copperfield.

"Cut to the chase," said Cole. "What exactly are we being paid to do?"

"The Apollo Cartel exports all the gemstones that are extracted from any world within twenty light-years of Bannister II," said Copperfield. He sighed deeply. "I could have told them not to locate there."

"Why not?" asked Forrice.

"Because it's right in the middle of the territory controlled by a very minor warlord who has taken the name of Genghis Khan, who controls Bannister and its neighboring systems with an iron hand. He was there five years ahead of them, so it can hardly be a surprise that he's causing them problems."

"Is he human?" asked Cole.

"With a name like Genghis Khan he'd have to be," said Christine.

"Don't bet on it," said Cole. "Out here they change names the way you and I change clothes."

"But his name—" she began.

"Is David human?" interrupted Cole.

"I'm human where it counts," said Copperfield with dignity.

"Fine," said Cole. "Just don't point to where it counts." Then: "So is Genghis Khan a Man?"

"To tell the truth, I have absolutely no idea what race he belongs to," said Copperfield. "I don't know anyone who's ever seen him."

"All right," said Cole. "Someone or something called Genghis Khan thinks he owns the Bannister system, and the Apollo Cartel wants him gone. That explains why they want the *Teddy R*. But how does it get Val her ship?"

"Khan sends a representative once a week to collect what I think you would call protection money," said Copperfield. "This representative travels without any enforcers or bodyguards, because no one in the system, or indeed anywhere in the sector, dares to stand up to Genghis Khan." He shot Val a smile. "He doesn't get to Bannister by flapping his arms."

"Too easy," said Cole. "No one's going to pay us a million pounds to kill a lone man, especially if it's not Genghis Khan himself."

"Of course not," said Copperfield. "I was answering your question about replacing dear Olivia's late lamented vessel. *That* is where she'll get her ship, if she's so inclined. As for earning the million pounds, that will require the elimination of Genghis Khan and his followers— or should I call them his horde?—as a threat to the Apollo Cartel."

"How many ships has he got and where are they located?" asked Cole.

"I don't know," said Copperfield with an eloquent shrug.

"Ask the Platinum Duke," said Cole.

"He's just a middleman," replied Copperfield. "The commission is being offered by the Cartel, which I gather has never even seen the self-styled Emperor Khan, let alone his headquarters."

"David," said Cole, "how do I know this isn't another assignment that sound easy until we learn that the enemy's got twenty ships all armed with pulse torpedoes?"

"I truly don't know, my dear Steerforth," said Copperfield. "I am merely relating an offer. We are opportunists. This is an opportunity. It is my job to report it, to put us together with opportunities. That does not mean you have to accept it."

"All right, David," said Cole. "Let me think about it for a minute."

"I don't like the sound of it," said Forrice. "Every time we go in blind, we find we're up against a much greater force than we anticipated."

"I'm with Forrice," chimed in Sharon Blacksmith, who had been silent up to that point. "Besides, we need Val right here on the *Teddy R.*"

"We promised to help her get her ship back when she joined us, or to replace it with another one," said Cole. "Besides, with a second ship we can take on bigger assignments that will hopefully pay a little better."

"Oh, come on, Wilson," said Sharon irritably. "This guy will be coming in a one-man job, not a military ship. It won't do us a bit of good."

"There's an ancient saying from old Earth itself," answered Cole. "'Great oaks from tiny acorns grow.'"

"What's an oak, what's an acorn, and what does that have to do with what I said?" Sharon demanded.

"Did you ever go fishing?" asked Cole.

"Are you going to answer me?"

"I'm doing it right now. Did you ever go fishing?"

"Yes. So what?"

"What did you use for bait?"

"I don't know—worms, artificial flies, other things."

"What other things?"

"Fish, mostly."

"You used a little fish to catch a big one, right?" said Cole. "That's exactly what we're going to do with the muscle's ship."

"How?"

He turned to the Valkyrie. "Tell her."

"What happens when the muscle doesn't return or report in, when they can't raise him on subspace radio?" said Val, and then answered her own question: "They send a bigger ship to see what happened. And when *that* one doesn't return or answer any messages?" She matched Cole's smile. "They can't ignore it, so sooner or later they're going to send the ship I want."

"And when they do," continued Cole, "a ship that big is going to have star maps, computer codes, *something*, to tell us where Genghis Khan is headquartered."

"And then we attack him?" asked Christine.

"Not in the *Teddy R*," said Cole. "But they don't figure to to fire on their own ship."

"You know," said Forrice, "between your deviousness and Val's total lack of morality, we could end up owning the galaxy."

"Since we left the Republic nothing's ever been quite as easy as it sounded," said Cole. "Let's settle for owning the million Far London pounds and another ship."

"I'll drink to that," said Val.

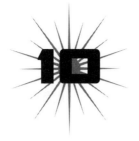

Bannister was a class-G star with six planets. The second of them had an oxygen atmosphere. There were a few life-forms on the planet, none of them yet approaching sentience. But there were deposits of gold, platinum, and fissionable materials, so a mining industry had grown up, and because the planet was so well located and able to grow enough food to sustain itself, it gradually, over a period of two centuries, became a commercial center specializing in the gem trade.

There were three continents, but only one city, which had grown from a ramshackle Tradertown to an almost-cosmopolitan metropolis of a third of a million men and another fifty thousand aliens. The tallest building—it was only seven stories, but land was not at a premium—housed the Apollo Cartel, and it was in the president's office that Cole and Val found themselves, seated comfortably on plush chairs that floated a few inches above the ground and rocked them very gently.

"You're sure they're due today?" Cole was saying.

"It's a he, not a they," answered the president. "And this is the day of the week that he always shows up for what he calls his protection money."

"And he always comes here, not to the comptroller's office?"

"That's right."

"Does he just walk in," continued Cole, "or does he register somewhere? Does someone announce him?"

The president shook his head. "There was some difficulty with one of our security guards last year. Since then I've instructed everyone to let him pass through unhindered, since he's going to reach this office one way or another."

"And he parks his ship in your private spaceport—the one where we landed our shuttle?"

"Yes."

"Is it always the same man?"

The president nodded. "For the past year, anyway."

"Okay," said Cole. "We'll take it from here—unless you have anything further to add?"

"Just make sure that whatever you do works," said the president. "I hate to think of what Khan will do to this entire planet if you fail." He got to his feet and walked to the door while Cole's and Val's chairs swiveled in the air to face him. "Does she speak?" he asked, indicating Val.

Suddenly there was a burner in Val's hand. "With this," she said.

The president made a hasty exit.

"You've been watching too many bad holos," remarked Cole as she bonded the laser pistol to her hip again.

"They made two about me during my pirate days," she replied. "I said that in one of them. Never said it in real life, so I thought I'd say it now and make it legitimate." She paused. "How do you want to handle it?"

"We'll play it by ear."

"Why not just kill him the second he enters?" she said. "It's not as if we're going to let him contact Khan."

"He's been making his pickups with no problem for over a year now," said Cole. "Maybe it's softened him up a little. Maybe he *likes* being alive."

She shook her head. "It's a waste of time. You don't send weaklings out on a job like this."

"We have a little time to waste," said Cole.

She shrugged. "You're the boss."

"I'm the Captain," he corrected her.

"Same thing." She glanced at some cabinets. "Do you suppose they keep any drinkin' stuff in here?"

"Forget it. I want you sober."

"I could drink *you* under the table and still be sober," said Val.

"I suppose you could," agreed Cole. "But don't drink anyway."

She stared at him. "What's the real reason?"

"I don't want to put him on the defensive the second he walks into the office," said Cole. "In a minute or two you're going to leave here and set up shop in that empty office across the corridor. Once he gets mad enough, you're going to have about three seconds to burst in here and disarm him. I want to be saved, not avenged, and I want to make sure your reaction time is what it should be."

"All right," she said. "No booze. I'll save you for your Security Chief. But when we're done, if any executive on this floor has got a bottle of Cygnian cognac, I plan to appropriate it."

"That seems fair enough," said Cole. "I don't imagine Khan will be paying Bannister II a second visit before tomorrow."

"Sir," said a disembodied female voice. "He has entered the building."

"Thanks," said Cole. He tossed a tiny earphone to Val. "Okay, get going and listen in on this. You'll know when I want you."

She caught the earphone, nodded, and walked out into the corridor while Cole moved to the chair behind the president's desk.

A little more than a minute later a tall, burly man entered the office.

"Who the hell are you?" he demanded.

"What does the sign on the door say?" responded Cole.

"So they've got a new president?" he said. "Did the one you're replacing tell you about our arrangement?"

"Why don't you tell me, just so I'm absolutely clear about it," said Cole.

"It's nice and simple. Genghis Khan and his organization provides protection for your operation for twenty-five thousand Far London pounds a week. In cash."

"Twenty-five thousand?" repeated Cole.

"Right." The man frowned. "Didn't he tell you?"

"Yes, he did."

"Well?"

"It's not enough," said Cole.

The man frowned. "What are you talking about?"

"Twenty-five thousand. It's not enough."

"Are you crazy?" demanded the man.

"No, I'm just a businessman," said Cole. "I think we'll make it fifty thousand."

"You want to pay us fifty thousand pounds a week?"

Cole shook his head. "No."

"Then what—?"

"I want you to pay us fifty thousand pounds a week for the privilege of protecting us."

"You're crazy!" bellowed the man.

"You're welcome to think so," said Cole easily.

"You've got thirty seconds to come up with my money!"

"Val," said Cole without raising his voice, "I believe that's your signal."

"What the hell are you talking about?" demanded the man as the door irised to let the Valkyrie pass through it.

He heard her enter, spun around to face her, and reached for his burner, but she was too fast for him. Her left hand shot out, grabbing his wrist, and a moment later even Cole could hear it crack from across the room.

He howled in rage and anguish and took a swing at her with his other hand. She ducked, stepped in, and gave him two quick karate chops, one to the throat, one to the groin. He collapsed, gasping for air, and before he could get back on his feet she had disarmed him.

"You can't get away with this!" he roared.

"I think we just did," said Cole pleasantly.

"I'll be back," he promised. "And I'll have enough men with me to handle you and this she-devil."

"You mean if we let you live and return to your ship, you'll come back in force?"

"You bet your ass! You haven't seen the last of me!"

"If you really mean that, we'd be pretty foolish to let you live, wouldn't we?" said Cole.

Suddenly the man's demeanor changed. He took one look at Val and began backing away. "You can't kill me!" he said desperately. "This is murder!"

"Correct me if I'm wrong, but isn't that just what you threatened to do to us?"

"We can deal!"

"I was hoping you'd say that," said Cole. "Just tell me where Kahn is and what codes will get us past his defenses, and we'll let you live. I won't let you go until I know the information is valid, but once it proves out, you'll be released."

"I can't tell you!" said the man. "He'll kill me!"

"And we'll kill you if you don't," said Cole. "Maybe you should consider who's closer to you at the moment."

The man, panic in his eyes, made a sudden break for the door, but Val was too quick for him. A quick, crunching kick to his knee sent him sprawling and moaning to the floor, and an instant later he passed out from the pain.

"He's going to have a limp for a long time," noted Cole.

"No he's not," said Val, aiming her burner at him. "He's going to be dead in ten seconds."

"No!" said Cole.

"Damn it, Wilson!" she said. "If the positions were reversed *he'd* sure as hell kill *us*."

"If we have to kill him, we will," said Cole. "We don't have to."

"Look," she said, "I know everyone else on the *Teddy R* is Navy, and I'm just a pirate who latched on to you, but you're letting this Good Guy/Bad Guy stuff color your judgment. He's an enemy. He wants to kill us. If he was a soldier in the Teroni Federation, what would the Republic's Navy do to him?"

"Kill him if we had to, and take him prisoner if we didn't."

"Maybe you think killing an unconscious man is a sin?" she said. "Fine. Step aside and let me take the sin unto myself. Hell, it can keep all my other sins company."

"It's not a sin," said Cole. "It's just not necessary."

She glared at him. "A son of a bitch like this holds a grudge, especially when he spends the rest of his life with a new wrist and an artificial leg. One of these years you and your Security Chief are going to have a kid, and this is just the kind of bastard who'll bide his time and someday slit the kid's throat."

"Spare me your predictions," said Cole. "He lives until I say otherwise. That's an order."

She shrugged and sighed deeply. "You're the Captain."

"I'm glad you remembered," said Cole. "They've got to have a hospital around here somewhere. It's too big a city not to. Get an ambulance to take him there, then have Bull come down on a shuttle and stand guard. Once they patch him up, no one but the doctor goes into his room, and he doesn't send or receive any messages. Then, once he's taken care of, hide his ship. I'll have Apollo's president use his influence to erase any record of it landing at the spaceport. By nightfall I want every trace of this thug's presence eradicated." He paused for a moment. "Change that. I want Domak watching him, not Bull."

"Why?" she asked.

"Because we're not going to shoot the place up. I just want someone there to discourage anyone from trying to talk to him—and Domak is a warrior-caste Polonoi. Her appearance, with all that natural spiky armor, will scare off more cops and hospital attendants that Bull's muscles."

"Anything else?"

He considered for a moment. "No, that should do it. The next move is up to them."

And it came the next afternoon, when a subspace message came through to the president's office.

"We haven't heard from our representative" was the demand. "Where is he?"

"I've no idea," answered Cole. "We were expecting him yesterday, and he never showed up, never even sent a message saying he would be delayed."

"If we find you've lied to us . . ."

"Why would I lie?" asked Cole. "The money is right here, waiting for you. Of course, I could have it delivered if you'll tell me where."

"We'll pick it up at your office."

"You're sure it won't be inconvenient?"

"Just have it ready. And you'd better be telling the truth."

"Why would I lie to you?" asked Cole. "I'm paying you to protect me from everyone else. I'm not paying anyone to protect me from you."

"Keep a civil tongue in your head. We're on our way. We should be there in six hours."

"Fine," said Cole. "I look forward to it."

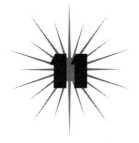

Cole sat at the desk, idly watching a murderball game that was piped in on the office's holo from the Quinellus Cluster and wondering why anyone would willingly play in a game that averaged seventy percent casualties, no matter how much it paid. He decided not to consider the casualty rate of mutineers, pirates, and mercenaries, because he was so far ahead of the game it was time the odds caught up with him and his crew.

He knew that Khan's representatives would be suspicious, and half expected them to prevent anyone from signaling him that they were on their way up to his office, but as they boarded the airlift the receptionist on the main floor alerted him to the fact that he was about to have visitors.

He deactivated the holo, made sure—for the third time—that his burner and screecher were fully charged, and waited.

Within a minute two men, a woman, and a Lodinite entered the office and confronted him.

"Who are you?" demanded the taller of the men.

"What do you care, as long as you get your extortion money?" responded Cole.

"*Protection* money," the man corrected him.

Cole shrugged. "Whatever."

"I don't like your attitude," said the man.

"I've heard that before," said Cole.

"What became of our representative?"

"How would I know?" said Cole. "I haven't left the building except to eat and sleep for the past two days. He never showed up, never sent a message, never sent a surrogate."

"I don't believe you."

"Look around," said Cole. "Do you see him anywhere?"

"Don't be clever with me!" snapped the man.

Cole was about to reply when he noticed the woman staring intently at him.

"I know you from somewhere," she said.

"I doubt it," said Cole. "We hardly travel in the same social circles. Besides, I'm sure if we'd met I'd remember you."

"I'll have it in a minute," she muttered, still scrutinizing him.

"Where's the money?" demanded the man, who seemed to be their leader, or at least their spokesman.

"In a safe place," said Cole. "Surely you didn't expect me to have it right here on my desk, where any thief could walk in and take it."

"Get it!" snapped the man.

"I don't believe you've heard a word I said," replied Cole.

"What are you talking about?"

"I just told you: I'm not leaving it right here for any thief to take—including you." He paused. "I'm afraid you're going to have to get yourself an honest job, and we're not hiring at present."

"I know who he is!" shouted the woman suddenly. "He's Wilson Cole!"

"This is our lucky day," said the man. "The Republic has put a ten-million-credit reward on your head."

"You might want to take a look behind you before you try to collect it," said Cole calmly.

The man and the Lodinite turned their heads and found themselves facing Val, who had a burner in each hand.

The second man, who had remained silent throughout, went for his pulse gun. A fraction of a second later he lay dead on the floor, a black bubbling hole between his eyes. As Val shot him, the Lodinite launched itself at her. She sidestepped and clubbed it across the back of the neck with her sonic pistol. There was a cracking noise, and the Lodinite fell to the floor, motionless.

"Does anyone else want to act stupidly?" asked Cole, getting to his feet.

"What the hell are you doing here?" demanded the man. "You're supposed to be on the lam from the Navy."

"I am."

"So now you're holding up businesses?"

"Just one," said Cole. "Yours. Where can I find Genghis Khan?"

"What do you want with him?"

"Everything he's got," said Cole.

"You're a fool," said the man. "He's Genghis Khan. He'll squash you like a bug."

"If that's the case, then you can't have any objection to telling me where he is."

"What's it worth to you?"

"Wrong question," said Cole.

The man frowned in puzzlement. "I don't follow you."

"The question is: What's it worth to *you*?"

"We're not telling you anything."

"That's your choice—but I promise you it's going to prove to be a very painful choice."

Suddenly the woman went for her screecher. Val melted it with her burner, and the woman screamed in agony as she found herself with a handful of molten metal. She dropped it to the floor, then knelt down in pain, holding her hand.

"This one's a pirate called Jezebel or Cleopatra," said the man, jerking a thumb at Val. "What the hell is she doing working for the Navy?"

"Her name's Val—this month, anyway—and as your friend noted, we're *not* the Navy anymore. Now why don't you make things easy on yourself and tell me what I want to know?"

"Not a chance," said the man. "You won't kill us. You do, and you'll never find out where Khan is."

"I won't begin to enumerate the logical fallacies in that statement," said Cole. "I'll simply repeat, for very nearly the last time, that I want you to tell me where I can find Genghis Khan."

"Go fuck yourself."

"Okay," said Cole, drawing his burner, "I'll ask you an easier question. Which one is your favorite testicle?"

"What?" said the man uneasily.

"I'm going to let you keep it," said Cole, aiming at his crotch. "At least I'm going to try. Now, which one can you spare?"

"You don't mean that!" said the man nervously.

"Do I look like I'm joking?" asked Cole.

"That's inhuman!"

"You come here to threaten and kill us, and *I'm* being inhuman?" said Cole with an amused laugh. "Now either tell me which one you can do without, or I'll have to guess."

"No!" screamed the man. He suddenly charged at Cole, oblivious of the burner that was trained on him, but before he could reach him Val stepped over and tripped him, sending him plunging headfirst into the desk. He was unconscious before he hit the floor.

"Thanks," said Cole.

"Would you really have shot him?" she asked.

"Of course not. I just wanted to scare him into talking. I don't shoot unarmed men."

"*I* would have."

"I know," said Cole. "That's why I'm the one who made the threat."

"So what do we do now?"

"Same as before," replied Cole. "Have the hospital send an ambulance and a pair of airsleds." He stared at the woman who was still kneeling, holding her hand. "She's in shock. Let them know that she needs immediate attention."

"And the two dead ones?"

"I don't want anyone to see the bodies leaving the building, so we can't bury them. Have Bull Pampas and Luthor Chadwick come down from the *Teddy R* and move them into the basement or some storage area. They're not going to turn into any nosegays, so have Bull bring a couple of body bags as well."

"I could do that myself."

"I know, but I want Bull and Luthor stationed down here anyway, so we might as well give them something to do. And have them bring Jack-in-the-Box with them."

"Jack-in-the-Box?" she repeated.

"Jaxtaboxl," answered Cole. "The Mollutei from the Gunnery section. His name's a pain in the ass to pronounce, so I exercised my captain's privilege and gave him a new one."

"All right," she said. "I'll get right on it."

The ambulance arrived in a few minutes, and the crew members Cole had requested made it within an hour. When everything he'd ordered had been done, he opened a visual communication with the ship.

"Hello, sir," said Christine, who was in charge of the bridge at the time. "I'm glad to see you're all right. Will you be coming back up soon?"

"Not for a while yet," said Cole. "Patch me through to Four Eyes. If he's asleep, wake him up."

A moment later Forrice's life-size holographic image appeared in front of Cole.

"I heard about your little adventure this afternoon," said the Molarian. "Congratulations, though without knowing the details I suspect the credit should really go to Val. I assume you're staying down there."

Cole nodded. "The next group isn't going to have any doubt that something's happened to their first two parties. One missing bag man is one thing; five are a little hard to ignore. After all, Khan's the biggest criminal kingpin in the sector; how dumb can he be?"

"So they'll be coming in force?"

"After a fashion," said Cole. "I don't imagine Khan himself will show up, not until he knows what happened to his men. For all he knows, a rival warlord with twenty ships is making the Bannister system his headquarters. But he'll send a much bigger force than this afternoon's."

"I want to come down to the planet before he gets there," said Forrice.

Cole shook his head. "I need you right where you are."

"Damn it, Wilson . . ."

"We can't have the Captain *and* the First Officer both putting themselves at risk away from the ship," said Cole. "If anything goes wrong down here, you're in charge of the *Teddy R*, and it'll be your job to attack whatever shows up before they can return to Genghis Khan's base and you have to face an even bigger force."

"But—"

"It's got to be you, Four Eyes. Christine's the best computer expert we've got, but she's got almost no battle experience, and you're the only two senior officers on board."

"So send Val up and let me come down," protested the Molarian.

"After all those years as a pirate, she's got more battle experience than you and me put together."

"She's worth three of you and ten of me in a pitched battle," answered Cole. "I need her down here."

Suddenly Sharon's image appeared a few feet away from Forrice's.

"May I make a suggestion?"

"Who told you to eavesdrop?" demanded Cole irritably.

"I'm the Chief of Security," she replied. "It's my job to monitor transmissions."

"I can already guess what your suggestion is," said Cole.

"Then why not come back to the ship?" she said. "Khan's going to send a force to Bannister whether you stay on the planet or not, and like you said, Forrice and Val are both better equipped to fight them than you are."

"This is my operation," said Cole. "I'm staying."

"Wilson, be reasonable," she said. "You're in fine shape for a middle-aged man, but the fact remains that you *are* a middle-aged man, and half the crew of the *Teddy R* can beat you in a fair fight."

"Then I guess it's damned lucky for me that I don't fight fair," he responded. "Now, is there anything else?"

"Just that I've had two messages from the executive you're impersonating," said Sharon. "The Cartel is getting nervous. They're wondering what's to prevent Khan's men from bombing them from space."

"The *Teddy R* can stop anything they've got."

"Not from where we're hiding, Wilson."

"You know it and I know it, but *they* don't know where the hell the ship is, or where it plans to be when the bad guys show up. Also, and more to the point, the Apollo Cartel is a prime source of income for Khan's organization; why the hell would he destroy it?"

"I don't think they're worried about his destroying the Cartel.

They're just afraid he might kill all the current officers who hired us."
She paused. "Maybe you'd better talk to them."

"All right," said Cole. "If you think it's necessary."

"It couldn't hurt."

"Okay. Anything else?"

"Just take care of yourself. I'd hate to go to the trouble of breaking
in a new bedmate, like for instance that gorgeous, sexy, young Bull
Pampas."

"Then I guess it's a good thing that I left you to him in my will,
isn't it?" he said, breaking the connection. He hunted through the
office for a source of coffee, couldn't find any, finally settled for some
whiskey that had been distilled on Pollux IV, and then contacted the
president.

"Captain Cole! I'm so glad to speak to you! We've been wondering
what steps you've taken to protect the Cartel's executives now that
Genghis Khan will have no doubt that we've hired someone to protect
us from him."

"We're on round-the-clock alert," answered Cole. "As soon as they
enter the system, the *Theodore Roosevelt* will plot their course and then
approach the planet from the far side, keeping it between us and
them."

"All they'll have to do is fly above the plane of the ecliptic, and
they'll spot you."

*Damn!* thought Cole. *I'd have sworn you'd never think of that.* Aloud
he said: "The *Theodore Roosevelt* is a Navy ship. Whatever the hell
Khan's got, our range is probably twice as great. If need be, we can
monitor him from Bannister III. Besides, let's be realistic; why would
he kill a cash cow like the Apollo Cartel?"

"I'm not worried about the future of the Cartel, just its leaders,"
came the acerbic reply. "After all, you've had your chance with five of

his henchmen and you still don't know any more about him than when you arrived."

"I know one thing," said Cole.

"Oh? What is it?"

"I know he can't ignore or tolerate what we've done. A man in his line of business can't show any weakness or his days are numbered. He'll be back, and we're ready for him."

"*You're* ready for him," said the president unhappily. "But are *we*?"

"Look," said Cole, starting to lose his patience. "We took this job to earn a million Far London pounds. If you want to call it off, that's fine with us. Just pay us off and we'll leave."

"And leave us to bear the brunt of their reprisals?" demanded the president. "Never!"

"Then go do whatever you were doing, and let us do our job," said Cole, breaking the connection.

He didn't know how soon Khan's men would arrive, and he hadn't eaten all day, so he went to the executive restaurant on the building's top floor, where he found Val, Bull Pampas, and Luthor Chadwick seated at a table and joined them.

"Where's Jack-in-the-Box and Domak?" he asked.

"Domak's still at the hospital," said Val. "The police are there, of course, but she doesn't trust them to stand their ground if there's an attack. Personally, I'd rather be protected by one warrior-caste Polonoi than a dozen human cops. The last time I checked, Jaxtaboxl was off trying to find some Mollutei food, but it's been half an hour now; he should be back any second."

"Have we got any medical reports on the three survivors?"

"I stopped by the hospital on the way here," said Pampas. "The woman's going to lose her hand; Sharon Blacksmith told me to have them bill the Apollo Cartel for her prosthetic hand and for the two men's treatment. Colonel Blacksmith also told Lieutenant Domak to have the hospital keep them sedated until we told them otherwise."

"Good idea," agreed Cole. "I should have thought of it myself."

"Have you got any idea what we're expecting, sir?" asked Chadwick.

"Not really," said Cole. "But it's got to be something a few levels of magnitude more powerful than the last group. Khan still has no idea who we are or how powerful we are, so he's not going to increase the size of his force gradually. If we can kill or capture one man and four men, probably we can kill or capture six or ten or a dozen, and he's got to have a limited number of men to spare, so I imagine this time we'll see something a lot more impressive."

No sooner were the words out of his mouth than Sharon's image appeared above the table.

"I hate to disturb the Captain when he's busy telling dirty jokes," she announced, "but you've got company."

"How big?"

"Eight laser and pulse cannons, crew of twenty-seven that we've been able to pick up with our sensors so far."

Her image vanished, to be replaced by a ship only a bit smaller than the *Teddy R*, displaying no insignia. Even as it appeared, its bay opened and disgorged a shuttle, capable of holding fifteen armed men, which promptly headed down toward Bannister II.

"Well, Val," said Cole, getting to his feet, "there's your ship. Let's get ready to take it."

Cole watched the shuttle as it touched down at the nearby spaceport. Ten Men, three Lodinites, and two Mollutei emerged from it, all heavily armed. They approached the Apollo Building, then fanned out. Only two men actually entered.

"They're getting smarter," remarked Cole to Val, Pampas, Chadwick, and Jack-in-the-Box. "They've already figured out that their previous parties made it this far and none of them came back, so they're not all going to walk into the same trap."

"You want us to keep out of sight at the start, like the last two times?" asked Val.

Cole shook his head. "Don't bother. They have to know I'm not alone. We'll handle the ones who come in here, and I've asked the police to help us round up the rest of them. They won't have any idea what's happened up here or how many of us there are, which should certainly put them at a disadvantage."

"Weapons out or in?" asked Pampas.

"If you're holding weapons in your hands, it'll just encourage them to do the same," said Cole. "And if that happens, someone's going to start shooting."

"That's what we're here for," said Pampas. "We'll win, sir."

"I don't doubt it," said Cole. "But they can't tell me what I want to know if they're dead."

"They're not going to tell you, period," said Val.

Cole shrugged. "You never know."

"You've got something up your sleeve, don't you, sir?" said Chadwick.

"Just his arm," said Val. "I say kill them the second they walk in, and then go after the others."

"Then what?" said Cole. "If we destroy their ship, you're still without a vessel and we haven't earned our money, since he'll probably send his whole fleet here, guns blazing."

"We have to face them sooner or later," said Val. "I prefer sooner."

"Oh, we'll face them, all right," agreed Cole. "But let's see if we can reduce their firepower first."

"One at a time or all at once, it makes no difference to me," said Val.

Suddenly Chadwick chuckled and Cole turned to him. "What's so funny?"

"It reminds me of something Commander Forrice is always saying after he and you discuss some problem," answered Chadwick. "Something to the effect that the problem was a whole lot simpler when it only had him thinking about it."

"That's Four Eyes, all right," said Cole.

"They're coming, sir," said Jack-in-the-Box softly.

"Whatever happens," said Cole, "no one shoots or does anything else until I give the signal." He stared directly at Val. "That's an order."

A few seconds later two leather-clad men, one bearded, one clean-shaven, entered the office. Both were heavily armed. The smooth-faced one had a pulse gun in his hand, and immediately trained it on Val, Pampas, Chadwick, and the Mollutei.

The bearded one stared at Cole for a moment. "I should have known those spineless cowards would hire help."

"I'm pleased to make your acquaintance too," said Cole.

"I know who you are, Wilson Cole," said the man. "I've seen your face on enough Wanted posters and holocasts. Why is the most decorated officer in the Republic hiring out as a mercenary?"

"Because I'm not in the Republic, in case you hadn't noticed," said Cole. "But there's no need for us to be enemies. Possibly Genghis Khan is looking for an ally."

"Why should he want to deal with the notorious Wilson Cole?"

"There's no reason why we can't be allies."

"We need no allies."

"Why not fly me up to the shuttle and let me send a subspace message to him?" persisted Cole. "I'd do it from here, but I don't have the necessary access codes."

"You don't need the codes," said the man. "Besides, they only respond to my voiceprint. And you're not going to live long enough to contact him."

"It's a pity," said Cole. "We could have been friends."

"We don't want any friends."

"What can I offer you as a show of good faith?"

"Keep your good faith," said the man.

"We're wasting time," said the smooth-shaven man. "Let's take care of business and get the hell back to home base."

The bearded man stared at Cole. "I'm only going to ask once: Do you have the money?"

"Yeah, I've got it. I don't suppose you'd care to split it down the middle? You take half, we take half, nobody shoots anybody, and we all walk away a little richer."

"Nobody shoots anybody," said the man sarcastically. "I think we'd rather have the money and take our chances."

"Don't do it, Bull," said Cole to Pampas, who had been standing absolutely still. "This man you're facing is Demon Jack Devereaux.

He's killed twenty men. Maybe twenty-five. You don't want to go up against him."

"You sure as hell don't," agreed the bearded man. "But I'm Black-beard Strahan. Never heard of this Devereaux."

"He's a pirate," said Cole. "Weapons or freehand, you'll never find anyone tougher. And he's got a little eight-man ship that could prob-ably blow that big vessel of yours right out of the ether."

"The eight-man ship's never been created that could harm the *South Star* in battle."

"It's *that* formidable a ship?" asked Cole.

"If we don't come back with the money, it's got orders to blow this whole city away. We could demolish it in ten minutes' time."

"What would it take *not* to blow it up?"

"Just pay us our money and we'll leave the city alone," said Strahan. "Until the next time. Now, are you going to pay up or not?"

"Not, I think. And this conversation has gone on just about long enough." He nodded almost imperceptibly to Val. She edged over to Chadwick and gave him a sudden shove with her hip. He wasn't expecting it, and careered into Jaxtaboxl, who grunted and spread his arms for balance. The unbearded man immediately trained his weapon on the Mollutei, and as he did so Val's long leg lashed out and kicked the pulse gun from his hand as Pampas launched himself at Strahan. Within seconds both men were on the floor, Pampas sitting atop one, Val with her boot in the middle of the other's back.

"One last chance," said Cole. "Will you tell me where I can find Genghis Khan?"

"Do your worst!" rasped Strahan. "We're not talking!"

"I can *make* them talk," said Val.

"Forget it," said Cole. "We've got thirteen men and aliens to dis-able. Put these two out of commission—that does *not* mean kill them

—and get to work on the others. If you need help, Domak's over at the hospital. Probably you won't; you may be outnumbered, but you know who they are, and they have no idea who you are—except maybe for Val; people don't forget nine-foot-tall redheaded giants."

"I'm not even seven feet tall," she said, putting both men to sleep with a pair of karate chops to the backs of their necks. "If I was nine feet, I'd own the universe."

"I can believe it," said Cole. He gestured to the two bodies. "How long will they be out?"

"A couple of hours," she replied. "And by the way, I've spent fifteen years on the Inner Frontier, and there's no Demon Jack Devereaux."

"I must have been mistaken," said Cole easily. "Now I think it's time for you four to go out and take care of the rest of Strahan's landing party." He knelt down and trussed his prisoner's hands and feet with glowing manacles. "Remember, the police will lend a hand if you need them."

"You're not coming with us?"

"I've got my own work to do," said Cole. "Report back when your mission's been accomplished. And don't kill anyone you don't have to kill."

"Our brig can only hold three or four of them, sir," said Chadwick.

"I've arranged for the city to provide them with accommodations in the local jail."

"Not if they think there will be reprisals from Genghis Khan," said Chadwick.

"There won't be," said Cole. "Now get going."

The four of them left, and Cole immediately contacted the *Teddy R*.

"Yes, sir?" said Malcolm Briggs.

"Where's Christine?" asked Cole.

"Her shift ended, sir," said Briggs. "I believe she's in the mess hall."

"Patch me through to her."

A moment later he was facing Christine Mboya's image.

"What can I do for you, sir?" she asked.

"I'm going to transmit some captured audio to you," said Cole. "I want you to edit it as follows."

He spent the next five minutes telling her what he wanted.

"I'm sure I can do that, sir."

"It's got to sound natural, and pass a voice ID test."

"That shouldn't be a problem, sir."

"Okay," said Cole. "After you send it back down, I want you to supply me with codes that will enable me to choose each sentence in the order I want it, based on what is said at the other end."

"That will be the easiest part of all."

"Good. If I was paying you anything to start with, I'd give you a raise."

"Thank you, sir. I think."

He had her transfer him back to the bridge and uploaded the captured audio of everything Strahan had said, then broke the connection, went to the executive restaurant on the top floor for a sandwich and a beer, and returned to the office.

He wasn't worried about his team. He wouldn't be surprised if Val alone could take out all thirteen of the enemy, and he had total confidence in the other three as well, plus Domak if they needed her (and he was sure they wouldn't need her *or* the police). He found himself idly wishing that some of the modern weapons made a loud bang like the pistols of old, so he could try to follow the battle by the number of gunshots and the direction they were coming from, but though he ordered the windows to remain open not a sound came to his ears.

Then, almost an hour after they left, Luthor Chadwick returned alone.

"How did it go?" asked Cole.

"We killed four and captured nine, sir," said Chadwick. "Val and

Bull are escorting the captives to jail, and they've had Domak tell the hospital to transfer the ones Val put there to jail as soon as they're healthy enough."

"What about Jack-in-the-Box?"

"He took a pulse burst to his leg, sir," said Chadwick. "He's at the hospital, though I don't know if they have any experts in Mollutei physiology."

"How bad did it look?"

"I don't think he'll keep the leg, sir."

"All right. Tell the hospital to bill the *Teddy R* for his treatment and his new leg."

"The *Teddy R*, not the Apollo Cartel?" asked Chadwick.

"The *Teddy R* takes care of its own. And it'll come to the same thing, once we collect from the Cartel."

"*Will* we collect, sir? I know we took care of the landing party, but the planet's no safer and we're no closer to Genghis Khan than we were a week ago."

"That's true," said Cole. "Temporarily."

"Temporarily, sir?"

"Ask me again in an hour. In the meantime, contact the jail and tell them to collect these two," he concluded, indicating the manacled Strahan and his companion, who were still lying unconscious on the floor.

Val and Pampas showed up a few minutes later, and Cole listened as they gave their accounts of the battle.

"Okay," said Cole. "The bad guys are dead or jailed, and the hospital's doing what it can for Jack-in-the-Box. I suppose it's time to get to work."

"I thought that was what we just finished doing," said Val.

"You were doing a preliminary exercise," replied Cole. "Christine has been preparing the next phase."

"Christine?" said Val, surprised. "Is she down here?"

Cole shook his head. "No. She's at her station on the *Teddy R*, doing what she does best." He contacted the ship, and Christine's image appeared. "All set?"

"Yes," she replied. "I've just downloaded everything to your computer. The first thing you'll see are the identifying codes you asked for."

"Thanks," said Cole. He broke the connection and brought up the codes on a holographic screen, each attached to a read-out of the sentences he wanted.

"What's all this?" asked Val.

"This is everything Strahan said," answered Cole. "Though not quite in the order he said it."

"So *that's* why you kept him talking!" said Pampas. "You recorded him and rearranged all his words!"

"Christine rearranged them. They'd spot it in two seconds if I'd done it. I don't have her skills." He stared at the codes. "Okay, let's try it out."

He sent a signal to the *South Star*.

"Identify yourself," said a voice.

"This is Blackbeard," said Strahan's voice.

"I can't see your image, sir."

"Check my voiceprint."

"The computer confirms that it's you, sir. I assume the battle's over?"

"There was no battle," said Strahan's voice. "We've become allies."

"Allies?"

"I'm going to bring them to the *South Star* as a show of good faith."

"Then you don't want us to destroy the city?"

"Leave the city alone."

"Yes, sir. Will we be staying here awaiting further orders or returning to home base?"

"We're going to get the hell back to home base," said Strahan's voice.

"How soon shall we expect you, sir?"

"In ten minutes' time."

"We'll be ready, sir," promised the voice, and then the connection was broken.

"Do you think it worked?" asked Pampas.

"They know he's on the planet," said Cole. "They can match his voiceprint. They know he's just fought a pitched battle, so they should be able to buy that he can only transmit his voice and not his image. They can assume that mercenaries would sooner join up with Khan than fight him. Yeah, I think it'll work." He walked to the door. "We'll know in nine minutes. Let's go."

The shuttle encountered no opposition as it reached the bay of the *South Star*. As the hatch slid open, Val strode out and aimed her burner directly at the Lodinite who had come down to receive them.

"What's going on here?" demanded the Lodinite as his T-pack took all the emotion out of his tone while translating it into Terran.

Cole emerged from the shuttle and confronted the Lodinite. "Keep quiet and there's an excellent chance that you'll live through this. Do you understand?"

The Lodinite made a gesture with his head that Cole took for an affirmative.

"Bull, take his weapons away from him."

Pampas disarmed the alien.

"Now, to coin a phrase," said Cole, "take us to your leader."

The Lodinite led them to an airlift.

Cole stopped and stared at the airlift. "Have you got any stairs?" he asked.

"Yes, but the airlift is faster."

"I lost all faith in these things a few months ago," replied Cole, recalling how he had tricked a pirate named Windsail into entering one of the *Teddy R*'s airlifts and then cut off the oxygen and gravity.

"This way," said the Lodinite.

They followed him up the narrow, winding stairs, then burst onto the bridge, weapons at the ready, surprising the eight men and aliens who were on duty there.

"Nobody moves, nobody gets hurt!" said Cole as Pampas, Val, and Chadwick spread out.

"Who the hell are you?" demanded the captain.

"We're the people who are going to put your boss out of business," said Cole.

"The four of you?" said the captain, arching an eyebrow in obvious amusement.

"We're very ambitious," said Cole.

"Being very lucky would serve you even better," remarked the captain, showing no sign of fear. "Genghis Khan is not known as a forgiving man."

"He'll have to learn to live with his inadequacies," said Cole. "Bull, you and Luthor get their weapons. Val, kill anyone who resists."

"Why don't we just kill them all anyway?" she asked.

"You must have had a very embittered childhood," said Cole. "We're not killing them because we're civilized men and woman—and more to the point, now that we own two ships, we need some more crew members."

"*Them?*" she said contemptuously. "They're just common thugs."

"And I'm a common mutineer, and you were a common pirate, and the two Men and the Pepon we picked up on Cyrano were just common murderers. We're mercenaries, not pacifists."

Val snorted in amusement. "That sounds like something *I'd* say."

"What inducement can you offer us to join you?" asked the captain.

"The very best," said Cole. "If you don't, we're going to load the lot of you into your shuttle and program it to take you down to Bannister II, where they will immediately put you in jail and prosecutors will be lined up around the planet to make sure you never get out. Do you doubt that?"

There was no answer.

"You have only one alternative," continued Cole. "Swear your allegiance to me, and most of you will be transferred to the *Theodore Roosevelt*, where you will join my crew. I should tell you up front that, regardless of our differences with the Republic and its Navy, we are a military vessel and we demand military discipline. The choice is yours. I'll give each of you five minutes to make it."

"You say *most* of us will be transferred," said the captain. "What about the rest of us?"

"The rest will stay right here. This beautiful lady, whose name is Val until she decides to change it again, will be your captain, and she'll need a few crew members who are familiar with the ship." He paused. "You've probably figured it out already, but your first action will be to attack the remainder of Genghis Khan's fleet."

"I've got no love for Khan," said the captain. "But he pays me well. How much will *you* pay me?"

"Considerably less," said Cole.

"That's not much of an incentive."

"I'm being as honest as I can," said Cole. "And your choices are still the same."

Val had been walking around the bridge, surveying the computer and weapons stations. "It'll do," she announced. "It's not the *Pegasus*"—her lost ship—"but it'll do."

"It had damned well better do," said Cole. "We need it. I'll loan you Christine and Briggs long enough for them to find all the hidden codes and messages, but once we know where Khan is, the *South Star* is going to lead the attack, since you'll be able to approach him with impunity."

"I'll need more than this warmed-over batch of losers," said Val.

Cole smiled at the ship's crew. "She's so tactful," he said.

"I'm serious, Wilson," she continued. "I'll take two or three of them, but this ship needs at least twenty crew members, probably more, and I'd rather have twenty who didn't surrender without a shot being fired." She paused for a moment, considering her options. "I want Forrice."

Cole shook his head. "You can't have him. He's my First Officer. If we're a fleet of two, the *Teddy R* is our flagship, and if anything happens to me, he's got to be there to take it over."

"I assume I can't have Christine or Slick, either?"

"No."

"Then give me Bull and Luthor."

Cole looked at the two men and seemed to consider it.

"Damn it, Wilson! You've got to give me *someone* I can trust, and they're here already."

"You heard the lady," said Cole. "Do either of you have any objections?"

"No, sir," said Pampas.

"Neither do I, sir," chimed in Chadwick.

"Okay," said Cole. "When I choose some more of the *Teddy R*'s crew to send over, I'll have them bring your gear."

"And mine," said Val.

Cole turned back to the *South Star*'s crew members. "Your five minutes are up."

To nobody's surprise, each of them volunteered to serve aboard the *Teddy R* or the *South Star*.

"How many more people are on the ship?" asked Cole.

The captain smiled. "I was wondering when you'd think of that."

"I thought of that the second we reached the bridge," said Cole. "The door to the stairs is locked, and I've had one of my weapons trained on the airlift."

"Good," said the captain.

"Good?" repeated Cole curiously.

"If I'm going to serve with you, it's nice to know that you're not a fool." He reached out a hand. "My name is Perez."

Cole took the man's hand and shook it. "Got a first name?"

Perez shook his head. "Left it behind in the Republic, along with my officer's commission."

"You were in the Space Service?"

"Second Officer aboard the *Sophocles*."

"The *Sophocles*?" repeated Cole. "Didn't we—?"

"Save our asses when the Teronis had us englobed?" said Perez. "Yes, you did, Commander Cole."

"It's Captain Cole these days. What the hell are you doing here on the Frontier?"

"Pretty much the same as you," said Perez. "Only I didn't have the luxury of taking my ship and crew with me. I killed an officer who was torturing a Canphorite prisoner for the sheer hell of it, and I had to leave in a hurry. Captain Bienvenuti looked the other way while I borrowed a shuttle. He was a good man."

"What were you doing with scum like that bearded thug you sent down to the planet?" asked Cole.

"This is the Frontier," answered Perez. "You take what you can get." He paused. "Probably you'll say no, but until I can get another ship of my own I'd like to volunteer to stay on the *South Star*. I know her better than anyone else."

"The *South Star* is Val's ship," answered Cole. "It's up to her."

"He can stay," said Val.

"I won't try to take it back," said Perez. "At least, not without warning."

"Best life insurance you could have," said Cole. "You really don't want to make that redhead mad at you. Now suppose you tell the rest of your crew what their options are."

"All right," said Perez. He walked to the airlift. "I'd better do it in person," he added. "They might not trust a holo projection."

"By the way, what's the breakdown?" asked Cole.

"Nine Men—six males and three females—plus four Lodinites, a Mollutei, and a pair of Molarians."

"Are the Molarians females?" asked Cole. "We may have to keep them under lock and key."

"Males."

"Okay, go talk to your crew. Luthor, use the ship's radio to contact Four Eyes and tell him to bring the *Teddy R* over here, that we're going to be making some personnel changes."

"Yes, sir," said Chadwick. He spent a moment looking for the subspace transmitter, found it, and opened communications with the *Teddy R*.

"What's the least number you can run this ship with?" asked Cole.

"I want a full crew," said Val.

"I didn't ask what you wanted," replied Cole. "You'll get your crew. But right now the *South Star* is going to be the ship that attacks Khan, because once you know all the codes and protocols he'll let you approach him. I don't want to risk any more lives than we have to."

She looked around the bridge. "We don't have a pilot like Wxakgini, so I'll need a navigator, plus four gunnery officers and someone to work the ship's defenses. I need someone familiar with the computer and radio complex. I don't like traveling without an engineer, but if all we're doing is going back to the ship's home base and firing on Khan, I suppose we can do without one for the time being. I can't imagine a ship like this has much of an infirmary, and you still haven't got a medic on the *Teddy R* so I can't borrow one." She paused, considering all her needs and options. "I think it carries about forty at capacity. I can get by with eight, but I'd rather have a dozen. If they're going to be shooting at us, I want to make sure I have some backups."

"Okay, eight at the minimum, and I'll try to get you a few more."
He paused. "Do you trust this Perez?"

"He seems minimally more honorable than the men he sent down
to the planet," she replied. "Besides, he'd better be more concerned
about me than I am about him. In case you're not aware of it, I can take
care of myself."

"I've noticed," Cole responded dryly.

"Sir?" said Chadwick, looking up. "I just spoke to Commander
Forrice. He's sending Christine Mboya and Malcolm Briggs over on
one of the shuttles, which will then transport you and such crew members of the *South Star* who will be joining you back to the *Teddy R*. He
asks if you know yet who, if anyone, you're transferring here permanently, besides Val, Bull, and myself?"

"Not yet."

Chadwick returned his attention to the small holograph of Forrice
that floated before him.

"That name's got to go," said Val.

"What name?"

"The *South Star*," she replied. "It's so dull just saying it could put
you to sleep."

Cole shrugged. "It's your ship now. Call it whatever you want."

"The *Sphinx*," she said after a moment's consideration.

"You're the head of it, and you've got flaming red hair," said Cole.
"How about the *Red Sphinx*?"

"I *like* it," said Val. "I'll tell the crew, as soon as I decide who's *in*
the crew, and I'll have all the computers reprogrammed so that the
ship and radio respond to that name instead of"—she made a sour
face—"the *South Star*."

"Just remember that you're still the *South Star* when you approach
Khan, or this is going to be the shortest-lived sphinx on record."

Cole was sitting at his usual table in the *Teddy R*'s mess hall, sipping from a cup of coffee, when Sharon Blacksmith sat down opposite him.

"Are they all processed?" he asked her.

"Most of them should be okay, though I'd expect at least half to desert the moment they get shore leave," she reported. "You've got two, though, a Molarian and a human woman, who are what I would call borderline psychopaths."

"You're sure?"

She nodded. "I think you'd better ship them down to Bannister."

"I can't," said Cole. "I offered them a choice. I can't go back on my word."

"Wilson, trust me," said Sharon. "You *really* don't want these two on your ship."

"All right," he said. "We'll set them off on an oxygen world."

"There's one three light-years away—an agricultural planet called Greenbriar."

He shook his head. "If they're too dangerous to keep on board, I can't turn them loose in a farming community. Assign one of your men to watch them around the clock, until we come to a world with at least a rudimentary law enforcement agency."

"All right," she said. Then: "You know, we could give all the crew that came over from the *Red Sphinx* a mock medical scan, and then say that we found something suspicious or contagious in these two and that we're confining them to quarters until we reach a medical facility."

"And nobody else who has been living in confined quarters with them has it?" said Cole. "Nobody'll buy it."

She smiled at him. "Nobody *has* to. You're the Captain. Your word is law. If you tell them that *you* believe the findings and order them confined, then it doesn't matter what anyone else thinks."

"I'll consider it," said Cole, taking a sip of his coffee. "Run 'em through your phony test. We might as well get that done, no matter what I decide."

"When we're through talking," said Sharon, "I'll have Vladimir Sokolov join me in the infirmary and see what we can devise that looks legitimate. How's Val doing with the ones who stayed behind on her ship?"

"I spoke to her an hour ago, and everything seemed to be going smoothly. This Perez, the guy who captained it, seems pretty capable."

"Capable of taking it back?"

"From *her*?" he said.

"Silly question," said Sharon. "Forget I asked it."

"He was showing her how and where to access all the protocols when I spoke to her," remarked Cole. "It probably wouldn't hurt to see how she's coming along." He pressed a button on the table, and a small holograph of the bridge suddenly appeared. "Rachel?"

A pretty blonde woman stared at his image, which took shape in front of her. "Yes, Captain?" said Rachel Marcos.

"Patch me through to Val again."

The bridge instantly disappeared, to be replaced by Val's full-sized image.

"Do you have what you need yet?" asked Cole.

"Just about. Khan's got eight more ships, and they're all in the Cicero system."

Cole frowned. "The Cicero system?" he repeated. "I thought that was nothing but gas giants."

"That's right." Val smiled. "He figures it's the last place anyone would go looking for him."

"He was right, until a few minutes ago," said Cole. "I assume your weaponry is all functional?"

"Bull says one of the pulse cannons is useless, but everything else is working."

"Have you got enough ammunition for a pitched battle?"

"Yes."

"How soon are you ready to go?"

"As soon as I learn my crew's names," said Val.

"And how long will it take your ship to get to Cicero?" asked Cole.

She looked to her left, and he could hear Perez's voice say: "Maybe four days in normal space, about five hours through the Bannerman Wormhole."

"Thanks, Perez," said Cole. "How far from the system will you be when you emerge from the wormhole?"

"Maybe half a light-year. It's collapsing a few light-years further on, and spitting you out at the other end of the Inner Frontier, but our navigator thinks it's safe as far as the Cicero system."

"Will you have warning if he's wrong?"

"We should," said Perez. "Who the hell knows with wormholes?"

"That's why every ship should have a Bdxeni pilot," said Cole. "Contact ours and run your route past him."

"What's his name?"

Cole shrugged. "Ask someone who can pronounce it, or just call him Pilot."

"They're part of the Republic," replied Perez. "You don't find them out here very often, and when you do, you can't afford them anyway."

"I assume we're approaching Cicero alone?" said Val. "If the *Teddy R* is anywhere near me, he's likely to blow us both apart without asking any questions."

"I agree," said Cole. "Let me think for a minute."

"Take two minutes," said Perez's voice. "I'd like to live through this."

"All right," said Cole after a pause. "The *Teddy R* is going to head off to Cicero right now. We'll either go through normal space, or if Pilot can find us a wormhole—not the Bannerman—that will deposit us a few light-years beyond it we'll use that. But let's assume he can't, and that it'll take us four days to get there."

"Okay, I'm assuming it," said Val. "Now what?"

"Use the Bannerman Hole and show up there in four and a half days. You've got the ID codes and protocols, and you've got Perez if anyone needs visual confirmation of who's on the ship. Then, when you're close enough so there's no chance of missing, blow Khan and his ship to kingdom come."

"That'll be about sixty thousand miles," said Val. "Fifty, to be on the safe side."

"You're not going to offer him the same deal you offered me?" asked Perez.

"No," said Cole. "Kingpins don't settle for second place, and I don't know how loyal some of the men and ships are to him."

"So much for what you said on my ship about being a civilized man," remarked Perez.

"It's *my* ship!" snapped Val.

"True," admitted Perez. "But it was my ship when he said it."

"And to respond to your comment," said Cole, "there's a difference between being a civilized man and a civilized fool."

"What will you be doing while I'm taking Khan?" asked Val.

"Once you've disabled or destroyed his ship, I'll offer amnesty to any ship and crew that will join us—and the *Teddy R* will pick off any ship that tries to escape. They're going to have two options—join us or fight us. Running away is not a third option." He paused. "Perez?"

Perez's holograph appeared beside Val's. "Yes?"

"You know the ships, their captains, and their personnel. How many are likely to stand and fight?"

"Against the *South Star* . . . excuse me: the *Red Sphinx?* Most of them. Against the *Theodore Roosevelt*—maybe half. Some won't want to try matching firepower with a Republic warship, even an ancient one like yours, and some will simply want to serve with Wilson Cole after having taken orders from Genghis Khan."

"Anything you can say to them once we dispose of Khan will be appreciated," said Cole.

"I'll be honest," said Perez. "Most of us are in this for the money, and I'm sure they'll come to the same conclusion I came to: that we'll do much better serving under Wilson Cole that we would either under Khan or on our own. You have quite a reputation."

"Yeah," said Cole sardonically. "There are rewards for me on every world in the Republic."

"The very things that make you a fugitive in the Republic accrue to your benefit out here on the Frontier," replied Perez. He stared at Cole's face curiously for a moment. "There's just one thing I don't understand."

"What is it?"

"You haven't asked anything about Khan. Don't you want to know what he's like?"

"Not especially," said Cole. "No matter what you can tell me, he's not going to live long enough for me to use it."

"You know," said Perez, "you're polite and well mannered and reasonably soft-spoken, but you're one cold son of a bitch."

Val smiled. "Why do you think I agreed to serve with him?"

"The subject at hand is Khan's ships, not my personality," said Cole. "Shall we get back to it?"

"I think we've taken care of it," said Val. "Go back to your Security Chief. If there's anything else I need to know, I'll contact you."

She broke the connection, and Cole turned back to Sharon. "What do you think?" he asked.

"Of Perez? I didn't see and hear enough to tell. Of the mission? Khan will never know what hit him."

"*Am* I a cold son of a bitch?"

"Not between the covers," she said with a smile. "As for the rest of the time, it goes with being the Captain. And when was the last time you weren't facing an enemy who wanted to kill you—including certain select officers of the Republic's Navy?"

"It's been a while," he admitted.

"Half a lifetime?"

"More." He got to his feet. "I suppose I'd better go speak to Pilot and tell him where we're going."

"Then what?"

"Then we relax until we get there, and hope everyone involved is as smart as Perez and that we don't have to fire a shot."

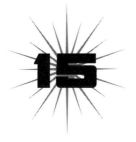

Usually battle plans that are months in the making and cover every conceivable detail tend to go wrong, so it was only just and fitting that Cole's plan, conceived in less than five minutes, ran like clockwork.

The *Red Sphinx* used the protocols it had been given by Khan's security officers, approached to within thirty thousand miles of his ship, and opened fire. Khan's ship was reduced to rubble in seconds.

Cole, who had spent four days training his new crew members (and dumping three of them who simply would not or could not follow orders onto an oxygen world), transmitted his message of amnesty to the *Red Sphinx* and had Val broadcast it to the eight remaining ships. Two tried to flee and the *Teddy R* shot them down, as it had threatened to do. Two more chose to fight, and the *Red Sphinx* and the *Teddy R* each accounted for one. The other four agreed to Cole's terms. He had each captain transferred to the *Teddy R*, where he explained what was expected (or, more accurately, demanded) of each, and then returned them to their ships.

Two days later Cole and his six ships docked at Singapore Station, where he hunted up the Platinum Duke, ready for bigger and more lucrative assignments.

"Remarkable!" commented the Platinum Duke. "Just remarkable! In truth, you should be paying the Apollo Cartel, not charging them. You went out a ship, and you came back a fleet!"

"Yeah," said Cole, somewhat less impressed. "Three hundred million more ships, and we can meet the Republic on even terms."

"You know," said Sharon as the waiter brought her a sizzling steak from the mutated cattle of Borimor III, "I could get into owning a casino."

"It's more trouble than it looks like from here," answered the Platinum Duke, sitting at his table with Cole, Sharon, David Copperfield, and Perez. "There are approximately seven hundred men and aliens in the building right this minute, and I guarantee that at least two hundred of them are trying to cheat the house."

"It's only fair," commented Perez. "The house has a ten percent edge."

"My dear man, the house has overhead," explained the Duke. "The players don't."

"I don't care about gambling," said Sharon. "All I know is the house has one hell of a chef."

"He doesn't belong to the house," said the Duke. "He's mine. And he only cooks for my friends."

"I didn't know I *was* your friend," said Sharon.

"You're sitting at my table. It would be rude to eat while you sat and watched." The Duke looked around. "Where is the remarkable Valkyrie? I have a couple of players who have been beating the house far too often this week. I'd like her to check them out."

"She's running our ships through their training exercises," said Cole. "Except for the *Teddy R*, which is restocking at one of the cargo docks right now. Also, we put out the word that we're looking for medics, and Sharon will check out the credentials of the four who showed up. Only two are human; I hope to hell one of them passes muster." He paused. "When the ship's ready to go in another day or two, Four Eyes will take over the training and Val can grab some shore leave while Perez here takes over the *Red Sphinx* for a while."

"That was *your* ship?" the Duke asked Perez.

"Yes."

"Don't you resent her commandeering it?"

"Fortunes of war," answered Perez. "I didn't have much choice in the matter—and Captain Cole has promised to find me a ship of my own." He turned to Cole. "Although I understand that with Val on her own ship there's an opening for a Third Officer aboard the *Theodore Roosevelt*."

"You'll be more use to us running your own ship," answered Cole.

"Let me guess," said the Duke. "You used to be in the Navy."

"A long time ago," said Perez.

"What happened?"

"I got out of the Navy."

"What a shame," said the Duke. "I was hoping that you were going to vilify Susan Garcia, and then you and I would split a bottle of my finest Cygnian cognac."

"Are you talking about Fleet Admiral Garcia?" asked Perez.

The Duke nodded. "Of course, I knew her when she was just a minor tyrant. I believe Mr. Cole has met her on a number of occasions as well."

"A few," said Cole.

"And?"

"I can't say we hit it off," replied Cole, "but she gave me some medals."

"'Some' medals," said the Platinum Duke in amused tones. "She gave you the Medal of Courage on three different occasions."

"Begrudgingly."

"Of course," said the Duke. "You made the Navy look bad."

"I served that Navy all of my adult life," said Cole. "I won't say anything against it."

"*I* will," offered Sharon. "They were more concerned with not looking incompetent than with winning the goddamned war. *That's* why they court-martialed him."

"And this surprised you?" asked the Duke with a smile.

"He saved five million Men," continued Sharon bitterly, "and got thrown in the brig for it. The captain he deposed, the one who was about to kill our own citizens, is still an active officer in the Navy."

"Why do you think I left the Republic?" said the Duke with a smile.

"One word from Susan Garcia and we could be back fighting the *real* enemy," continued Sharon.

"Poor deluded child," said the Duke. "The Republic *is* the real enemy. Hell, the Teroni Federation has never done me any harm; I can't say the same for the Republic."

"Neither can I, come to think of it," put in Perez.

"Complaining isn't going to help," said Cole. "The Republic's got a war to fight. They can't waste their time worrying about us. We're never going back, so you might as well change the subject."

There was a momentary silence, which was broken by David Copperfield.

"That steak smells exquisite," he commented.

"Would you like one?" asked the Duke.

"Alas, I am on a diet," said Copperfield.

"Can't metabolize it, eh?"

"I have never denied my limitations," said Copperfield with all the dignity he could muster, "but it is extremely ungracious of you to refer to them."

"If you can't eat it, you can't eat it," said the Duke. "It's no big deal. Just tell me what you'd like and I'll have my chef prepare it."

"I'd *like* a steak," said Copperfield unhappily. "I will settle for an Alphard brandy."

"I could have sworn I saw you eating a steak aboard the *Teddy R*," remarked Sharon.

"Soya products, made to look like a steak," said Cole.

"You knew all along?" said Copperfield, surprised.

"It's my job to know everything about my crew."

"But I'm not your crew," replied Copperfield. "I'm your old school chum and your business manager."

"You're all of that," agreed Cole. "But when you're on my ship, you're also my crew."

"All right," said Copperfield. "I can accept that."

"I can't tell you how relieved I am."

"Now, now, Steerforth," said Copperfield. "Sarcasm is unbecoming in a well-bred Englishman."

"The mind boggles with replies," said Cole. "In the interest of peace, I'll keep them all to myself."

Suddenly Cole's communicator came to life.

"He's gone again, sir," said Idena Mueller, who was sitting at the bridge's computer console.

"Four Eyes?"

"Yes, sir."

"To the Molarian whorehouse?"

"I believe so, sir."

"Well, what the hell," said Cole, "it could be years before he finds another receptive Molarian. Let's cut him a little slack."

"But he's in charge of red shift, and it starts in another forty minutes."

"He'll be back in time," said Cole.

"What if he's not?"

"I've known him for twenty years, Lieutenant," said Cole. "He'll be back."

He broke the communication.

"Your Molarian contingent is making me rich," remarked the Platinum Duke.

"They've got nothing else to spend it on," said Cole. "You own the whorehouse, I presume?"

"Not exactly," replied the Duke. "I told you: I run Singapore Station. In practical terms, it means I get a little percentage of almost every business in lieu of rent."

Suddenly David Copperfield stood up. "If you will excuse me, I believe I see an old friend across the room. I really must go over and say hello to him."

"He owes you that much?" asked Cole with a smile.

"I do not recall the immortal Charles endowing you with a sense of humor," replied David with dignity. "Therefore, I will assume that remark is not funny, but merely in poor taste." He bowed to Sharon, and then began walking through the Men and aliens that were crowded around the gaming tables.

"What's with him?" asked Perez. "He's an alien, he dresses like a Victorian dandy from three thousand years ago, he thinks he's a Dickens character and that you're another . . ."

"He was the biggest fence on the Inner Frontier," explained Cole. "He fell in love with the works of Charles Dickens, to the point where he dresses like he does, calls himself David Copperfield, and was living in a Victorian mansion when I first met him. In fact, the easiest way to gain entrance to his house was to introduce myself as Steerforth, David Copperfield's friend at school. He risked his life and his business to help us. He kept his life, but he lost the business."

"His collection takes up three cabins aboard the ship," added Sharon.

"Collection?" asked Perez.

"Of Dickens books," she said. "Thousands of editions and translations."

"Interesting character," said Perez. "I think I'm going to like working for you guys. I heard of Val when she was calling herself the Queen of Sheba. She was one hell of a pirate. How did you ever convince her to join you?"

"A confluence of circumstances," replied Cole. "I'm sure she'll tell you all about it, putting a properly heroic spin on the events."

"Right," added Sharon. "It wouldn't do for people to know that the Hammerhead Shark stole her ship while she was sleeping off a drunk. We helped her get it back."

"Then why—?"

"It was disabled in the process," said Cole.

"So was the Shark," added Sharon.

David Copperfield made his way back to the table and seated himself.

"That was a short visit," commented Cole.

"But, I hope, a fruitful one," said Copperfield.

"Let me guess: he has a leatherbound copy of *Bleak House* for sale."

"Don't be facetious, Steerforth," said Copperfield. "Besides, if he did, do you think I'd have returned here without it?" He paused. "What do you know of New Calcutta?"

"Never heard of it," said Cole.

"I have," put in Perez. "About four hundred light-years from here, in the direction of the Core."

"The very place," said Copperfield. "Oxygen world, ninety-seven percent Standard gravity."

"Okay, it's an oxygen world toward the Core," said Cole. "So what?"

"Bear with me, my dear Steerforth," said Copperfield. "After all, did the sainted Charles ever reveal the entire plot on page one?"

"The sainted Charles was getting paid by the word," said Cole. "You're not. Now, what about New Calcutta?"

"There is a dealer in merchandise of questionable ownership . . ."

"A fence."

"A fence," agreed Copperfield. "I knew him in my former life."

"Your former life?" interrupted Perez, frowning.

"He means, when he was a fence himself," said Sharon.

"Precisely," said Copperfield. "Anyway, New Calcutta is ruled by Thuggees . . ."

"Hold it right there," said Cole. "There hasn't been a Thuggee in close to three millennia. I don't mind you being David Copperfield if it makes you happy, but don't go inventing whole planets from Kipling."

"Oh, it exists all right," Copperfield assured him. "So do the Thuggees. They're not humans, of course, and they do not practice the obscene secret rituals of the original Thuggees, at least so far as I know. They are an alien race, once known as the Drinn, who took the name of Thuggee when they found out what New Calcutta was named for. They found that calling themselves Thuggees brought them instant respect from Men."

"Let me guess," said Cole. "Your friend the fence is languishing in the Black Hole."

"I have no idea what color hole it is, but the poor man has done something to offend the Thuggees and they have incarcerated him. He would surely trade his kingdom for a horse, and failing that would doubtless pay half his kingdom to be rescued." He learned forward. "Steerforth, he's worth almost twenty million credits!"

"Hold on a minute, David," said Cole. "We may have six ships instead of one, but we're not strong enough to take on a whole planet."

"I'm not suggesting that you attack it," said Copperfield. "If you go in with guns blazing, either the Thuggees will kill you or you'll inadvertently kill Quinta."

"That's the fence?"

"Yes."

"All right," said Cole. "Have you ever been to New Calcutta?"

"A few times," answered Copperfield. "A very pleasant world, except for the climate and the dust and the insects and the diseases and the Thuggees."

"I'm sure it's a fair-sized planet, and we'll be looking for one particular jail cell," said Cole. "If we decide to undertake this job, we're going to need a guide. Do you think you can lead us to where they're keeping him?"

"I'm afraid not," said Copperfield.

"I thought you said you've been there."

"I have."

"Well, then?" demanded Cole.

"The last time I was there I had to leave in rather a hurry," said Copperfield uncomfortably. "They've actually had the audacity to put a price on my head."

"*I've* been there," said the Platinum Duke. "I won't go back again, but I can supply you with a map of the place, including their major city, which is where they'll likely be keeping him."

"I assume you're not offering this out of the goodness of your heart," said Cole.

"One-sixth," said the Duke.

"That seems a lot for just for a map."

"Okay," said the Duke. "Find it without a map, and good luck to you."

"One-sixth," said Cole, reaching out and shaking the Duke's metal hand.

"You're really going to pay it?" asked Sharon, surprised.

"There are two million Thuggees on the planet," replied Cole. "Without some notion of where they're holding Quinta, what do you think the odds are of breaking him out? Besides," he added, "the Duke's cut is coming out of the half we leave to Quinta, not our half."

"Bravo!" said Copperfield. "You're thinking more like a mercenary each day!"

"David," said Cole, "go tell your friend that if we agree to do it, it's going to cost the fence five-sixths of whatever he's got."

"It's not up to him," answered Copperfield. "He just told me, friend to friend, that Quinta has been incarcerated. He's not Quinta's agent. It's up to Quinta, and considering the alternative, I'm sure he would agree now."

"Even if he disagrees after we break him out," predicted Sharon dryly.

"All right," said Cole. "We'll put Christine, Briggs, and Domak to work finding out what they can about the planet and the Thuggees, and then make a decision.

"You'll go," said Copperfield.

"What makes you think so?"

"I can tell by the look on your face. You're thinking of all that money."

"No, my old school chum," said Cole. "I am thinking of all those empty Thuggee ships."

Since rescuing Quinta was clearly going to be a covert operation requiring a landing party rather than massive firepower from space, Cole decided to take just the *Teddy R* to Calcutta, and leave the five new ships at Singapore Station to have their weaponry and defensive capabilities upgraded. He transferred Val and Bull Pampas temporarily to the *Teddy R*, and left Perez in charge of the other ships with instructions to take them out and test their new capabilities when the re-outfitting was accomplished. Then the *Teddy R* set off for Calcutta.

The planet was a real piece of work. The humanoid natives had allowed Men to colonize it just long enough to learn their language, learn how to read their books and computers, and learn how to use their weapons. Then they slaughtered the entire colony.

That had been four hundred years ago. Somewhere along the way they decided they could frighten Man off and stop them from recolonizing by calling the world Calcutta and themselves Thuggees, though no one knew quite what they had against Men. As it turned out, whatever it was, it extended to Canphorites, Setts, Domarians, Lodinites, and half a dozen other races, all of whom were promptly set upon and slaughtered when they landed.

The Thuggees had no dreams of conquest in terms of their solar system or the galaxy at large, but there were five continents on Calcutta, and the government of each was constantly at war with the other four. It was then that they decided that trading with beings whose weaponry had improved over the past four centuries might help them conquer their enemies, and so each country allowed one or two traders—or, in the case of David Copperfield's friend, fences who temporarily functioned as traders—to land long enough to deliver newer and deadlier weapons. The planet didn't have much of value to outsiders, but it was home to a type of mollusk that produced a geometrically perfect sixteen-sided pearl-like growth that was much sought after by the jewelers of the Republic and the Inner Frontier.

"And that's it, sir," said Briggs as he concluded his brief history of Calcutta. "Since they've been closed to trade and immigration for more than four hundred years, we know almost nothing about how their society has evolved, or even about the current political situation, other than that there are five large nations, they don't like each other very much, and they like intruders even less." He paused. "We don't even know if they speak or understand Terran."

"They did once," noted Val.

"Yes, but languages change and evolve. Even if they comprehend Terran, it might be a very archaic form of it. Or they might not understand it at all. After all, there hasn't been a colonist there in four centuries."

"What about David's fence?"

"He's not human," said Copperfield. "Humanoid, yes, but human, no. He's a Thrale: the right number of arms and legs and such."

"Is that what *you* are?" asked Briggs.

David Copperfield drew himself up to his full, if unimpressive, height. "I, sir, am a British gentleman," he said haughtily.

"What David is or isn't is not at issue here," said Cole. "What we need to know, first of all, is where the particular Black Hole we're looking for is located. I don't suppose the Platinum Duke supplied that little tidbit of information." He turned to Copperfield. "Did your friend give you any hint whatsoever?"

"I never spoke to him directly," answered Copperfield. "You know that."

"Well, we're sure as hell not going to invade five warring nations looking blindly for him," said Cole. "In case it's slipped anyone's notice, we *still* don't have a goddamned doctor on board."

"I thought we had a number of candidates, sir," said Briggs.

"Four," answered Cole. "But none of them were knowledgeable in all three of the main races we have on board, and we can't carry three medics." He turned to Copperfield. "What kind of weaponry would your friend have been trading or selling?"

"I don't know," said Copperfield. "As I keep reminding you, I never spoke to him."

"Can you find out?"

"Whatever it is, it probably can't harm us," offered Forrice. "Not if he didn't need half a dozen ships to deliver the components."

"We're not worried about being shot down," answered Cole. "We're worried about finding David's friend. And since no one's going to tell us where he is, we're going to try to buy a little help. Now, since they never leave their planet and they don't belong to any federation of like-minded worlds, they obviously mint their own currency, always assuming they use currency at all, and it's pretty clear that neither credits, Maria Theresa dollars, Far London pounds, or any of the other common currencies will interest them. Since the only reason they let traders touch down on Calcutta is to buy or trade for weapons, we need to offer some weapons in exchange for information—and we don't want to offer anything more powerful than what they're already got."

"That could still be some mighty powerful firepower," said Briggs.

"We'll rig them to go bad in a week's time," replied Cole. "They could be decades getting spare parts, once they find out what's wrong." He turned to Copperfield. "David, can you contact anyone who works for your friend and find out what kind of weaponry he was selling?"

"Yes, Steerforth," said Copperfield. "I shall do so immediately." He walked over to the subspace radio and began sending a message.

"Mr. Briggs, Lieutenant Domak, do either of you know which of the five nations is the most dominant at this moment?"

"Punjab," said Domak promptly, pointing to the continent on a holographic map.

"Why the hell do they name themselves and their countries after a race they won't allow on the planet?" mused Val.

"That's a question for an alien sociologist," said Cole. "We're mercenaries. Our question is: Which of the other four nations is holding David's friend?"

"Why not Punjab?" asked Val.

"Which side do you think would pay more for your weapons—a nation that needs them to become dominant, or a nation that would merely like to have them?"

"You'd better be right," said Val dubiously.

"If I'm not, then Four Eyes can mount a rescue party to save me *and* David's pal."

Sharon's image popped into view. "You're not going anywhere!" she said.

"Another party heard from," said Cole. "I appreciate your concern, but I'm going down with the rescue party, which will consist of me, Val, Lieutenants Sokolov and Mueller, and crewmen Nichols, Moyer, Braxite, and Bujandi."

"This is enemy territory," persisted Sharon. "The Captain doesn't leave his ship in enemy territory."

"Besides, you've already chosen your landing party," noted Forrice.

"I selected them to come *with* me, not to go *for* me," responded Cole.

"Almost every member of the *Teddy R* willingly gave up his career and made a commitment to spend his life as a hunted criminal on the

Inner Frontier in order to continue serving with you," said Forrice. "You have no right to endanger yourself over some fence we know next to nothing about."

"I'd like to volunteer to go in your place, sir," said Rachel Marcos.

"Ensign Marcos, are you twenty years old yet?" demanded Cole.

"I'm twenty-two, sir."

"And have you ever seen any action?"

"Certainly, sir."

"Other than on the bridge?"

She paused.

"The truth," said Cole.

"No, sir."

He turned to Sharon's image. "You see?"

"I have the records of every member of the crew," said Sharon. "Would you like to know how many of them *have* seen action against the enemy?"

"You know she's right, Wilson," said Forrice. "We're in the mercenary business, not the hero business. Your place is aboard the *Teddy R*, overseeing the operation, not risking your neck like some foot soldier."

"Val's got her own ship too," said Cole irritably. "I notice you're not demanding that she stay aboard it."

"Tell me that you can't see any difference between your physical abilities and hers, and I'll insist that she stay behind too," said the Molarian.

"Shut up," said Cole. He looked over the bridge personnel. "All right, Rachel," he said. "Go get blooded."

"Thank you, sir," she replied.

"We still need to know where to land, sir," Briggs pointed out.

"We'll start by contacting the party that's most likely to help us."

"Who would that be?" asked Briggs.

"Some higher-up on Punjab," said Cole. "It's the least likely nation for David's friend to have traded with—or at any rate the least likely to pay the highest price, since they're already the dominant power here—and once they find out he's trading weapons to their enemies, they should be willing to tell us where he is."

"*They're* going to want weapons, too," said Forrice. "I can have Mr. Odom begin rigging some to go bad in a week."

Cole nodded his approval. "Okay, but first we'll try it without offering anything. We have to leave ourselves a little negotiating room."

"Just a minute," said Sharon. "Why the hell will Punjab care if the fence is in jail on some other continent? Isn't that better than setting him free so he can trade with them again?"

"They won't," said Cole. "Until we sweeten the pot."

"Just by offering weapons?"

Cole smiled. "That's just the first step, to get them listening."

"And what's your ace in the hole?" asked Sharon.

"Once we pinpoint the jail where he's incarcerated and break into it, we don't just set the fence free," explained Cole. "We empty out the whole damned prison, give them arms, and point them toward their keepers. *That* should cause enough havoc for Punjab to jump at the deal."

"What if they don't think Val and the others can pull it off?" asked Forrice.

"Then it'll mean that they've picked up some weapons for nothing, and the guy who was arming their enemy is still in jail," answered Cole. "From their point of view, it's a no-lose situation."

"You see?" said Forrice, emitting a hoot of laughter. "*That's* why we need you on the ship! No one else has such a fiendishly devious mind."

"I may be the one to think of the plan," said Cole, "but Val and her team are going to have to carry it out in an enemy city with almost no help from us. This rescue isn't accomplished yet, not by a long shot."

"Don't you worry about *us*," said Val firmly. "Save your sympathy for anyone who tries to stop us. And you, Blondie"—she gestured toward Rachel—"just make sure you stay close by me when the fighting starts."

David Copperfield returned from the subspace radio desk. "I've got the information you need, Steerforth," he announced. "Quinta was selling them Level 3 thumpers."

"All right," said Cole. "No Level 3 pulse cannon is going to get through the *Teddy R*'s defenses, so the ship's in no danger. Four Eyes, have Mr. Odom rig a couple of Level 4 burners to permanently lose power a week from when we activate the batteries. Tell him not to just drain the batteries, but to make sure no one can charge them again."

"I'll take care of it."

"Are there any other questions before Christine and I start contacting the Thuggees?"

Silence.

"All right," said Cole. "Before you return to your duties, I want to say that I'm not unmoved by your desire to protect your Captain from harm. I will overlook the fact that my First Officer and my Security Chief publicly disagreed with a command decision." He paused and stared at each of them in turn. "But if anyone ever argues with or disobeys an order once a military action has begun, that person is history."

It was common knowledge that Cole was closer to Forrice and Sharon than to anyone else on the ship, probably to anyone else in his life—yet only Val and David Copperfield, who had joined the *Teddy R* after it had reached the Inner Frontier, seemed at all surprised by his statement. And Val, for her part, strongly approved of it.

"David, you do the talking."

"Me?" said Copperfield, surprised.

"You've got a reputation as being one of the biggest fences on the Frontier," said Cole, "and given that Calcutta doesn't welcome visitors, they probably haven't heard that you've taken on a new profession as business agent for the *Teddy R*. They're more likely to listen to you than to a warship's captain."

"All right, Steerforth," said Copperfield. "I want you to know I wouldn't do this for anyone else."

"No one else on the ship would ask you," said Cole. "Christine will tell you when to start. If you're nervous, I'll have everyone else leave the bridge."

"I'm not nervous," replied Copperfield. "You've already convinced me that they can't harm the ship. I just don't know if they'll believe me."

"And if you don't contact them now, we still won't know an hour from now," said Cole.

Copperfield shrugged an alien shrug that began at his waist and simultaneously worked its way up to his shoulders and down to his ankles. "All right, I'm ready," he announced. Suddenly he held up a hand. "Everyone else can stay, but Olivia Twist must leave the bridge."

"I keep telling you—that's not my name," said Val. "And I'm staying."

"My dear lady," said Copperfield, "they probably don't know the name of Wilson Cole and they may not have heard of the *Theodore*

*Roosevelt*, but everyone on the Inner Frontier knows of the beautiful redheaded pirate, no matter which name you're using on any given day. I don't know the extent of their communication technology, but if they can scan the bridge, I think it would be detrimental to our cause if they see you."

"He's got a point," agreed Cole. "Go on down to the mess hall."

Val gave Copperfield a furious glare and stalked off to the airlift.

"Are there any other conditions, David," asked Cole, "or do you think we can get this show on the road?"

"I told you: I'm ready."

"Christine," said Cole, "you might as well put this on the broadest wavelength possible, since we don't know quite who we're going to be dealing with. Mr. Briggs, is there a way to make sure the other four continents can't read or receive it?"

"Probably, sir," said Briggs, uttering orders to his computer in what seemed to Cole to be an incomprehensible coded language that sounded vaguely like Atrian. A moment later Briggs nodded, and Christine signaled Copperfield to speak.

"My name is David Copperfield," he began, "and I have information that a good friend of mine, a Thrale named Quinta, is being held prisoner somewhere on Calcutta. I want to know where he is, and I am prepared to pay or trade very handsomely for that information."

Cole ran his finger across his throat, signaling Christine to break the transmission.

"That's all they need for now," he said. "Send it every two minutes until we get a response."

"Should I put the response through to you or to David?" asked Christine.

"Pinpoint the source, capture the message, break the connection, and play it for the whole ship," answered Cole. "We'll decide who answers it and what do to once we hear what they've got to say." He turned and headed to an airlift.

"Where are you going, sir?" asked Briggs.

"I'm off to grab a bite of lunch," said Cole. "I'm hungry, and they figure to spend a few hours fashioning a response. If I'm wrong and they reply immediately, just patch it through to the mess hall as well as the rest of the ship."

Val was sitting alone at a table when he arrived, and he joined her, quickly ordering a sandwich and a beer.

"Don't worry," she said. "I'll keep your little blonde girlfriend alive."

"She's not my girlfriend," replied Cole.

"She wants to be."

Cole grimaced. "I don't know what to say to twenty-two-year-olds."

"It's not talk she's after."

"She's doomed to be disappointed," said Cole. "Now drop the subject and start thinking about which shuttle you're going to take down to the planet. When the time comes, assemble the rescue party down in the shuttle bay."

"Right," she said. "And I want to take Bull Pampas, too."

"I've already chosen the landing party."

"Come on, Wilson," she continued. "After me he's the best freehand fighter we've got and you know it."

"Let me think about it."

"What the hell's the problem?"

"He's also one of our two best weapons experts," replied Cole. "I hope your party comes away clean, but if anything goes wrong I can replace a good freehand fighter a hell of a lot easier than I can replace a man who's spent the past four years working on the *Teddy R*'s weapons systems."

"First of all, nothing's going to go wrong if I'm in charge of the landing party," she said firmly. "Or do I look like cannon fodder to you?"

"No, you don't," said Cole. "But it's my job to consider every possibility."

"Second," she went on, "he's not a member of the *Teddy R* anymore. He's the Second Officer of the *Red Sphinx*, in case it's escaped your notice."

"And you're both aboard the *Teddy R*," said Cole. "You don't own him, Val. Any time I need him back for a week or a month, he'll come back."

"Damn it, Wilson!" she said furiously. "I trust him to protect my back!"

Cole stared at her for another long moment, then sighed. "All right. You can have him."

"Thanks," she said. "You won't regret it."

"I already regret it."

Christine's image suddenly appeared above the table. "Sir," she said, "I've just captured their response."

"That's very fast," noted Cole. "They must really be worried about what Quinta has been supplying the other Thuggee nations. Well, one other nation, anyway. Patch it through, Christine."

The holograph of a tall, incredibly slender alien, covered with glistening brown scales, suddenly appeared. He was humanoid in form, with two arms, two legs, and a bulbous head with wide-set oval eyes, two slits for nostrils, no discernible ears, and a broad mouth. He had three fingers and a pair of opposing thumbs on each hand, and was naked except for a sash around one shoulder that displayed an array of symbols that might or might not be military medals.

"My name is Rashid," he said in thickly accented Terran, "and I am authorized to speak on behalf of the Punjab. We know that the alien

Quinta has been supplying weapons to our enemies, and we know where he is currently incarcerated in durance vile. What we do not yet know is why we should have any dealings with you." He flashed them an alien smile of anticipation. "Perhaps you will enlighten us."

"That's it, sir," said Christine as the alien vanished. "There isn't any more."

"'In durance vile?" repeated Cole. "They must be reading the same books that David reads." He paused. "All right. Christine, transmit my image to the bridge." He waited until she had done so. "David, I want you to reply to them. Tell them we know that Quinta's been supplying their enemies with Level 2 thumpers—make that pulse guns; they may not know the slang for them—and Level 3 laser cannons, and that we're prepared to trade two Level 4 laser cannons for the information we want."

"What if they want more than two cannons, Steerforth?" asked Copperfield.

"We'll explain that these are a gesture of goodwill, and that if their information proves accurate, we're prepared to trade them a lot more."

"And if he asks—?"

"Don't worry about it," interrupted Cole. "We're going to capture this and send it, just the way we sent the first one. He won't be getting it in real time, and you won't be having a live dialogue with him." He paused. "Mr. Briggs?"

"Yes, sir?"

"We know they reply with some degree of haste, so be ready. I want the location of these transmissions pinpointed, and we're only going to receive two or three more."

"Yes, sir," said Briggs. "May I ask a question, sir?"

"Go ahead."

"Why do we care where the transmissions are coming from?" asked

Briggs. "I thought we were going on the assumption that Quinta is being held prisoner not by the citizens of Punjab, but on another continent."

"Because if they lie and try to set us up, we're going to leave one hell of a big hole in the ground where they used to be," answered Cole.

He nodded to Christine's image, and she ended the transmission.

"They're not going to set us up," said Val. "Not if they think the two cannons are just a down payment and that there's more coming."

"Probably not," agreed Cole. "But they're aliens, and they think like aliens, which is to say that if they're not Molarians I have no idea how they think. They might think that two Level 4 burners will keep them dominant for a decade or more, and not want to be bothered by any more visitors."

"Ain't going to happen," replied Val.

"I agree," said Cole. "But I still have to consider the possibility."

"Forrice is right," said Val. "You *are* a devious son of a bitch. That's why I decided to stay with the *Teddy R.* I've got to learn to start thinking like that!"

"Take it easy in the beginning," said Cole dryly. "It'll make your head hurt."

"Thanks," she said angrily. "I compliment you and you insult me."

"It wasn't an insult," explained Cole. "I meant it. I joined the service to beat the Bad Guys. It's been a few years now since I even knew who the Bad Guys were. And now I've got the crews of six ships living or dying based on my decisions. You don't think all of that can give you a headache?"

"I don't know why it should," said Val. "I never gave a damn what happened to my crew."

"That's probably why they sold you out and joined the Hammerhead Shark."

"All right, all right!" she said in exasperation. "You win!"

"I don't care about winning with you," said Cole, getting to his feet. "My job right now is to win against the Thuggees. And since I need to be at my sharpest to do so, I'm going to take a nap."

When he got to his cabin he went right to his bunk, lay down, and was asleep within a minute. It was Sharon's voice that woke him an hour later.

"Yeah?" he said, swinging his feet to the floor. "What is it?"

"There's a transmission coming in from the planet," she said. "I figured you'd want to be wide awake when Domak patches it through to you."

"Domak? What happened to Christine?"

"White shift is over. We're been on blue shift for forty minutes."

"Right," said Cole. "Don't worry—my brain'll be functioning in another few seconds."

"I still don't know how you can sleep or eat at times like this."

"I learned a long time ago that you don't get much chance to do either once the shooting starts, so you grab your meals and your sleep when you can."

"Here it comes," said Sharon. "Talk to you later."

Her image vanished, to be replaced by Domak's.

"Are you awake, sir?" said the Polonoi officer.

"Yeah, patch it through."

The alien Rashid's image appeared in front of him. "We have the information you want, and we find your offer to be of some minimal interest. How can we ascertain that it is legitimate, and that the laser cannons are functional?"

The image vanished.

"That's the whole thing?" asked Cole.

"Yes, sir."

"Has Mr. Briggs pinpointed the source of the transmission?"

"Mr. Briggs's shift is over," replied Domak, "but Ensign Jacillios is working that station now and tells me that he has the exact coordinates should you require them."

"Not yet, but log them and have Four Eyes program them into one of the Level 4 burners, just in case. And tell David his job is done. I'll take over talking to them now."

"Yes, sir," said Domak, signing off.

"No sense bothering you now," said Sharon, her holograph appearing again. "You're off to the bridge."

"The hell I am."

"I just heard you say—"

"I don't have to be on the bridge to transmit a message," said Cole. "Besides, just because *they* appear eager doesn't mean *we* have to. Let 'em wait four or five hours."

"Well, as long as you're already on your bed, you want a little female company?"

"Sure," answered Cole. "Send Rachel Marcos over."

"Seven thousand, three hundred and six," said Sharon.

"What's that?"

"The number of nights you're going to be sleeping alone for that remark."

"Belay that request," said Cole, "and send me a woman of the older-but-wiser persuasion instead." He paused. "What does that do to the seven thousand days?"

"You've still got 'em," said Sharon.

"I do?"

"Yes," she said. "But they don't have to start for another century. I'll be there in five minutes. Fall asleep before then and you're a dead man."

It was three hours later that Cole got out of his bed and put on his uniform. Sharon was sleeping, but the rustling of his clothing woke her.

"Where are you going?" she asked.

"I'm off to talk to the King of the Thuggees, or whatever the hell he is," replied Cole. "I've decided it'll look more official from the bridge."

"Have fun," she said, rolling over and starting to go back to sleep.

"I just *had* fun," he said. "Now I've got important things to do."

"Gee, you really know how to flatter a girl."

Then he was out the door and walking to the airlift. A moment later he reached the bridge.

"Think we've made 'em sweat long enough?" he asked as he approached Forrice.

"I don't know. We could play a quick game of *bilsang* first."

"There's no such thing as a *quick* game of *bilsang*," answered Cole. "How long has it been since we received their last message?"

"Just over three Standard hours," said the Molarian.

"Yeah, I guess it's time," said Cole. He looked to see who was operating the communications console. "Mr. Briggs?"

Briggs looked up from his various computers. "Sir?"

"I want to send a communication to our friend Rashid," said Cole.

"Canned or live, sir?"

"Live, this time."

"Whenever you're ready, sir."

"Now's as good a time as any," answered Cole. He waited an extra few seconds until Jaxtaboxl nodded his massive head. "Rashid, this is Wilson Cole, Captain of the *Theodore Roosevelt*. We are ready to deliver your two laser cannons. This is a live transmission, so please respond. I have to know where to send them."

The Thuggee's image suddenly appeared a few feet away from Cole and Forrice.

"So you are through speaking to me through underlings," said Rashid.

"Spare me your petulance," said Cole. "Calcutta is a very minor planet, and the planetary wars that occur there are of no interest to me. I want my friend, but I'm not going to waste a lot of time bargaining for him. You have the information I want. I have the weapons you want. Now, are we trading, or do I go to Plan B?"

The Thuggee blinked his eyes rapidly, as if trying to comprehend. "What is Plan B?"

"Trust me: you won't like it at all," said Cole. "Do we have a deal?"

"Yes, we have a deal," said the Thuggee after a moment's hesitation.

"I will send a shuttlecraft down to the planet to deliver your laser cannons. You will feed the landing coordinates into my ship's computer. I will give you four Standard hours to check them out and make sure they are functional, at which time you will tell us exactly where the Thrale named Quinta is being incarcerated." He paused. "I would consider any abrogation of our agreement an act of war. I am ending the transmission from this end; give our computer the coordinates and then break the connection."

Briggs signaled to Cole that he was no longer sending words and images.

"Well, so much for playing the bully," said Cole. "Mr. Sokolov, as soon as we know where they want the cannons, put them on a shuttle and take them down to the surface. Take Lieutenant Domak with you; she's probably the most formidable-looking member of the crew."

"Yes, sir."

"And Vladimir?"

"Sir?" said Sokolov.

"Under no circumstance are you or Domak to set foot on the planet."

"That means the Thuggees will see the inside of the shuttle when they pick up the cannons," said Sokolov. "We've got a lot of advanced equipment in there—advanced as far as the Thuggees are concerned, anyway. Are you sure you want them to see it?"

"If things go as planned, they'll never see it again," said Cole. "But the one club I've got to hold over their heads to make them reveal Quinta's location to us is the fact that we can annihilate them from orbit. I lose that threat if they have you and Domak as hostages."

"That wouldn't stop a lot of commanders, sir."

"It wouldn't stop me either, if it was a matter of saving the ship and the crew, but it's not and they know it's not. Just make sure you stay on the shuttle. I want you to attach a micro-holocam to your shoulder. Once they approach the shuttle, start transmitting back to the ship. Don't mention that you're doing it; their holo transmitters probably don't look at all like ours, and there's no reason for them to know they're being monitored. Oh, and one more thing—don't stand within fifteen feet of each other. Got it?"

"Yes, sir," said Sokolov.

"Sir?" said Jaxtaboxl. "We've got the coordinates."

"Okay, Mr. Sokolov," said Cole. "Get to work. And before you leave, have Mr. Odom check them over and make sure you've loaded the right cannons."

"Yes, sir." Sokolov saluted and walked briskly to the airlift.

"Jack-in-the-Box," said Cole, "just how far is the landing site from their transmitting site?"

"About eighty miles," answered Jaxtaboxl.

Cole smiled a satisfied smile. "I guess I made an impression."

"Sir?"

"Tell him, Four Eyes."

"They don't know we've pinpointed their sending station," explained Forrice. "They also don't know that we're not about to demolish an entire city if they decide not to tell us where Quinta is being held. So they want the one location we *do* know—the spot where we deliver the cannons—to be a safe distance from where they're sending their transmissions to us."

"Ah!" said Jaxtaboxl happily. "I see now."

"How did *you* know it, sir?" asked Braxite.

"Fifteen years with the Captain will corrupt *anyone*," answered the Molarian.

"You're just mad because I took you away from your whorehouse," said Cole.

Forrice shrugged. "The last of them was going out of season anyway."

Sokolov's image popped into being. "They're loaded, sir, and Mr. Odom has confirmed they're the right ones."

"Okay," said Cole. He turned to Jaxtaboxl. "Is Domak with you?"

"She's already inside the shuttle."

"Then let's get this show on the road."

"Yes, sir."

The image vanished. "Jack, track them down to the planet. Four Eyes, let's go grab some coffee."

"I don't drink coffee."

"Fine. You watch me drink, and I'll try not to watch you drink that foul stuff you're so fond of."

"Sir?" said Jaxtaboxl.

"Yes?"

"It's still blue shift, and we still have no Third Officer. If there is a problem, who do I report it to?"

"Val's the Third Officer as long as she's on board the ship," said Cole. "Once she's joined the landing party, report to me, and if I'm not handy, report to Mr. Briggs."

Cole and Forrice went down to the mess hall and sat at Cole's regular table.

"Well," said Cole. "What do you think?"

"I think it's a far cry from fighting the Teroni Federation," replied the Molarian.

"You're just being moody because you're oversexed," said Cole. "What do you think of our chances of pulling David's friend out of durance vile?"

"We'll get him," said the Molarian. "After all, the Frontier desperately needs another fence."

"What's bothering you, Four Eyes?"

"Seriously?"

"Am I smiling?"

"We're too good for this, Wilson," said Forrice. "I know, I know, it's better than piracy, but we shouldn't be cleaning up the Frontier one villain at a time. And this time we're not even doing that; we're rescuing a fence so he can sell more illegal weapons to more outlaws that we'll eventually have to face. Doesn't that strike you as just a bit idiotic?"

"No more so than life," answered Cole. "The Navy demoted you because you refused an order to kill a helpless prisoner you knew to be a double agent. They incarcerated me for saving five million lives. Was life really more meaningful in the Republic than it is out here?"

"Not when you put it that way," admitted the Molarian. "But when we were in the Navy, we at least had the *illusion* that we were doing something meaningful, something that made a difference."

"Take a minute and consider our situation," said Cole. "The Teroni Federation tried to kill us. The Republic tried to humiliate and jail us. Out here Captain Windsail's pirate crew tried to kill us. The Hammerhead Shark tried to annihilate us. Genghis Khan would have killed us if he'd been able to. As far as I'm concerned, our primary responsibility is to the crew that gave up their homes and their families and their careers for us."

"I tell myself that every day," said Forrice. "And sometimes I even believe it. But never for long. You and I were the best the Navy had, Wilson. What are we doing out here fighting petty little warlords for money?"

"Do you really want to be part of a Navy that treats the best they have the way it treated you and me?" asked Cole.

"No," said Forrice.

"Well, then?"

"I want to be part of a *better* Navy!"

"And I want to be twenty-three years old with my whole future ahead of me and someone like Rachel waiting for me in my cabin," said Cole. "I think we're both doomed to be disappointed, so we'll make the best of what we've got."

"Do you expect to be doing this five years from now?"

Cole shrugged. "Who the hell knows anymore? Two years ago I didn't expect to be a pirate. Last year I didn't expect to be a mercenary. I've given up guessing what the future holds. I'm just taking it one day at a time."

"I know," said Forrice. "I just get depressed sometimes."

"That's because there's not two cents' difference between Men and

Molarians," said Cole. "At least, not in the things that count. You're the only other race with a sense of humor. Maybe you're the only other one that gets depressed, too."

"Probably," agreed Forrice.

"You've been my closest friend for a dozen years," said Cole. "I want you to feel free to talk to me any time you're feeling this way."

"I appreciate that."

"There's a corollary."

"I know," said the Molarian, his mouth twisted into an alien smile. "Don't talk to the crew about it."

"You got it."

There was a brief pause.

"Do we have any business to discuss?"

"Nothing we didn't have on our plates yesterday," said Forrice. "We still need a permanent Third Officer now that Val's got her own ship."

"When the right candidate comes along, we'll know it," said Cole. "Too bad she's keeping Perez with her. The man has qualities."

"You just like anyone who's on the run from the Navy," said Forrice.

"Can you think of a better qualification?" replied Cole wryly.

Forrice was about to answer when Jaxtaboxl's image appeared.

"Everything went smoothly, sir. The shuttle landed, the cannons have been offloaded, and Lieutenants Sokolov and Domak are on their way back to the ship."

"Good," said Cole. "Let me know when we have the location we need. It'll be coming sometime in the next four hours."

"And if it doesn't?"

"It will," said Cole with absolute certainty.

He was right. It took the Thuggees just over three Standard hours to field test the laser cannons. Then, satisfied, Rashid fed the location of the prison that was holding Quinta into the *Teddy R*'s computer.

"It's on a continent called Jaipur," announced Jaxtaboxl. "I've shown all the data to Val, who has selected the *Edith* to carry the landing party."

"Okay. See if you can piggyback some local computer and find out whatever you can about Jaipur. Four Eyes, make sure every member of the landing party stops by the armory and draws a burner, a screecher, and a pulse gun. Is it day or night where they're landing?"

"Twilight, sir," said Jaxtaboxl.

"Night-vision contacts for everyone," ordered Cole.

"We don't have any for Pepons," said Forrice.

"All right. Bujandi will just have to make do. Where's David?"

"In the officers' lounge."

"Patch me through." Cole raised his voice. "David, get over to the shuttle bay."

"Why?" asked David, seated on a chair in the tiny room.

"Because we don't know what Quinta looks like and you do."

"He's a Thrale."

"What if they have three Thrales in the damned prison?" said Cole.

"Then *ask* which one is Quinta."

"David, stop giving me a hard time and get your ass down to the bay."

"I can't, Steerforth!"

"I read the book too," said Cole. "Are you trying to tell me that David Copperfield was a coward?"

"He was a survivor!" said Copperfield.

"You'll survive. Just get down there."

"Your team are just mercenaries, doing a job," said Copperfield desperately. "The Thuggees know that. But I'm a fence—or at least I was. And we're here because of what they do to fences."

"Just tell them you're not a fence anymore."

"Why should they listen? I'll be the one who identifies Quinta."

Val's image appeared to the right of Copperfield's. "I've been listening," she said. "Let him stay. I don't want any cowards serving with me."

"I'm not serving at all!" shouted Copperfield. "I'm a businessman and a Victorian gentleman!"

"Keep him," said Val.

"You're sure?" asked Cole.

"The soiled pants might give us away."

"I resent that!" said Copperfield.

"Okay, come along then," she said.

"I said I resented it," said Copperfield morosely. "I never said I denied it."

"We're just about ready to go," announced Val. "We'll have the party loaded and be on our way in less than a minute."

"Once you touch down on the planet, leave one member of your party aboard the *Edith*," said Cole.

"Why?"

"To make sure it's still there when you get back."

"All right," she agreed. "It makes sense."

Her image vanished, and Cole decided he had nothing further to say to David so he broke the connection.

He watched the viewscreen on the shuttle through the holocam on Sokolov's shoulder. Val had elected not to approach the city directly with the *Edith*, but to fly toward the ocean separating Jaipur from its sister continents. *Curious*, he mused, *that all their nations and continents are named after Indian cities, but nothing is named India.*

The shuttlecraft got to within two hundred feet of the ocean's surface, then leveled out and headed west toward Jaipur. Once there it went lower still, avoiding all conventional radar and sensing devices, and finally, about twenty minutes later, it touched down about two miles beyond what was obviously the city where Quinta was incarcerated. The team silently emerged from the shuttle and began moving stealthily toward the outskirts of the city, keeping to the shadows along the poorly lit minor streets.

*Damn it!* thought Cole, as he watched them through Sokolov's camera. *Val's too big! She stands out.*

The party made its way deep into the heart of the city through the crazily winding streets, around oddly shaped buildings, with Val constantly checking her wrist computer. Then, finally, she gave the signal to halt, and using more hand signals began dividing her party and scattering them around a massive stone building, and Cole knew they had reached their destination. One by one they vanished into the building—

—And then, suddenly, Cole could hear an ear-shattering alarm. The scene on Sokolov's holocam became too blurred to follow, as he spun, ran, avoided a laser blast, disabled a Thuggee at close quarters, and dove for cover amid more beams of solid light. Cole could hear Val's bellowed curses over the hum of lasers, the buzz of screechers, even the thunderclaps of projectile weapons.

"I don't know if you can hear me, sir," said Sokolov's voice, "but we've got a bit of a situation here. I think we're—"

And then the transmission stopped as an old-fashioned bullet tore through the holocam.

"Vladimir!" shouted Cole. "Can you hear me?"

There was only silence at the other end.

"*Shit!*" muttered Cole. "Who's on the *Edith?*"

"Lieutenant Mueller."

"Patch me through," said Cole. "Idena, this is Cole. Take off this instant."

"But sir," said Idena Miller's voice. "I'm waiting for—"

"No arguments! Just do it!"

"Yes, sir."

"We've got to help them, Wilson," said Forrice.

"I know. Pilot, take us down to within half a mile of the surface, and hold us steady directly above the jail."

Forrice headed off to the airlift. "I'm going down to Gunnery," he said. "Give me half a minute to get there, then tell me what you want and where you want it aimed."

"Will do. Someone get Christine up here!" ordered Cole.

"She's sleeping," said Jaxtaboxl.

"Then wake her. I want her up here."

"But—"

"I don't mean to hurt your feelings," said Cole, "but our people are in danger down there, and I want the best I've got." He turned to Wxakgini. "Pilot, how's it coming?"

"Another twenty seconds," replied Wxakgini.

"Where's Briggs?"

"I'm not sure, sir," said Jaxtaboxl.

"Find him and get him up here, on the double!"

"I've summoned him."

"When he gets here," said Cole, "put him on the armory console."

"I thought Commander Forrice was handling the weaponry, sir," said Jaxtaboxl.

"He's on offense," said Cole. "If they start shooting back, I need someone to do nothing but handle our defenses. That's Briggs."

"We have arrived at the location you requested," announced Wxakgini.

"All right. Four Eyes, can you hear me?"

"Yes," answered the Molarian.

"Home in on any building you like within a city block of the jail, and blow it away. If you can find one with all the lights out, one that looks empty, so much the better, but don't waste any time."

"Weapon?"

"Level 3 laser. Let's let 'em think we're no better armed than they are, so they'll concentrate on shooting us down. If we give 'em any time to consider their situation, they'll hit on the notion of holding our people hostage."

"Done," announced Forrice. "I just took out a building thirty yards northwest of the jail."

"Are there any vehicles in the street?"

"I think so," answered the Molarian. "They're not like any I've ever seen, but they're clearly not dwellings, and they *are* outside. Wait! One's moving. Yes, they're definitely vehicles."

"Do whatever it takes with the lasers to set half a dozen of them on fire."

"Four . . . five . . . all done, that's six."

"*That* should convince them there are more important things to worry about than the jail."

Christine came onto the bridge and walked immediately to her station.

"Sorry to wake you," said Cole. "Monitor any transmissions coming from the jail or the city and let me know what's happening. Where the hell is Briggs?"

As if in answer, Malcolm Briggs reached the bridge.

"What's going on, sir?" he asked.

"The landing party's in trouble, and we're doing what we can to divert the Thuggees' attention. If we're successful they're going to start shooting at us. It's your job to make sure nothing gets through."

"Yes, sir," he said, rushing to the armory console. "Do you want me to take over the offensive weaponry as well?"

"No, Four Eyes is on it," answered Cole. "Just make sure they don't hit us."

"Yes, sir."

"What about me, sir?" asked Jaxtaboxl, who was now without a station.

"Put together another party," said Cole. "Eight members, all armed, and get down to the shuttle bay."

"Yes, sir. We can be ready to attack in five minutes."

"You're not attacking anyone. We can do that just fine from up here. But if we've got any survivors at all, we're going to have some walking and nonwalking wounded. They can't go through two miles of hostile territory to get back to the *Edith*, and besides, it's not there anymore. Once we soften up the opposition, you'll land the shuttle right at the jail and evacuate them."

"Yes, sir," said Jaxtaboxl, hastening off to gather his landing party.

"They're firing back, sir," announced Briggs. "Level 2 thumpers and Level 3 burners. Nothing we can't handle."

"Four Eyes," said Cole, "pinpoint where the thumpers and burners are and blow them away."

There was a brief silence.

"They're history," announced Forrice.

"Christine," said Cole, "any word from Sokolov or the others?"

"Nothing, sir."

"How about the enemy's brass? What are they saying?"

"They know they're under attack, but they don't know who's doing it or why," answered Christine.

"*Someone* had to give the order to fire on us," said Cole. "Can you pinpoint him and put me through to him?"

"Not yet, sir."

"Work at it."

"Yes, sir."

"And patch me through to Mr. Odom."

"Done, sir."

The image of Mustapha Odom, the ship's engineer, suddenly appeared on the bridge.

"Yes, Captain?" asked Odom.

"You've doubtless noticed that we're in a minor action," said Cole. "It's nothing the *Teddy R* can't handle—Level 2 thumpers and Level 3 burners. But I may have to send the *Kermit* or one of the other shuttles down to the surface. Can it withstand them?"

"The burners are no problem, not below Level 4," answered Odom. "But the thumpers are another matter. They can blow the shuttle off course, which is easily correctable . . . but it's also possible they could pound it with such force that the shock does serious harm to the passengers even while not destroying the *Kermit* itself."

"Thank you, Mr. Odom," said Cole. "Jack-in-the-Box?"

"Yes, sir?" came Jaxtaboxl's voice.

"Stand ready, but that shuttle doesn't budge without my express order, is that understood?"

"Yes, sir."

"Have they fired again, Mr. Briggs?"

"No, sir. I don't think they will, now that they know they can't harm us and we can take out their weapons as fast as we spot them."

"Christine—anything yet?"

"Possibly, sir," she said. "I can't guarantee this is the person you want, but I have one that most of the military seems to be reporting to."

"All right," said Cole. "Let's see if we can end this without another shot being fired. What's the name of the Thuggee we traded the weapons to? Rashid?"

"Yes, sir."

"Have his holograph on standby, and put me through."

"I can't pinpoint just the leader, sir," said Christine apologetically. "You're going to get anyone standing near him as well."

"That's fine. Just do it."

And suddenly Cole was facing the image of three Thuggees, one seated, two standing behind him. All three were dressed the same as Rashid—naked except for a single sash bearing their rank and insignia.

"I am Wilson Cole, Captain of the *Theodore Roosevelt*."

The seated Thuggee looked straight ahead, obviously staring at Cole's image. "I am Nasir, Commandant of the city of Jamata. Why have you attacked us?"

"You are holding a prisoner named Quinta, a member of the Thrale race," said Cole. "We want him."

"I assume those were your representatives who tried to force their way in?"

"That's right. I want them, too. Alive."

"You break our laws and fire upon our appointed peacekeepers, and you expect me to bargain with you?"

"There's not much of a bargain involved. I want them back, and you're going to give them to me."

"I may very well do that, but not alive."

"I think you will," said Cole. "You haven't heard my offer yet."

"What do I care about your offer? Obviously you will threaten to kill us if we don't comply, and clearly you have the power to do it, but that will not get your crew back alive. If your weapons don't kill them as well as us, then we will kill them before you annihilate us."

"I'm all through firing from space," said Cole. "That was just to get your attention, and I deeply regret any harm we may have caused to any of your citizens. But I really think you should listen to my offer. I'm only going to make it once, and it's nonnegotiable."

"All right, Captain Cole," said Nasir. "Let me hear it, and then pray to your deity for your crewmen."

"I'm going to send a shuttlecraft down to the planet. It will land directly in front of the jail, and will evacuate my crew members and the prisoner Quinta. You will not harm or hinder them in any way."

"You are delusional, Captain Cole."

"You didn't let me finish," said Cole. "If my conditions are not met, my ship will not fire another shot or harass you in any way. But . . ." He turned to Christine and lowered his voice. "Send down the holo of Rashid." He raised his voice again. "But I will *give*, not sell, ten Level 5 pulse cannons and ten Level 5 laser cannons to my friend Rashid, of the nation of Punjab, whose image you can now see. The *Theodore Roosevelt* has no interest in conquest or annexation. If we were to punish you for killing our crew and your prisoner, we'd kill some of your leaders, we might even take out your entire city if you inflicted additional suffering upon our crew members, but that would be the end of it. The rest of your nation would continue to go about its business. I don't think you can count on the leaders of Punjab to have such short attention spans." He paused for the consequences to sink in. "You have two Standard minutes, Nasir."

It didn't take two minutes. It didn't even take thirty seconds. Nasir knew when he was beaten.

"Send your shuttle down," he said after a very brief hesitation. "We will not harm it."

"It's on its way," said Cole. "We lost contact with our landing party a few minutes ago. If anyone's still shooting inside the jail, tell them to end it. *Now!*"

"If it's still going on, it will stop," promised Nasir.

Cole nodded to Christine, who broke the connection.

"Jack-in-the-Box?"

"Yes, sir."

"Get moving. Theoretically no one will bother you, but be prepared for anything. It's always possible that Nasir can't get word to the Thuggees inside the jail."

"We're heavily armed and ready, sir," said Jaxtaboxl.

"Four Eyes?" said Cole.

"I know," answered the Molarian. "I'll cover them all the way down and all the way back."

"Christine, announce to the crew that the second the shuttle's back the *Teddy R* is heading for the nearest medical facility."

"Yes, sir."

"All right," said Cole as the shuttle took off for Jaipur. "Now we wait."

It took seventeen minutes for the *Kermit* to land, evacuate the crew members and the prisoner, and return to the *Teddy R*, followed by the *Edith*, which had taken up a high orbit around Calcutta. Cole sent Slick and two others down to the bay to help move the wounded to the infirmary.

"What's the body count?" he asked after the shuttle had been emptied.

"The good news is that Val is unscathed, sir," reported Slick.

"That figures," said Cole. "Give me fifty like her and I could probably overthrow the Republic. Now how about the bad news?"

"James Nichols is dead," said Slick. "Dan Moyer and Vladimir Sokolov have serious wounds. Idena Mueller, Rachel Marcos, Eric Pampas, Jacillios, and Braxite have minor, or at least non-life-threatening, wounds. The Thrale seems to be fine."

"All right," said Cole. "See to it that they're made as comfortable as possible. Sharon's got the combination to the medical supply cabinet. We've got some alphanella seeds stashed away there. Give one seed each to Moyer and Sokolov to chew, and then make sure you lock the damned thing up again."

"I'm ahead of you," broke in Sharon. "I'll have the seeds waiting when they get to the infirmary."

"Thanks," said Cole.

"Aren't alphanella seeds illegal even for medical treatment?" asked Christine as Cole broke the connection.

"Yeah, back in the Republic," answered Cole. "Nothing much is illegal on the Inner Frontier. I confiscated the seeds the first month I reported for duty here. I thought we'd use them to trade for information when we were in the pirate trade, but the opportunity never arose. Just as well. It'll put Moyer and Sokolov in dreamland quicker than any legitimate drug I know. Patch me through to Sharon again."

"Yes, Wilson?" said Sharon.

"I know you're not a doctor or a nurse," he said, "but you have to know how to tie a tourniquet. If anyone's bleeding badly, do what you can to stanch the flow. Commandeer all the help you need."

"Right."

"Pilot, how long until we can get to a planet with a hospital?"

"I am searching the nearby wormholes," answered Wxakgini, as he and the navigational computer to which he was connected scanned the star maps.

"Don't search too long. We've got a couple of men who are in a bad way."

There was a brief pause.

"There is a medical facility orbiting Prometheus between the third and fourth planets, which have both been colonized, sir," announced Wxakgini. "I can traverse the Kurasawa Wormhole and have us there in eighty Standard minutes."

"Okay, get us there."

"It's not an exceptionally large hospital, sir."

"Just do it."

Cole left the bridge and walked to the officers' lounge, where he found David Copperfield.

"It's over," he announced. "We got Quinta out."

"I know," said Copperfield. "I've been following it. Our headmaster would be proud of you, Steerforth."

"I just hope your friend was worth the effort."

"I'm sure he'll be properly grateful."

"He'd better be," said Cole. "He's going to pick up the tab for all the medical bills we're about to acquire."

"Surely we can afford it ourselves, given what we've just earned," replied Copperfield.

"Fine," said Cole. "It'll come out of your share."

For just a moment David Copperfield was speechless. Then he frowned and slammed a fist down on the arm of his chair. "That ingrate will pay for it or we'll send him right back to Jaipur!"

Cole smiled. "You know, David, I think our headmaster would be proud of you too."

Four days later the *Theodore Roosevelt* docked at Singapore Station. A skeleton crew was drawn by lot to patrol the ship for twenty-four hours, then traded places with another group. Moyer and Sokolov were still in the hospital orbiting Prometheus IV; early reports were that Sokolov would be able to rejoin them in ten days, Moyer in about thirty.

Perez reported that the upgrades to the other ships had just been completed, and they were ready to go out on maneuvers. The captains of the four smaller ships were unhappy about not sharing in the profits from the Calcutta mission until Cole explained that the profits were what was paying for the upgrades.

Cole was sick of the close confines of the ship. He stuck it out for three days. Then, like most of the crew, he chose to rent a room in one of the multitude of hotels on the station. He was rapturously discussing his accommodations with David Copperfield and the Platinum Duke in the casino when Forrice, looking considerably less tense, walked over to their table, which was barely large enough to hold their drinks.

"I never thought a ten-by-ten room with an eight-foot ceiling would give me such a sense of freedom," Cole was saying. "I've been cooped up on the *Teddy R* and other ships too damned long. Hell, I've spent half my life in places where I couldn't extend my arm straight up above my head. I even paid the extra fee for a bath with real water instead of taking a Dryshower." He looked up to see Forrice carrying a smoking blue drink over. "Hi, Four Eyes. Have a seat."

"Thank you," said the Molarian. "Perez and I have just been working with the other ships again."

"And?"

"They're starting to function as a unit. Remember, none of their captains was ever in the military. They're all freelancers." He paused. "This Perez is a good man. He ought to have a ship of his own."

"He will. Give us a little time."

"By the way, I spoke to Vladimir Sokolov just before I came over. They seem to be taking good care of him. He's lucky they didn't have to clone any of his internal organs. Nothing but major burns and a few broken bones. He's optimistic about returning to duty soon."

"He is?" said Cole. "He must have a six-and-a-half-foot ceiling and no windows. What else could make him want to go back to his cabin aboard the *Teddy R?*"

"I think your Captain is getting a serious case of cabin fever," noted the Duke in amused tones, his human lips smiling in his metal face.

"It's just nice to be able to stretch—arms, legs, everything—once in a while," said Cole. He turned to Forrice. "I've hardly seen you the last three days. You can't be spending *all* your time working with the ships and patronizing that whorehouse."

"I found a game that appeals to the intricacies of the Molarian mind," replied Forrice.

"Then it must be simpler than blackjack," said Cole with a laugh.

"It is incredibly complex," answered Forrice. "But the rewards once it is mastered are considerable."

"Well, you're sure not playing it here at Duke's Place," noted Cole. "Like I said, I haven't seen you."

"No, I've been playing at a casino called the Glowworm. I had to have Mr. Briggs explain the name to me."

"The Glowworm?" said the Duke, sipping his drink through a

straw as usual, so as not to let any of it stain his metal chin. "Then I know what you're playing. *Stort*, right?"

"Yes," said the Molarian. "Fascinating game. You play an opponent as well as the house, and there are cards, tokens, and four levels."

"Of difficulty?"

"Of space."

"Why not play it here?" asked Cole.

"I don't run a *stort* game," answered the Duke. "It only has a two percent break for the house."

"Only two percent?" said Cole. "I don't blame you. How much have you made so far, Four Eyes?"

"Actually, I'm down almost three thousand Far London pounds," said the Molarian uncomfortably. "There are more subtleties than appear at first. But I'm mastering them. Another week and I'll own the place."

"Remind me someday to tell you what gets born every minute," said Cole.

"I've been thinking, Steerforth . . ." began Copperfield.

"Don't," said Cole only half-jokingly. "Every time you do you almost get us killed."

"I resent that!" said Copperfield. "I was going to suggest that we should invest some of our earnings."

"David, by the time I pay all the crew members their share—and there are six ships' worth of crew members these days—and refresh the nuclear piles and replace armaments and ammunition, there's not a hell of a lot left to invest. Besides, we go into action a lot more often as mercenaries than we ever did in the Navy. It would be unrealistic to suggest that we'll win every time, and since none of us has any family out here, who will we leave those investments to?"

"You're brighter than that, Steerforth," said Copperfield. "Stop thinking like some common crewman."

"We don't have any *common* crewmen," said Cole irritably.

"You know what I mean," persisted Copperfield. "Surely you can see the advantages of having an investment that will continue to grow."

"It's not *my* money, David. It's *our* money. Ask Four Eyes if he's willing to skip two trips to the whorehouse every shore leave so that he can have an extra hundred pounds ten years from now, after they've shot his balls off. Ask Val if she'll be a teetotaler for five years now so she can hang one on in fifteen years. Ask Bull Pampas if he wants to make do with half the torpedoes we usually carry so he can afford better weapons in twelve years." Cole paused. "I understand the principle of investing as well as you do, David, but it doesn't apply to people who put their lives on the line every day, have no dependents, and have reasonable expectations of not seeing their old age."

"You'll have to excuse my friend," said Forrice. "He's such an optimist."

"I'm not an optimist *or* a pessimist," responded Cole. "I'm a realist. It dates back to the days when we were still Earthbound: today's mortal enemy is tomorrow's cherished friend, today's cherished friend is tomorrow's mortal enemy, and nothing ever changes. We've been at war with *someone* since the first caveman cracked another one over the head with his club. Better to live for the moment."

"It depends on the moment," said the Molarian. "I can think of a lot of moments I wouldn't care to revisit."

"None of them in the past two hours, I presume," said Cole dryly. "Well, David, does that answer your question, such as it was?"

"You don't mind if I invest *my* money, do you?" asked Copperfield.

"Why bother? We both know you've got millions stashed all over the Frontier from the days when you were the biggest fence in the business."

"Half from my business, half from my investments."

"What'll you do with it if we go back into the Republic?"

"I'll wish you Godspeed and use a tiny portion of it to pay for shipping funeral wreaths, my dear Steerforth," answered Copperfield.

"No one's going back to the Republic," put in the Duke. "While you were gone, a Teroni ship managed to get through the Navy's defenses, and destroyed four agricultural worlds."

"Why bother?" asked David. "The average farm world has less than one hundred people on it. They're worked by robots."

"They each feed anywhere from five to ten worlds that can't grow their own crops," said Cole. He looked across the table at the Duke. "Let me guess. Word got out, and now the colonists are shooting down anything that moves."

The Duke nodded. "According to my information, aggressivly programmed planetary defense systems have shot down seven Navy ships, two cargo ships, and a spaceliner." He paused. "This is definitely *not* a good time to consider returning to the Republic."

"We're never going back," said Cole firmly. "They shot all those other ships by accident. When they shoot us, it'll be on purpose."

"There's nothing back there for us anyway," added Forrice. "Every crew member of the *Teddy R* who left with us is wanted dead or alive. There's a ten-million-credit reward for Wilson, three million for me, and an even bigger bounty on the ship itself."

"Still, if you've heard any further news, I'd like to pass it on to the crew. Never going back doesn't mean they're not still interested in what goes on there."

"You mean the war?" asked the Duke.

"Both sides want to kill us. No one gives a shit about the war. Give me some sports results, a copy of new holos we can stick in the ship's library, touches of home."

"I shall obtain what you want," said the Duke.

"Don't *you* miss your home world?" asked Forrice.

"Singapore Station *is* my home world now," replied the Duke. "I haven't been off it for close to thirty years, and I have no intention of ever leaving it again."

"At least you *have* a home world, however artificial it is," said the Molarian. "Ours is a century-old ship."

"This is getting morbid," said David. "What we need are some dancing girls."

"Would they appeal to you?" asked the Duke curiously.

"I am a Victorian gentleman, sir," replied David heatedly. "Of course they would. Do only platinum women appeal to you?"

"No offense intended," said the Duke. "To change the subject, I am still being swindled over at the *jabob* table. Where is the redheaded giantess?"

Cole shrugged. "Beats me. She's got her own ship now, so she's not answerable to me until we take off again. But a guess is that she's drinking or fighting not too far from here."

"Why doesn't she join us?"

"She's probably afraid you'll disturb her drinking by asking her to spot how people are cheating you," answered Cole.

"Ask and ye shall receive," intoned Copperfield.

"What are you talking about?" asked the Duke.

"Take a look," said Copperfield, pointing to the entrance, where Val had just appeared.

Cole waved to her and she approached the table.

"Come have a drink with us, dear lady," said Copperfield.

"Been drinking all day," she replied, sitting down. Then: "Just a short one."

"What can I get for you?" asked the table.

"The one I taught your bartender the other night," said Val. "A Purple Flame."

"That is not in my data bank," said the table.

"Ask the barkeep. He knows how."

"We have seventeen bartenders" was the reply. "Can you identify which one?"

"Human, male, maybe six feet tall, bald on top, gray on the sides, looked like he had a prosthetic left hand, two teeth missing on the top right. Probably in his fifties."

"Damn, that's good!" muttered Forrice.

"That would be Gray Max, true name Archibald Token. He is currently off-duty and unavailable."

"All right," said Val. "Start with three ounces of Crystalblue rye, then add an ounce of Benitaris III sillywater, an ounce of New Barbados rum, a pinch of bitters, and an ounce of any citrus from Laginappe II. Now make one for me and put it in your memory."

"That's a *short* one?" said Cole, wondering for the hundredth time how she kept her fabulous figure.

"Straight or on the rocks?" asked the table.

"Straight."

The drink appeared thirty seconds later.

"You've got to train your hired help better," Val told the Platinum Duke. "Imagine leaving without filing all that away first! A person could get damned thirsty waiting for Gray Max to tell the bar computer what goes into a Purple Flame."

"Damned good thing the bar computer can't give you its opinion of that thing," offered Cole.

"You should try one before you knock it," said Val.

"I value my stomach too much," answered Cole.

"I'll be glad when Sokolov gets out of hospital," said Val. "He and Briggs are my drinking buddies. *Were* my drinking buddies," she corrected, "before I moved to the *Red Sphinx*."

"I'm sure you can find more drinking buddies on Singapore Station than you can shake a stick at," said Cole. He noticed a slight swelling around her left eye. "Though it looks like you've been shaking a stick at some of them already, and one of them shook back."

She shook her head. "That was one of the androids in the whorehouse," she said with no show of self-consciousness or embarrassment. "He got a little enthused." She paused and looked thoughtfully at her bruised knuckles. "I'm sure they'll have him functional in two or three days."

"If the Republic had you in the Navy they'd have won the war ten years ago," said Copperfield admiringly.

"You wouldn't like it," said Val.

"I'm afraid I don't follow you, dear lady."

"If they won the war ten years ago, they'd have taken over Singapore Station by now. Then where would you go to relax and hunt up business?"

"She's got a point," agreed the Duke. "Men have always hungered for new worlds. I'm sure if they didn't have the Teroni Federation shooting at them they'd hunger for mine."

"They've got their hands full right where they are," said Cole.

"Who gives a damn about them?" said Val. "Let's talk some business. I'm all refreshed and ready to go back out again."

"Out of here?" asked Copperfield, confused.

"Out into the Frontier," she replied. "Have we got another job lined up yet?"

"We haven't even discussed it," said Cole. "I thought everyone could use a little shore leave."

"We've *had* a little shore leave," said Val decisively. "Time to head out again."

"Soon," said Cole.

Val finished her drink and got to her feet. "I'm going to make the rounds and see what's going on," she said. "Catch you later."

"Look at her," said Forrice as she walked to the front door of the casino. "Straight as an arrow. How can she put so many stimulants into her system and remain so clearheaded?"

"She's a remarkable lady," agreed Cole. "Be glad she's on *our* side."

"I've held off putting the word out," said the Duke. "But if you're ready to take on another assignment . . ."

"Don't go twisting any arms just yet," said Cole, "but if you hear of one that's interesting and lucrative enough, let David know about it."

"Will do," said the Duke.

"And now," said Cole, standing up, "I think I'm going to go get some dinner."

"Just tell me what you want and I'll have my private chef cook it for you," offered the Duke.

"Thanks, but I'm out of the ship so infrequently that I'd like to see a little more of your world, even if it *is* just a few miles long."

"All right," said the Duke. "I can appreciate that. Will I see you later?"

"Yeah, I'll probably stop in again before I hit the sack." He turned to Forrice. "You're welcome to come along. We'll find a joint that serves all species."

"I think I'll try my luck again," replied the Molarian. "I'm still developing a system. Pick me up at the Glowworm in two hours."

Cole sighed deeply. "Men and Molarians—they never learn."

"I just have to get a little better understanding of the subtleties and complexities," said Forrice. "I'm getting close, I know I am."

"Why don't you just pay another visit to your whorehouse?" suggested Cole. "You'll enjoy your money a hell of a lot more over there."

Forrice made a face. "I pay, they accommodate me, and it's no challenge at all."

"What are you more interested in—satisfaction or a challenge?"

"Stop complicating things," said Forrice. "You're going to give me a terrible headache." He walked off toward the door. "Just pick me up in two hours."

Cole watched the Molarion leave, swirling out in his surprisingly graceful three-legged stride. "You wouldn't believe he's the brightest and most loyal member of my crew, would you?" he said at last. "Ah, well, I'll be back in a couple of hours."

He left the casino, wandered the narrow streets, still feeling a bit claustrophobic since the next level was only twelve feet above him and there were no windows or viewscreens. He passed a trio of Lodinites, a pair of human women, a huge Torqual, a few species he'd never seen before, even a Teroni who paid him no attention on this neutral world in the middle of a galactic No-Man's Land.

Finally he came to a restaurant that caught his eye, one that advertised the beef of mutated cattle from Pollux IV. He was about to enter when a bistro farther down the block captured his attention. There was music coming from it, real jazz played by a human band, and when he walked over and looked in he saw that a pair of human women were performing a slow, sensuous dance on a small, makeshift stage. Then he noticed that menu consisted entirely of well-disguised soya products.

He stood, undecided, between the two for a long moment. Finally his appetite for food beat out his appetite for entertainment, and he entered the first restaurant, where he dined on a thick and wildly expensive slab of real beef. Since he was eating alone he was done in twenty minutes, and decided to kill some time before going to the Glowworm.

The streets were more like wide sidewalks, since they didn't have to accommodate any traffic. A narrow slidewalk ran in each direction for those who disdained walking. All cargo transports ran along the middle level on a monorail; the human habitations were on the top levels and the alien on the bottom, though that was an arbitrary definition based on the artificial gravity. Every street corner had either a ramp or an airlift to the next levels up and down. Cole had seen a lot of the human levels, so he decided to spend an hour walking around one of the alien levels.

When he got off the airlift he didn't notice any difference at first, but soon he began to see doorways that were wider, or taller, or shorter; windows that were so heavily tinted or polarized as to be opaque to the human eye, though some alien species were clearly looking through them; restaurants with odors he'd never encountered before; aliens speaking to each other in their native tongues, rather than Terran or the translated Terran of the omnipresent T-packs. He looked in store windows that displayed items that made absolutely no sense to him, side by side with items that were clearly of human origin or based on human design.

He couldn't really say that it was enjoyable—it had been quite a while since he'd actually *enjoyed* anything other than an occasional non-soya meal and his time in bed with Sharon—but it *was* interesting. Most of his experiences on alien worlds were limited to attacking the enemy or defending himself; very rarely did he have time to explore the world he was liberating or assimilating.

Finally he decided it was time to head over to the Glowworm. It was in the human section, so he took an airlift back up, stepped out, and walked to the casino where Forrice was engaged in the *stort* game. The place possessed a certain trendy seediness, and Cole made his way among the human and non-human gamblers until he was finally able to spot his tripodal First Officer.

"How's it going?" he asked.

"Don't distract me," said Forrice. "I'll be just a minute."

"Your call," announced a Hesporite who seemed to be a dealer or croupier.

"All right," said Forrice. "Warrior to level two, lane three, and"—he slapped an octagonal card down on the table—"I play the purple empress."

The croupier studied what Forrice had done, and waited for two others to move pieces in ways that were incomprehensible to Cole and play cards that he could not identify. Finally the croupier rolled a twelve-sided pair of dice that had icons rather than spots on their faces, studied them, and pronounced Forrice to be the winner of this round. The Molarian emitted a hoot of triumph.

"You see?" he said as he collected his winnings. "I told you that I just needed a little more time to work out the subtleties."

"It looks like one hell of a complex game," noted Cole.

"They all do—until you start playing them."

"So how do you stand compared to the house?"

"I'm about two hundred pounds ahead."

"That much that fast?" said Cole, impressed.

"Why not?" replied the Molarian. "I lost it just as fast."

"Okay, you've got a point. Let's go over to Duke's and you can buy me a disgusting stimulant and then watch me destroy my health by drinking it."

"Fine," said Forrice. "Now that I've doped it out, I can come back here and break the bank any time."

"Don't make it look too easy and don't brag about it," cautioned Cole, "or they'll find a way to ban you from the tables."

"You think so?"

Cole nodded. "Societies have been penalizing excellence ever since there *were* societies."

They left the Glowworm and walked over to Duke's Place. It was crowded, as usual, and Cole sensed a certain tension in the room as he and Forrice made their way to the Duke's table.

There was a Teroni sitting at it—tall, lean, with the piercing golden eyes that were so distinctive to the species. Like most Teronis he wore wide boots over his splayed feet, the rust-colored jumpsuit that formed the standard Teroni military uniform, and the usual weaponry bonded to hips and midsection. Teronis had thick, glistening hair that always reminded Cole of worms, and this one was no different. Cole looked for an insignia of rank, but they had all been removed.

"Come join us, Wilson," said the Platinum Duke. "There's someone I'd like you to meet."

Cole walked over and stood before the Teroni.

"Captain Cole and Commander Forrice," said the Teroni in lightly accented Terran. "We meet again."

"Again?" said Cole, frowning. "I don't recall ever seeing you before."

"We have not met in the flesh, Captain Cole, but we have communicated."

"We have?" asked Cole.

"The Cassius Cluster?" suggested Forrice.

The Teroni nodded. "I am Jacovic, Commander of the Fifth Fleet. I believe we spoke to each other mere moments after you deposed your captain."

Cole stared at him silently for a moment, and Jacovic and the Duke both grew visibly tense—and now Cole understood the tension in the room. Two captains who had previously met as enemies were in the same room for the first time since that meeting.

Finally Cole smiled and extended his hand.

"Allow me the privilege of shaking your hand, Commander," he said. "It's a human custom, but I hope you'll honor it."

Jacovic, visibly relieved, took Cole's hand.

"Honor isn't confined to any one race," Cole said, "and you displayed it in abundance."

"What are you referring to?" asked the Duke.

"The *Teddy R* was sent to patrol the Cassius Cluster, an exceptionally isolated area. Our sole duty was to protect a pair of fuel depots and not allow the enemy access to them. It was just a way to get us out of the brass's hair. No one ever expected the Teronis to actually show up there." He paused, recalling the situation. "Then suddenly the Fifth Teroni Fleet entered the Cluster. We were one ship, and Commander Jacovic had perhaps two hundred."

"Two hundred and forty-six," Jacovic put in.

"Our captain, a Polonoi named Podok, knew that she couldn't hold the Fleet off, so she interpreted her order to mean that we were to prevent them from appropriating the fuel at all costs." The muscles in Cole's face tightened inadvertently. "So she turned our cannons on one of the two planets, killing about three million inhabitants, just to make sure that Commander Jacovic couldn't make use of the fuel. She was about to do the same to the second planet and kill five million Men in the process when I relieved her of command."

"I knew you had mutinied," remarked the Duke. "I never knew why."

"Anyway, I contacted Commander Jacovic and told him he could have the fuel if he would promise not to harm the inhabitants. He agreed, he kept his word, and he gave us safe passage out of the Cluster."

"Actually, you told me that I could accept your terms or *you* would destroy the planet as your captain had destroyed the first," said Jacovic. "From what I have learned of you since that day, I do not believe you would have done so. But I would like to hear it from your own mouth. Were you bluffing?"

Cole smiled. "Possibly."

Jacovic returned his smile. "I am very glad to finally meet you, Captain Cole."

"What are you doing here?" asked Cole. "And why are you traveling incognito?"

"I am not traveling incognito," said Jacovic. "I am no longer a member of the Teroni Navy, or even the Teroni Federation."

"What happened?" asked Forrice.

"I opened my eyes."

"I beg your pardon?" said Cole.

"You probably have not yet heard of the Battle of Gabriel," said Jacovic.

"No, not much news of the war makes it to the Inner Frontier, and what gets here is usually pretty old."

"It took place some forty days ago, and it lasted for twenty-two days."

"Where *is* Gabriel?" asked Forrice. "I'm not familiar with it."

"There is no reason why you should be," answered Jacovic. "Why *anyone* should be. The Gabriel system—that is your name for it; we have another—consists of seven uninhabitable gas giants circling a class-M star that is neither in the Republic nor in our Federation."

"So who won?" asked Forrice.

"Let me guess," said Cole, studying Jacovic's face. "No one did."

"That is correct," said Jacovic. "By the time it was over, we had lost fifty-three ships and the Republic had lost forty-nine. One hundred and two ships, and perhaps twelve thousand Teronis and Men, and for what? For a system that did not possess a single habitable planet, or anything either side could possibly use. It was then that I realized the idiocy of this war, the utter madness that led each side to sacrifice thousands of lives for a totally useless system simply so the other side could not lay claim to it—and on that day I tore the insignia from my uniform and made my way to the Inner Frontier."

Cole turned to Forrice. "I told you a year and a half ago that he had more sense then any of the politicians and admirals on our side."

"Commander Jacovic has just arrived here at Singapore Station in the past hour," the Duke informed them. "I gather he brought no one with him."

"Each Teroni is free to make his own decision," said Jacovic. "I have made mine. And do not call me Commander; I am just Jacovic now."

"What are you going to be doing with yourself?" asked Cole.

"I haven't had time to consider that yet," replied Jacovic. "I have spent my entire adult life in the military. I shall have to discover what else I am good at."

"Not necessarily," said Cole.

Jacovic looked at him questioningly.

"I know a former military vessel that's in need of a competent Third Officer," continued Cole. "And a Captain who'd be proud to have you serve with him."

"Who is this military vessel at war with?" asked the Teroni.

"Fate."

"That is the perfect answer," said Jacovic. "I am more than willing to take up arms against Fate. I will be honored to join the crew of the *Theodore Roosevelt*."

This time it was Jacovic who extended his hand, and Cole who took it. But it didn't really matter who reached out first. It was the first time in twenty-three years that a Man and a Teroni had willingly touched each other in friendship.

Cole had just finished giving Jacovic a tour of the *Theodore Roosevelt*, and now they stood on the bridge of the almost-empty ship.

"Well, what do you think?" he asked.

"It's old."

"So are you and I," said Cole with a smile.

"Not *this* old," replied Jacovic, returning his smile. "When was the last time it was re-outfitted?"

"Probably before a few of my younger ensigns and crewmen were born."

"Still," said the Teroni, "old or not, it is probably the most famous ship in the galaxy."

"The most notorious, anyway," said Cole. "By the way, you seem comfortable with the air content and gravity here and on Singapore Station. I can give you a cabin in the human quarters, or if you're simply being stoic, we can adjust any of the alien rooms to your speculations."

"The oxygen content is fine, but I think I would like a greater gravity."

"All right. Our Security Chief, Colonel Blacksmith, will debrief you when you're ready to move your gear aboard. I'll tell her to give you a cabin on Deck 5, and to adjust it to your specifications. How about dietary needs?"

"I can give a list to your Colonel Blacksmith."

"Fine. If there's anything else you need, come to me if I'm available, or to Four Eyes or Colonel Blacksmith if I'm not."

Jacovic frowned. "Four Eyes?"

"A bastardization of Commander Forrice's name," said Cole. "We're old friends. I've been calling him that for years. Besides, he *does* have four eyes."

"Will there be much resentment, not just at having a Teroni commander who used to be your enemy, but at making me your Third Officer?"

"Probably," said Cole. "They'll get over it."

"I hope so."

"They didn't think much of the officer you're replacing when I brought her aboard," said Cole. "Within a month she was the most popular person on the ship. You'll have an even easier time of it. Almost all of them were aboard the *Teddy R* when you spared the citizens of New Argentina and gave us safe passage out of the Cassius Cluster."

"Any reasonable commander would have done it," said Jacovic.

"Our own captain was prepared to destroy the whole damned planet before I took over the ship," said Cole. "Reasonable commanders are in shorter supply than you might think. Otherwise, why would we both be on the Inner Frontier?"

Jacovic's jowls fluttered as he sighed. "You have a point, Captain Cole."

"Call me Wilson."

"I'd better continue to call you Captain Cole," said the Teroni. "I might forget in front of the crew."

"They're welcome to call me anything they want, though most of them do stick to Captain."

"Might I ask why? On the surface it seems like a lack of discipline, but I am sure you have a reason for it."

"It's to remind them that we're not in the Republic or the Navy any longer," said Cole. "I insist on obedience and competence, but I never saw any reason for saluting each other. It's some holdover from a

couple of thousand years before my race even developed space travel."
He paused. "I suppose the gist of it is that we're here forever. No one's
tour of duty will ever be up, we can never go back to the Republic, and
of course we'll draw instant fire if we enter the Teroni Federation, so I
want them to be as comfortable as they can be, since they're stuck here
for the rest of their lives."

"Now I understand, and I approve," said Jacovic. "But I think I'll
still call you Captain Cole."

"Only on the ship and Singapore Station," said Cole.

Jacovic stared at him curiously.

"If I join my crew on a covert mission," continued Cole, "a salute
or a 'sir' tells the other side who to shoot first."

The Teroni smiled. "I never left my ship, and I would never have
thought of that. Now in the future I will know better."

"Well, you'll be leaving the *Teddy R* more than I do. I've got some
officers who are convinced that their job is to protect me, even more
than protecting the ship."

"Clearly they care for you."

"I could do with a little less care and a little more servility," said
Cole.

"You don't mean that, of course."

"No, I suppose I don't," said Cole. He looked around. "Okay,
you've had the cook's tour. I suppose we might as well get back to the
station. I guarantee you'll get a better meal and a more comfortable
bed there than here."

The two walked to an airlift, took it down to the shuttle bay,
saluted Idena Mueller who was standing guard, walked onto the dock,
then caught a transport to the interior of the station. A few minutes
later they were back in Duke's Place, where Cole spotted Val, Forrice,
and the Duke all sitting at the Platinum Duke's usual table.

"Ah, Captain Cole and Commander Jacovic!" said the Duke. "Come join us!"

"Happy to," said Cole as the two of them sat down. "Val, have you met your replacement yet?"

"I've heard about him," she said. "Welcome to the madhouse."

"Thanks," said Jacovic. "And you are . . . ?"

"I'm Val this month. If you've got a name you like better, I'll probably answer to it."

"You've had other names?" he said, surprised.

"I'm not Navy," she replied.

"I don't understand," said the Teroni.

"You've only been on the Inner Frontier for a few days," said Cole. "What you're going to find out is that the people here change names the way you and I change clothes. For example, I'll lay odds that our host wasn't always known as the Platinum Duke."

"I am now, and that's all that counts," said the Duke.

"As for Val, she went a little overboard on names," continued Cole.

"There are so many good ones, why stick with just one?" said Val.

"Or ten, or twenty," said Cole.

"Well, once they put a price on your head, you'd be crazy to keep the same one."

"So she's been Cleopatra, and Jezebel, and Salome, and the Queen of Sheba, and the Dowager Empress, and a dozen others," said Cole. "She was Dominick, which is a man's name, when I met her."

"I was working my way through my lovers' names," said Val. "He was my eighth."

"And Val was your ninth?" asked Jacovic.

"No," she answered. "*He* gave it to me."

"Well, almost," said Cole. "I likened her to a Valkyrie. She shortened it."

"I've kept it for almost four Standard months now," she added. "It's past time for a change. If you know a nice Teroni name, tell me before we take off again."

"Why would you want a Teroni name?" asked Jacovic curiously.

"Why not?" she replied. Suddenly she got to her feet. "I see a spot opened up at the *jabob* table. I think I'll try my luck."

She began walking, and the crowd parted before her like the Red Sea before Moses.

"It must be nice to be that intimidating," said Forrice.

"It has its advantages," agreed Cole.

"Why am I replacing her?" asked Jacovic. "Has she done something to displease you?"

"No, not at all," answered Cole. "We captured five ships on our last job, and since she captained her own pirate ship for years, I gave her one."

"She was a pirate?"

"The most notorious," said Cole. "Well, one of the most notorious," he amended. "She wasn't kidding about all the rewards they posted for her death or capture."

"And yet you took this pirate and made her your Third Officer," said Jacovic. "That is surprising."

"If you're as good an officer as she was, and I expect you to be, everyone will be happy," said Cole.

"I must talk to her and learn more about how she adjusted to life on a ship that would have been her enemy if they'd ever met while you were still in the Navy."

"Fine," said Cole. "Two warnings."

"Yes?"

"Never gamble with her, and never get into a fight with her."

"Formidable?" asked Jacovic.

"Formidable is an understatement," put in Forrice.

"I'll add a third warning," offered the Duke.

"Oh?" said Cole.

"Never try to drink with that lady."

"Yeah, she's got quite a capacity."

"She has downed a bottle of Altarian rum, a bottle of Cygnian cognac, and close to a bottle of some hundred-and-thirty-proof whiskey from the Deneb system since she came in her. And look at her." He shrugged. "It'll probably hit her all at once."

"She holds it pretty well," said Cole.

"No one can hold that much alcohol," said the Duke. "It'll be a delayed reaction. We'll be cleaning up the table and floor here, and you'll be carrying her back to her ship."

Suddenly the Duke stopped speaking and tensed noticeably.

"What's the matter?" asked Cole.

"Nothing, I hope," said the Duke, staring across the casino.

"Who are you looking at?"

"Do you see that Djarmin?"

"I don't know," said Cole. "What's a Djarmin?"

"A native of Visqueri II," said the Duke. "Tall, burly, humanoid, biped, light blue skin, no visible ears, prehensile lower lip."

"Yeah, okay, I see him," said Cole. "Weird-looking. What about him?"

"Unless I'm wrong, that's Csonti."

"Who's Csonti? Should I know the name?"

"If you don't yet, you will soon enough. His full sobriquet is Csonti the Vengeful."

"Sounds like a bad cartoon."

"Well, you've got the 'bad' part right," said the Duke.

"Tell me about him."

"Not much to tell," answered the Duke. "He's a warlord, and he controls, oh, it must be forty worlds by now."

"Then he should be Csonti the Collector," said Cole lightly.

"Nothing lives on twenty-three of those worlds," said the Duke. "If a world resists, there is no bargaining, no accommodation. He destroys it."

"Sweet fellow."

"I just wonder what he's doing here," said the Duke. "He's said to be the best freehand fighter on the Inner Frontier. I hope he isn't a mean drunk."

"Well, if he is, he'd better not pick on Val," said Cole. "He'll never know what hit him."

"She's that good?" asked Jacovic.

"She's that good," said Cole.

"I wonder that you let her go."

"Why?" Cole seemed amused. "The only people she could fight on the *Teddy R* were the Good Guys."

"The *Teddy R*?"

"A term of endearment," explained Cole. "Teddy is a nickname for Theodore, and R is the initial for Roosevelt. So if you hear anyone referring to the *Teddy R*, as most of our crew will do, it's the *Theodore Roosevelt* they're talking about."

"I see."

"Where did he go?" said the Duke, looking across the room.

"Probably he's sitting down," said Forrice.

"Or answering a call of Nature," suggested Cole.

"No," said Jacovic. "He walked out the side door a moment ago."

"Just as well," said Cole. "If he and Val got into it, there wouldn't be much left standing."

"Why would he fight her of all people?" asked Forrice.

"Because if he started feeling aggressive, she's the one who wouldn't back down from him."

They ordered a round of drinks, alcoholic for the humans, other things for the Molarian and the Teroni.

"Where's David?" asked Cole. "I thought he'd taken up residence here."

"He was here about twenty minutes before you arrived," said the Duke. "He's around somewhere."

"Why does he dress like a Man and mimic human mannerisms?" asked Jacovic.

"He fell in love with a human author named Charles Dickens at an early age and never got over it," said Cole. "He dresses and acts, or tries to act, like a Dickens character; he took a Dickens character's name; he built his house to resemble a house Dickens once described; he even calls me by the name of another Dickens character." Cole paused. "If you want to know why I put up with it, it's because David put his life on the line for us a while back. It cost him his business—he was a very successful fence with outlets on half a dozen worlds—and damned near his life. The only place he was safe was on the *Teddy R*, and the *Teddy R* pays its debts."

"And of course," added Forrice, "like Val he has a lifetime of contacts on the Inner Frontier, which is pretty handy for a ship and crew that have only been here about a year."

"But he does cut quite a figure," said the Duke.

"You've known him longer than we have," said Cole. "Was he always . . . ?"

"More so," answered the Duke. "And here he comes now."

"Hi, David," said Cole when the dandified alien reached the table. "Pull up a chair."

"In a minute," said Copperfield. He walked around the table until he was standing next to the Duke. "He wants to see you."

"Who?" asked the Duke.

"Csonti."

Suddenly the Duke's entire demeanor changed. "What does he have against me?" he said. "I've never refused him docking privileges. He's always been welcomed in the casino. If he's been offended in some way, why didn't he just—?"

"It's none of that," Copperfield interrupted. "He says it's a business proposition. Given his business, I think there's every likelihood that you'll be passing it on to us, but he says this is your world and he insists on making it to or through you."

"Oh?" said the Duke.

"You want me to come along?" asked Cole.

"No," said the Duke, recovering his composure. "If it's just an offer of some kind, I'll be fine. Unless he wants to buy Singapore Station," he added with a weak laugh. "Where is he?"

"The hotel next door," said Copperfield. "This level, fourth room back on the right."

The Duke got up and walked off without another word.

"Why did he speak to you in the first place?" asked Cole as Copperfield sat down.

"I've done some business with him in the past," said Copperfield. "Rare carvings and paintings from the museum on Baskra III."

"Baskra III?" said Cole. "I remember reading or hearing about it." He lowered his head in thought for a moment, then looked up. "Isn't that the world that was blown to smithereens?"

"Oh, there's still a Baskra III," said Copperfield. "But it used to be Baskra IV, and now there's a new asteroid belt between it and Baskra II."

"Nice playmate you got yourself," said Cole.

"A fence doesn't ask people how they acquired their goods, my dear Steerforth," replied Copperfield. "Not if he wants to stay in business. Or in this case, alive."

"What's he like?"

"He grunts a lot," said Copperfield. "The strong silent type. Although when he's annoyed he can swear with the best of them."

"Well, let's hope he's not making an offer for Duke's Place."

Val sauntered back to the table and sat down. Cole noticed a strong odor of alcohol about her.

"How'd you do?" asked Forrice.

"Don't ask," she said. "I was up against a Picanta. Those bastards can outthink a computer, so I cut my losses and quit."

"But it wasn't crooked?"

"If it was, they'd have been carrying the Picanta's body out by now." She looked around the table. "Where's the Duke?"

"Off doing business," said Cole.

"Good for him," said Val. "He's sure not getting rich off our crews. Most of them hang out at Silver Monte's."

"What has Silver Monte's got that this joint doesn't have?" asked Cole.

"A lack of command personnel," replied Val. "They don't necessarily plan to misbehave, but if they wind up doing so, they don't want their officers around."

She downed another drink, they all spent a few minutes talking, and then the Platinum Duke rejoined them.

"Well?" asked Cole.

The Duke sat down, looking much relieved. "It was a proposition, all right." He paused. "Have you ever heard of a world named Prometheus IV?"

Cole frowned. "What about it?"

"He's spread a little thin, and he wants to hire some ships to help him."

"Help him do what?"

"Wipe it out."

"Why?"

"He didn't see fit to confide in me."

"Damn it!" said Cole. "We've got two men in the medical facility that's orbiting Prometheus IV. Is there any chance of talking him out of it?"

"I'm not aware of anyone ever talking him out of anything," said the Duke.

"He's not the reasonable type, Steerforth," added Copperfield.

"We're going to have to evacuate Sokolov and Moyer," said Cole decisively.

"I don't know if Moyer can be moved, Wilson," said Forrice.

"He'll have to be," said Cole. "We only need one ship for this, and we'll run on a ghost crew. Pass the word to Briggs, Christine, Idena, Jack-in-the Box, and Domak. I assume Pilot is still on board?"

"He's connected to the navigational computer," said Forrice. "It'll take major surgery to disconnect him."

"Okay," said Cole. "Get the crew I named ready to go in two hours' time."

"What was he offering?" asked Copperfield. "Just out of curiosity."

"Fifty million Maria Theresa dollars, to be divided evenly among any ships that sign on."

"Fifty million?" repeated Val with a low whistle.

"Ridiculous, isn't it?" said the Duke. "It's like play money to him. I guess you lose all sense of proportion when you own forty worlds."

Val turned to Cole. "Do you know what we could do with fifty million Maria Theresa dollars, Wilson?"

"I'll tell you what we can't do," said Cole. "We can't decimate a world that's never done anyone any harm."

"It must have done some to Csonti, or he wouldn't want it dead," said Val, reaching over and appropriating the rest of the Duke's drink.

"Probably it refused to pay him half its planetary wealth as a tribute," said Cole. "Forget about it."

"What do you mean, forget about it?" she said. "We're mercenaries. Someone is offering more for one little job than we could make in two years."

"We don't slaughter whole planetary populations," said Cole. "It's not what we trained for, it's not who we are. Let it drop."

"I'm getting sick of your orders and your moralizing!" snapped Val, her words starting to slur.

"Just how much did you lose at the *jabob* table?" asked Copperfield.

"You shut up too, you ugly little alien wart! We're mercenaries, damn it!"

"It's not how much she lost," said Cole. "It's how much she drank."

"That's none of your business, Wilson Cole!"

"When you're part of my crew, it *is* my business."

"You want to step outside and prove it?"

"Don't be silly."

She stood up. "Okay, we'll prove it right here!"

"I'm not going to fight you, Val," said Cole. "Go to your ship, sleep it off, and see how you feel in the morning."

"Fuck you!" she said. "Now you're patronizing me!"

"Val, the last time you fell off the wagon your crew sold you and your ship out to the Hammerhead Shark while you were sleeping it off," said Cole. "Don't make another blunder."

She blinked her eyes furiously, trying to get them to focus. "I've had enough of people telling me what to do. I was the Captain of the *Pegasus* for twelve years, and no one gave me orders. I've got another ship now, and no one's giving me orders again." She stared at the Duke. "Where is this warlord at?"

"Please, Val," said the Duke.

"Am I going to have to beat it out of you?" she said. "Don't look to these guys for help! They know better."

"Can't we just—?"

"*Now!*"

The Duke swallowed hard and gave her the location of Csonti's room, and she walked off, unsteadily at first but gaining grace and strength with each step.

"New orders, Four Eyes," said Cole grimly. "Shore leave is over in two hours. For everyone."

"The other ships too?"

"The four smaller ones, yes," said Cole. "And pass the word to the crew of the *Red Sphinx* that we'll find a spot on the *Teddy R* for anyone who doesn't want to stay there."

The Molarian got up and began spinning across the room with his surprisingly graceful three-legged stride.

Cole turned to Jacovic. "Well, you've been an officer of the *Teddy R* for almost three hours," he said with an ironic smile. "How do you like it so far?"

"Perhaps she'll feel differently when she sobers up," suggested the Teroni.

"I'm sure she will. But she's also got a code of honor, though it's a little better hidden than most. If she signs on with Csonti today, she'll honor it tomorrow." He grimaced. "I'll tell you something else."

"What?'

"I'd rather face ten Csontis than one of her."

The *Teddy R* and its four companion ships entered the Prometheus system and radioed ahead to the orbiting hospital.

"This is Wilson Cole, Captain of the *Theodore Roosevelt*," said Cole. "You've got two of my crewmen there, Vladimir Sokolov and Daniel Moyer. We're here to pick them up. Get them ready to go."

"I am not empowered to authorize that, Captain Cole," said the Lodinite official at the other end of the transmission.

"Then connect me to whoever's in charge of the facility."

"That's out of the question, sir."

"Listen to me," said Cole irritably. "The Prometheus system's going to be under attack within a Standard day, probably a lot sooner. Now put me through to someone in authority."

The Lodinite's image vanished, and for a moment Cole thought the connection had been broken, but then the image of a gray-haired woman popped into existence.

"I am Bertha Salinas, Administrator of the Prometheus Orbiting Medical Facility," she said. "What is all this about an attack?"

"A warlord named Csonti is going to be attacking one of the Prometheus planets, either III or IV," said Cole. "He's not coming after the medical station, but if it's in the way, he's not going to worry about saving it either. You have two of my men there. I want them ready to go in twenty minutes."

"Are you quite sure of your information?" said Bertha Salinas.

"Yes," said Cole. "I can't do a thing for the planets, and I'm sure they have their own defenses, but I can help evacuate the hospital if you can have your staff and patients ready to go in an hour."

"This is very sudden," she replied. "I'll have to discuss it with my staff."

"What you and your staff choose to do is up to you," said Cole. "But have my two men ready to go in twenty minutes. If Moyer is tied in to any machines, then put them on an airsled; they're coming with us. If we have to, we'll pick up a nurse or a doctor from the next inhabited system."

"I don't know if we can discharge your men on such short notice," she said. "After all, we have our regulations."

"Screw your regulations!" snapped Cole. "Don't you understand what I'm telling you? A war is about to break out in the Prometheus system."

"Even so . . ."

"I *offered* to help you evacuate the hospital. That's your decision. But I'm coming to pick up my men. That's nonnegotiable."

"Are you giving me orders?" she said haughtily.

"You're damned right I am," said Cole.

"And if we choose not to obey them?"

"Then you will suffer the consequences," said Cole. "The *Theodore Roosevelt* will not be a participant in the action to come, but we are a military ship carrying military personnel, and we will do whatever is necessary to take our men to safety, with or without your consent. If we have to add a few more patients to your wards as a result, the responsibility will be yours, not mine."

"I will require a few minutes to consider the situation," she said.

"We will be there in seventeen minutes," said Cole. "Just have our crew members ready to be evacuated. Whatever else you decide is up to you, but if I were you, I'd empty that hospital as fast as possible."

"I will give you our decision shortly," said Bertha Salinas. "Please keep this channel open."

Her image vanished, and Cole turned to Christine. "Keep it open, like she says. Four Eyes, put together a boarding party in case we have to forcefully extract Sokolov and Moyer."

"I'd like to volunteer to lead the party, Captain Cole," said Jacovic.

"I appreciate the offer," answered Cole. "But the answer is no."

"May I ask the reason why?" persisted Jacovic.

Cole nodded. "The men we're evacuating don't know that you have joined us. If they see a Teroni, they may be disinclined to go anywhere with you."

"Ah." Jacovic nodded his head. "I hadn't thought of that. I apologize for making the suggestion."

"There's nothing to apologize for," said Cole. "It was an honorable request."

"It was a foolish offer which, if accepted, could have had unfortunate consequences. A Third Officer should exercise better judgment than that."

Cole smiled. "We could use a few more officers like you on our side," he said. "Mr. Briggs, is there any sign of Csonti's fleet yet?"

"I have no idea of its size, sir," said Briggs. "So I'm checking all incoming traffic, and trying to spot the *Red Sphinx*. So far, nothing's come into the system except a two-man job and a trio of cargo ships."

"Keep watching," said Cole. "I don't think they'll show for another two or three hours, but we don't want to be sitting ducks, docked at the hospital, when they get here. Christine, any word yet?"

Christine Mboya shook her head. "No, sir. The channel's still open. She could pop into view any—"

As the words left her mouth, the image of Bertha Salinas reappeared.

"Captain Cole, your men will be ready in ten minutes. Crewman Moyer is indeed attached to a machine, which has been transferred to an airsled. Lieutenant Sokolov is mobile."

"Thanks," said Cole. "We'll be there is just over fourteen minutes."

"Is your offer to evacuate the station still in force?" she continued, trying unsuccessfully to hide her concern.

*I don't know who she talked to, but it must have been pretty damned convincing,* thought Cole. Aloud he said: "It's still in force. How many patients and staff have you?"

"Three hundred seventeen patients, and a medical and administrative staff of ninety-four," she answered. "Also, more than half the patients are tied in to various life-support machines."

"It'll be cramped, but we can probably take about eighty aboard the *Theodore Roosevelt*," said Cole. "My four other ships probably can't accommodate more than another forty or fifty. I think it makes more sense to start loading them into every available ship that's at the station. My five ships will ride shotgun for you until we get to a hospital in a neighboring system."

"And your two men?"

"If Sokolov's mobile, we want him. We'll leave Moyer in your care until we can get to a hospital in another system. Now I suggest you start moving those patients *fast*. I *think* you've got a couple of hours, maybe a little longer, but no one's going to stand in his way. If he's in a hurry to get here, he could show up any minute."

"We'll begin moving your crewmen immediately," said Bertha Salinas. "Your Lieutenant Sokolov will be waiting at the end of Dock H-3."

"We'll be there," said Cole, and signaled Christine to break the connection.

"Maybe we should have asked her where the nearest hospital is," said Forrice.

"She can tell us once we leave the system," said Cole. "I get the distinct feeling that not a lot of things get done without her express orders, and I don't want her to keep talking to us when she should be directing the evacuation." He walked over and stood next to Christine. "Contact the leaders of Prometheus III and IV—presidents, kings, chancellors, whatever the hell they are—and warn them what's coming. If they're as dense as Bertha Salinas and won't believe you, let Four Eyes take a shot at it."

"And if they will to speak only to the Captain?" she asked.

"My first thought is that if they're that distrusting and bureaucratic, let Csonti and Val blow them to kingdom come," replied Cole. He sighed. "I'll be in the mess hall, grabbing some coffee."

He walked to the airlift, then turned back. "Jacovic, you've only been a member of the crew for a few hours, and it would be unfair to put you in charge of blue shift, which is one of the Third Officer's duties. But once you learn the ropes and do take over blue shift, I don't want to see you, Forrice, and Christine on the bridge together except under my explicit orders. The reason we have shifts in the first place is so that one of the command personnel is always on duty, and that the ship is never under the active authority of anyone but the Captain and the first three officers. Christine, how long until blue shift?"

"Fifty-three minutes, sir," she replied.

"All right. In fifty-four minutes I want you and Mr. Briggs off the bridge and getting some sleep. Before you leave, inform Lieutenant Mueller that she's in charge of blue shift until otherwise notified. And have Braxite take over your station."

"Yes, sir."

Forrice went off to gather a boarding party as Bertha Salinas's image appeared again.

"Captain Cole, we have decided to accept your kind offer to help us evacuate the entire hospital."

"I said we'd provide protection, not that we'd help with the evacuation," said Cole. "If Csonti gets here while you're loading your ships, I need my crew right here to work the weaponry and hold him off."

"Semantics," she said. "As long as you provide us with military protection during our exodus, that is all we require of you."

"Freely given," said Cole.

He signed off and went down to the mess hall, where Sharon joined him a moment later.

"Do me a favor," said Cole.

"What?"

"That hospital can get along just as well with ninety-three doctors as ninety-four. Find us one who knows Men, Molarians, and either Polonoi or Mollutei."

"What can I offer him?"

"The same as we're offering our officers: room, board, and two percent of net. Always assuming we *have* a net profit one of these days."

"By the way," said Sharon, "I like this Jacovic."

"I always did," agreed Cole, "even when we were on opposite sides."

"He'll do us a lot more good than Val ever did."

"Don't underestimate her," said Cole. "If there's one person in the whole damned galaxy I'd want protecting my back, it's the Valkyrie."

"But she doesn't begin to understand what we're about," protested Sharon. "Once a pirate, always a pirate."

"Believe me, we're going to miss her."

"She was more trouble than she was worth."

"She had her share of rough edges," agreed Cole, "but she was worth every bit of trouble she put us to, and more."

Christine's image appeared above the table. "We've got an incoming message from the planetary government. They say they'll only speak to the Captain."

"You'd think they're doing *me* the favor," grumbled Cole. "Which planet?"

"The third one, sir."

"Okay, pipe it through."

A tall, lean, balding man suddenly appeared in Christine's place. "I am Marcus Selamundi, planetary President of Prometheus III."

"And I'm Wilson Cole, Captain of the *Theodore Roosevelt*. Was there something about our message you didn't understand?"

"I understood the message," said Selamundi. "I have but one question: Why should I believe the notorious Wilson Cole?"

"I have no reason to lie to you," said Cole. "I just thought you deserved a warning."

"Why do you want to attack us?"

"I guess you didn't understand the message after all," said Cole. "We're not attacking you. We're warning you—or, if you prefer, we're *alerting* you. Either you or Prometheus IV or both planets are shortly going to be under attack by a warlord named Csonti. I don't know who he's mad at or why. I just know he's coming in force, and he is not known for the quality of his mercy—or even the existence of it."

"We are quite capable of defending ourselves."

"There's a difference between being capable and being prepared," explained Cole patiently. "That's why I'm alerting you."

"Have you come to offer your services, then?"

"Not to you, no," said Cole. "We're helping to evacuate the orbiting hospital, and we'll see to it that they make it safely to a medical facility in another system."

"And you have no idea why this Csonti is attacking us?" persisted Selamundi.

"No," answered Cole. "I rather thought you might."

"No, none whatsoever."

"Well, if it's you that he's after rather than Prometheus IV, then you must have something he wants. If I were you, I'd guard it as heavily as possible."

"We will devise our own strategies, thank you," said Selamundi, breaking the connection.

"Sweet guy," commented Cole sardonically. "I get the feeling that no one in this system ever learned any manners from their mothers."

"Being rude is probably the way he hides his fear," suggested Sharon.

"I don't mind his being rude, but I have a feeling that he's going to be stupid as well. He seems to have total confidence in his planetary defenses." Cole paused. "Csonti didn't pick up an empire of forty worlds by not scouting his enemies and being prepared for everything they could throw at him. Oh, well, I've warned him; it's up to him to decide what to do next."

The *Teddy R* reached the hospital station a moment later. After docking, Forrice and his landing party found Sokolov, helped him into the ship, and then stayed on the station to supervise the evacuation and make sure that Moyer was one of the first patients to be loaded onto a ship.

"How long should this take?" Cole asked.

"Commander Forrice estimates close to two hours, sir," said Christine.

"That's cutting it awfully close," remarked Cole. "Why that long?"

"Some of the life-support machines are awkward to move," she replied. "And some cannot be disconnected, even for a minute or two, so they're finding ways to power them while moving them onto the waiting ships." She frowned. "Sir?"

"Yeah?"

"There's an urgent message coming in from Lieutenant Chadwick."

"From Luthor? Okay, let's have it."

Instantly Luthor Chadwick's image appeared, full-size, a few feet away from Cole.

"Hi, Luthor," said Cole. "How's life aboard the *Red Sphinx?*"

"I'm not sure," said Chadwick, frowning. "I need to hear it from you personally: Are you part of this military action Csonti is planning?"

"No, Luthor, we're not. We never were."

"Thanks," said Chadwick. "There was some confusion about it here."

"I hope that straightens it out," said Cole.

"Indeed it does, sir," replied Chadwick. "From this point on, I'm no longer a member of the *Red Sphinx*'s crew."

"You're deserting?"

"I don't view it as deserting, sir," said Chadwick. "I've served loyally aboard the *Red Sphinx*, but I will not be a party to any military action that might put us in conflict with the *Teddy R*, now or in the future."

"I'm impressed by your loyalty, Mr. Chadwick," said Cole. "But—"

"Damn it, sir!" exploded Chadwick. "I'm the one who unlocked your cell and got you to your shuttlecraft while you were awaiting your court-martial, and I've been your assistant Chief of Security ever since I got here. I didn't do that so I could fight for a woman who is clearly disobeying, if not your orders, then at least your wishes."

"You should have left when you got Four Eyes's message," said Cole.

"It wasn't passed on to us until after we took off."

"And just how do you plan to leave your ship when it's in full flight to Prometheus?" asked Cole.

"There's a two-man shuttle, sir. I plan to take it and join up with you."

"That may be a little difficult. We'll be on our way out of the Prometheus system in another two hours."

"That's just about when we'll be arriving there, sir."

"All right," said Cole. "Christine will feed you the codes to follow, and when you're close enough Mr. Briggs will give you our exact coordinates. What about Bull Pampas?"

"He says he's staying as long as the *Red Sphinx* isn't going to be in direct conflict with the *Teddy R*."

"Okay," said Cole. "That day is probably coming, but it's not here yet. Be very careful, Luthor; I don't think Val will take kindly to your leaving her ship."

"Log off, Luthor," said a familiar female voice. He did so, and Val's image appeared.

"You look a little more sober today," noted Cole.

"I am. I woke up sick as a dog, but I got rid of my last couple of meals, which were mostly alcohol anyway, and I'm feeling better. Weaker, but better."

"So what's the purpose of this conversation?" asked Cole.

"Just to tell you that Chadwick can leave any time he wants," she said. "The same goes for Bull. They were serving on the *Teddy R* and I appropriated them for the *Red Sphinx*. They're welcome to go back. But the rest of the crew never served under you. They stay—including Perez."

"Fair enough."

"And Bull says that as long as we're not fighting the *Teddy R*, he's willing to stay with me."

"Yeah, Luthor told me."

"God, I feel awful!"

"You served under me too, Val," said Cole. "If Luthor and Bull can come back, so can you."

"I can't, Wilson," she said. "I gave my word to Csonti."

"Let him sue you."

She smiled at the thought of the warlord suing the pirate. "I've got to see it through."

"That's up to you," said Cole. "But don't go after the ships that are about to leave the hospital. We're getting the sick and wounded out of the line of fire."

"I'll see to it that no one harasses you," she promised.

"Thanks."

"Aren't you going to wish me good luck?"

"Do you even know why you're attacking Prometheus?" asked Cole.

"No."

"When you know, and convince me that your actions are justified, then I'll wish you luck."

He broke the connection.

Forrice swirled into the mess hall a moment later.

"How's it going?" asked Cole.

"So smoothly you'd swear they do it every week," said the Molarian. "I pulled the landing party back. We were just in the way."

"How are Sokolov and Moyer?"

"Sokolov's back on board," said Forrice. "He's lost about twenty pounds, maybe a little more, but he seems reasonably healthy. No prosthetics that I could see."

"And Moyer?"

"I don't know. He's got a lot of tubes running into and out of him, and he was sedated while they moved him."

"He's with one of the medical ships, not with us, right?" said Cole.

"That's right."

"Then I guess they can begin the attack in another two hours."

"We'll be on our way in ninety standard minutes, maybe a little sooner," said Forrice. "I take it Val hasn't changed her mind?"

Cole shook his head. "She didn't stop Chadwick from leaving, though."

"But she's still coming with Csonti?"

"Yeah."

"You know, Wilson," said the Molarian, "if she sticks with him, it's only a matter of time before we find ourselves facing her in battle."

"The thought hasn't escaped me," said Cole grimly.

"Two more," announced Forrice as Cole came onto the bridge a day after they had evacuated the hospital station.

"Damn!" said Cole. "What's the total now?"

"Seven dead so far. The move was hard on the patients. It still is."

"What about the hospital on Clementis VI?" said Cole. "Any word from it?"

"They're short of supplies, they're short of help, and they're full."

"Jack-in-the-Box, what are the next three closest colonized worlds?"

Jaxtaboxl studied his computer. "Ramanos, Braechea II, and New Gabon, sir."

"Rachel?" said Cole. "What kind of hospital facilities have they got?"

"Checking, sir," replied Rachel Marcos. "Ramanos is a mining world, population two hundred eighty-six, no medical facility. Braechea II was colonized by the Canphor Twins and refuses to treat Men or any of Man's allies." She studied the holoscreens that had popped up in front of her. "New Gabon doesn't claim to specialize, and treats all species . . ."

"Great!" said Cole. "That's where we're going."

". . . but they're totally full," continued Rachel. "There is a minimum of a twelve-day wait for a bed."

"Goddammit, we can't wait for twelve days!" growled Cole. "Not at the rate they're dying." He lowered his head in thought. "I've been looking at this all wrong. They've got their entire medical staff on the ships; all we need is a hospital."

"I have a feeling that's not going to be enough, Wilson," said Forrice. "We'll need a world that can supply the proper medications, and the proper power for the various life-support machines the ships are carrying."

"How hard can it be?" asked Jaxtaboxl.

"You heard the report from New Gabon," said the Molarian. "What good is having medics and doctors if we can't get our people into a hospital?"

"As long as we have the medics and the machines, how about taking over a hotel?" suggested Jaxtaboxl.

"That's fine if everyone's stabilized," said Cole. "But what if we need an operating theater—or three operating theaters at once?" He muttered a curse. "That's the problem with colony worlds. They just don't have the populations to support a huge medical industry. They lack beds, they lack hospitals, they import all their drugs from the Republic—"

"Only their legal ones," put in Jaxtaboxl.

"Sir?" said Rachel, who was operating the communications system. "Another message from the *Portmanteau.*"

"That's one of the hospital's ships, right?" said Cole.

She nodded. "They need a sophisticated medical facility in the next thirty hours, or they're going to lose another five patients, possibly six. They need to perform surgical procedures that require stationary equipment that they left behind . . ." She continued listening. " . . . And one of them, a Lodinite, seems to be slipping away for no reason that they can determine."

"Maybe we should ask how many are going to survive," said Cole. He paused, lost in thought. "You know, if the shooting's over, maybe we can get permission from whoever won to bring them back to the hospital station."

"I'll check, sir," said Jaxtaboxl. A moment later he looked up. "The battle is over. I have no idea who won, but I know who lost. The station no longer exists."

"Great!" muttered Cole disgustedly. "Just great!" Another pause. "Jack-in-the-Box, are we close to any of the larger Inner Frontier worlds—Binder X, Roosevelt III, New Kenya, any of them?"

Jaxtaboxl checked his computer, uttered a few orders to it in a language only his machine could comprehend, and surveyed the results.

"Unless Wxakgini knows of some wormholes that aren't listed here, we're no closer than four days to any of them."

Wxakgini confirmed that there were no wormhole shortcuts to the major Frontier planets in their immediate vicinity.

"Damn!" muttered Cole. "I feel responsible for this. I'm the one who told them to evacuate. For all I know, Csonti would have spared the hospital station if he'd known there were patients there."

"You don't really think so, do you?" said Forrice.

"No, of course not."

"Then stop blaming yourself," said the Molarian. "There's nothing to be done. They'll just have to make do until we can get to a major world out here."

"We're not going to give up and let them die that easily," said Cole. "Jack-in-the-Box, what's the closest Republic world with a major hospital?"

Jaxtaboxl put the question to the ship's computer. "Meadowbrook, sir."

"Pilot, how long will it take to get to Meadowbrook?"

"Approximately six hours," answered Wxakgini. "We can reach the Chabon Wormhole in an hour. It will take two hours to traverse, and it lets us out just under three hours from Meadowbrook."

"And the hospital can definitely handle us?"

"I can't see why not. It looks like a small city, all by itself."

Cole frowned. "Something's wrong. Why would they build a

facility like that on the edge of the Republic, so far from the major population centers?"

"Good question," said Forrice.

"There's one person on board who might know the answer," said Cole. "Patch me through to Jacovic."

"Yes, Captain?" said Jacovic's image a moment later.

"What do you know about a Republic planet called Meadowbrook?" asked Cole.

"I've never heard of it."

"Jack-in-the-Box, transmit a holograph of that sector of the Republic to Jacovic, and highlight Meadowbrook."

"Done, sir."

"Ah!" said Jacovic. "I see. Meadowbrook is not only on the edge of the Frontier, but it's in the sector where your Admiral Kobrinski has recently engaged the Third Teroni Fleet."

"The Teroni Fleet has moved that far into the Republic?"

"You've been away for almost two years, Captain Cole."

"Thank you, Jacovic. You told me what I need to know."

He signaled Rachel to break the connection. "Obviously it's a military hospital," said Cole. "It's probably just a year or two old. Rachel, inform the senior officers that I'm holding a meeting in my office in twenty minutes. Attendance is mandatory—and make sure the four other captains and Bertha Salinas tie in holographically."

"Christine Mboya is sleeping, sir," said Rachel.

"Then wake her. Also, have Idena Mueller and Braxite take one of the shuttles to the hospital ship that's carrying Moyer, and bring him back to the infirmary. If Moyer's tied in to a machine, bring it along. If he's got to have a medic in constant attendance, bring the medic too. Whatever we do with the other patients, we can't leave Moyer on a Republic world. Even if they saved him, he'd just be court-martialed and executed." He raised his voice. "I assume you're monitoring this, Sharon. I want you there too."

"You don't have to yell," replied Sharon Blacksmith.

"It's the easiest way to get your attention."

"All right, I'll be there."

"Rachel, have we had any contact with Luthor Chadwick yet?" asked Cole.

"Not since we heard that he was leaving the *Red Sphinx*," answered Rachel. "Actually, we don't know for a fact that he's left it yet. He might very well be waiting for the best opportunity."

Cole shook his head impatiently. "Val gave Bull Pampas and him permission to leave."

"Permission is one thing," noted Forrice. "A ship is another."

"Okay, you've got a point."

Cole paced around restlessly for a couple of minutes, then went down to his office. Sharon arrived a moment later.

"Message from David Copperfield," announced Rachel, just before the image of the elegantly clad alien popped into existence.

"Hi, David. How's it going?"

"Steerforth, how can you possibly consider having a high-level meeting and not include me?"

"It's a meeting that has nothing to do with selling our services, which is your bailiwick," answered Cole. "This doesn't concern you."

"Everything about this ship is my concern," answered Copperfield. "Steerforth, you can't do this to me! You cut me to the quick."

"Believe me, David, you've got nothing to bring to this particular discussion, and once I decide upon a course of action, you'll be the first to know."

"All right," said Copperfield sullenly, his alien face coming as close as it could to a pout. "But I resent it, Steerforth. I resent it deeply."

"I'm sorry you feel that way, David," said Cole, breaking the connection. "Rachel?"

"Yes, sir."

"No more transmissions except from Bertha Salinas and the four captains until I say otherwise. Got it?"

"Yes, sir."

Cole sat down behind his desk and sighed deeply. "Who'd have thought they'd start dying like this?" he said at last. "I mean, hell, they're surrounded by their own doctors, we moved all the machines to the ships, we brought along their medications . . ."

"*Healthy* people don't handle stress too well," replied Sharon, "and we're stressing gravely ill people. And beings."

"I know," said Cole. "But we can't let them just keep dying three and four a day. Hell, if they're stressed and having trouble adjusting to the changes, they're going to start dying in *greater* numbers, not less."

Jacovic entered the office and saluted smartly. "I heard that we lost some more patients," he said. "I assume that's what this meeting and our recent conversation is about?"

"Yeah. We didn't get them out of the line of fire just to die as a result of our actions. We were well-intentioned, but evacuating them has turned out to be as dangerous to them as leaving them right where they were." He grimaced. "Well, *almost* as dangerous," he amended.

"I assume there are no medical facilities on any nearby Frontier worlds?" said the Teroni.

"None that can handle the quantity and diversity of the patients," said Cole as Forrice entered the office. "That's why I've called this meeting."

"Thanks for giving me five minutes to grab some lunch," said the Molarian.

"You're not starving," noted Cole. "You could just as easily have had it when the meeting's over."

"I've been to your senior officers' meetings before," replied the Molarian. "Somehow they have a way of ruining my appetite. I don't imagine this one will be any different."

The images of the captains of the four smaller ships suddenly materialized, followed by that of Bertha Salinas.

Christine entered the office, greeted everyone briefly, and leaned against a bulkhead.

"All right, we're all here," said Cole. "You all know the situation. We're four days from the nearest Inner Frontier world with a hospital that can accommodate the evacuees, and we have no idea how much time or space they can spare us. Everything else is either smaller or farther." He stared at each of them in turn. "Do we all agree that the patients are our responsibility?"

"I think you're taking an awful lot of guilt on yourself," said Sharon. "If we'd left them at the hospital station, they'd have been blown to bits."

"They're not our responsibility because of any decision we made or didn't make," said Cole. "They're our responsibility because they can't fend for themselves, they need us, and we're here. It's as simple as that. I know we're mercenaries, but we were trained to help the helpless, and you don't get much more helpless than these people."

"We're *trying* to help them, Wilson," said Forrice.

"We're not doing a very good job of it," said Cole. "We're going to have to try harder."

"How?" asked the Molarian.

"Clearly you have something in mind, sir," said one of the captains, "but I have no idea what it is."

Cole turned to Jacovic. "How about you, Commander? What would you do?"

"The very same thing you're going to do," replied Jacovic calmly.

"We're four days from a Frontier hospital capable of handling the evacuees. But I believe we're just hours from the Republic world of Meadowbrook. I assume it has a major medical facility. We're going to have to transfer the patients and their physicians there."

"*You* don't have to do anything," said Bertha Salinas. "Just give us the coordinates and we'll go there on our own. I can't believe that the Republic will refuse us."

"It's not the Republic you have to worry about," said Cole. "Meadowbrook is in a war zone. If you run into any Teroni ships, you are probably fair game."

"We'll display our medical insignia," said Bertha Salinas.

Cole turned to Jacovic. "Will the Teronis honor that?"

"If they would, I might not have left the Fleet," answered Jacovic.

"There's your answer," said Cole. "Hopefully there are no Teroni ships anywhere in the area, but you have absolutely no means of defense, and you're not built to outrun them. We're going to have to come along as protection."

"In a ship that's wanted all over the Republic?" she demanded. "You say you'll protect us. Who will protect *you*?"

"She's got a point, Wilson," said Forrice. "There's still a ten-million-credit reward on your head, and a twenty-five-million-credit bounty for the ship that destroys or disables the *Teddy R.*"

"That will make it more difficult," agreed Jacovic. "But there is no alternative if we wish to save most of the patients."

"He's right, you know," said Christine. "I wish he wasn't, but he is."

"I suppose so," said Bertha Salinas unhappily. "I'm not happy about it, but we *must* get to a facility, and if we're really entering a war zone, we have no choice but to accept your help."

"I *knew* it!" said Sharon. "That's why you called this phony meeting, isn't it? You were always going to go into the Republic. You just wanted Jacovic or someone else to suggest it so you could claim it wasn't a unilateral decision."

"Making unilateral decisions goes with being the Captain," answered Cole. "But things go more smoothly when you can see that I'm right, rather than simply being told that I am."

"I don't know that you are . . ." said the Molarian.

"Speak up, Four Eyes," said Cole. "This is an open forum, and everyone's free to speak their mind, encouraged even. That goes for you four captains as well," he added, because clearly they felt uncomfortable about speaking out so recently after joining him. "Until you leave the office. Then we all speak in one voice."

"I don't like it," said Forrice glumly.

"What's bothering you, other than the obvious?"

"The numbers," said Forrice.

"I know. The Navy has a couple of hundred million ships, and we have five. But it's a big galaxy, we'll only be in the Republic for a few hours, and most if not all of their ships will be in other battle zones or on military bases."

"Not those numbers," said Forrice. "If it was just you and me, I'd say sure, let's take a chance and enter the Republic. After all, we have three hundred patients who are seriously ill." He paused. "But it's *not* just you and me. I know we're running short-handed, but even without Val and her *Red Sphinx*, we still have about sixty-five crewmen on the *Teddy R* and the other four ships. So we're not risking two men to save three hundred. We're risking maybe sixty-five or more healthy ones to save three hundred sick ones, many of whom may be beyond saving. I don't think the reward-to-failure ratio holds up very well."

"I wish I could think of a way to make the numbers look a little better," said Cole, "but we can't wait any longer. When this meeting ends, Pilot's got to alter course and get us into the Republic by the shortest possible route. Even if some wormhole spits us out a thousand light-years inside the Republic, we have no choice. Christine, I'm sorry to keep you awake, but I want you running the communications until each ship has been informed of our route, especially if we find a wormhole that will serve our purposes. I know we've got Rachel at your station now, and she's good, but for this operation I want the best."

"Yes, sir," said Christine.

"And Commander Jacovic?"

"Yes?"

"If you would like to stay behind, I'll turn the *Kermit* over to you. I don't think it's an exaggeration to say that once we're inside the Republic the Commander of the Fifth Teroni Fleet will not be welcomed with open arms."

"Thank you for the offer," said Jacovic. "It is extremely considerate of you. But it is not necessary."

"You're sure?"

Jacovic smiled. "Do you think they're going to ascertain who is aboard the *Theodore Roosevelt* before they start shooting?"

"He's got a point," said Forrice.

"And if they *do* learn who's aboard," added Sharon, "who do you think they'll shoot first—Jacovic or Wilson Cole?"

"All right," said Cole. "I just felt I owed you the opportunity to say no." He looked around the room. "Are there any other questions? Captains? Administrator Salinas? No? Then the meeting is over." The five holographic images vanished. "Christine, tell Pilot to get us to Meadowbrook as fast as possible. And once he's got the coordinates, make sure Mr. Briggs passes them on to all the other ships."

"Yes, sir," she said, saluting and heading to the door. Sharon and Jacovic followed her out, while Forrice lingered behind.

"Are we going to argue some more?" asked Cole.

"No," said the Molarian. "You've made your decision. The time to talk you out of it was five minutes ago. I tried, I failed, it's over."

"Good," said Cole. "I didn't feel like another fight. What can I do for you?"

"I just wanted to explain something to you," said Forrice. "Probably I should have explained it a long time ago."

Cole looked at him curiously. "Go ahead."

"There are four other ships in our little fleet, not counting the *Red Sphinx*. Val has wanted a ship ever since she lost the *Pegasus*, and now she's got one. I can't imagine that Jacovic doesn't want one, not after commanding an entire military fleet, and of course he'll get one as he becomes more comfortable working with us. Perez use to be the captain of the *Red Sphinx*; doubtless he deserves one, too." The Molarian paused. "By rank, I should have had a ship ahead of everyone."

"I have no disagreement with that," said Cole. "Is that what you're leading up to."

"No," said Forrice. "If I wanted one, I've have asked for it."

"I've wondered about it from time to time," admitted Cole. "I figured you were just waiting for a better one, something more substantial than the *Red Sphinx*. I'd miss working side by side with you, but of course you've got one coming to you any time you want it."

"That's just the point," said Forrice. "I *don't* want it. I've watched what command does to you." He paused. "Every life-and-death decision you make affects not only you, but the crews of five ships—six if Val ever rejoins us. Just now you had to make a decision that will doubtless affect the lives, and possibly the deaths, of close to four hundred patients and medics."

"It goes with the job."

"I don't *want* the job, even the smaller job of commanding just one ship and crew. Oh, if we were still in the Navy I'd want my own command, if for no other reason than the extra pay and the prestige. But there would still be a chain of command, and I wouldn't bear the ultimate responsibility for the victories *or* the catastrophes." The Molarian paused again, ordering his thoughts. "Out here you're the top of the chain. I'm not. But I sleep well every night. Have you taken a good look at yourself in the mirror lately? You've got bags under your eyes, you're developing nervous tics and twitches, and you've lost a lot of weight." Forrice walked to the door. "I like the thought of commanding a ship of my own—but I like being able to sleep well every night even more."

Then Cole was alone. He sat there, wondering if he'd missed an alternative, wondering if he'd made the right decision. What if he got them to the hospital and they all died anyway? And what if the *Teddy R* got shot up on the way back? He'd have killed the one without saving the other. But on the other hand . . .

"Sir? Wxakgini has pinpointed the Chabon Wormhole—I gather it's moved since it was originally charted—and says we should be entering it in fifty-one Standard minutes."

"Good!" said Cole. "Give the coordinates to our four other ships and the hospital ships."

"Already done, sir."

Cole spent the next two hours walking the ship, inspecting the Gunnery section, conversing with the other ships, having the medics access blueprints of the Meadowbrook hospital so they'd know exactly where to go once they arrived. He tried to alert the hospital, but something about the structure of the wormhole prevented it. Wormholes were like that; some moved constantly, some were stationary, some were transparent to messages, some were opaque.

Then they were out of the wormhole and into the Republic.

It was exactly eleven minutes later that he got a message from

Jack-in-the-Box, who had replaced Christine at the communications center.

"Sir, we've been spotted," he said. "According to Lieutenant Domak, a fleet of twelve Navy ships is headed directly toward us."

*Damn!* thought Cole. *You were right, Four Eyes. I'm not going to get any sleep again today.*

"How much time have we got?" asked Cole.

"They should reach us in about two Standard hours, sir," replied Jack-in-the-Box. "Shall I get Christine up here?"

"No," said Cole. "I'm not going to wake her twice in one day. Is Four Eyes up there?"

"He says he's on his way, sir."

"Okay. Ask Pilot if there are any handy wormholes, not the one we just came out of, but one that'll get us around these ships and over to another Republic world with medical facilities."

A brief pause. "Sir, he says no. There are only two wormholes in our proximity: the one that will take us back to the Inner Frontier, and another one that will dump us off between a pair of blue giants with no habitable planets for close to two hundred light-years."

"It's going to be one of those days," muttered Cole. "How about Jacovic? Is he awake or asleep?"

"He's awake, sir. He's in the mess hall. He just asked me if his presence is required on the bridge."

"Tell him to stay there," replied Cole. "I need some coffee. I'm on my way."

He arrived a moment later and sat down across from the Teroni.

"You heard the news, I gather?" he said.

"Yes, Captain Cole," replied Jacovic. "I assume we're going to retreat. We can't possibly hold our own against twelve armed Navy warships."

"Hell, this old tub couldn't fight even one of them to a draw," said Cole.

"So we're retreating?"

Cole frowned. "I don't know."

"What is hindering us?"

"We've *got* to get those patients to a hospital. We came here because they couldn't go four days before reaching one. If we retreat and go back to the Inner Frontier, I've cost them another half day."

"But the alternative is to face twelve ships that have doubtless been ordered to destroy us on sight," Jacovic pointed out mildly.

"I figure that gives me half an hour to see if there are any other alternatives before I sound the retreat. And there's another consideration."

"Oh?"

Cole nodded. "If they're within two hours of us, they can probably chase us halfway across the Inner Frontier and claim hot pursuit."

"Can they catch us?"

"Probably," said Cole. "The *Teddy R* should have been decommissioned half a century ago. To the best of my knowledge, it hasn't even been re-outfitted since then."

Forrice's image suddenly appeared.

"What is it?" asked Cole.

"A transmission from one of the Navy ships. They've identified us and order us to surrender or face the consequences." The Molarian smiled. "I gave them a totally human answer," he continued. "I told them to go fuck themselves."

Cole laughed. "I approve."

"I knew you'd be proud of me. I've had Domak run a quick survey on what we're facing: an aggregate of more than one hundred and fifty cannons—half thumpers, half burners."

"Got any more cheerful news?" said Cole.

"Yes," said Forrice. "Our number four laser cannon isn't responding to computer controls."

"Deactivate it before it shoots one of the hospital ships," said Cole.

"Any further orders?"

"You'll be the first to know."

"I wouldn't wait too long, Wilson," said Forrice seriously. "They've got a couple of class-MV ships in that group—and those things are *fast*."

"I'll take that under advisement," said Cole, breaking the connection.

"Will the Navy fire on a convoy carrying patients to a hospital?" asked Jacovic.

"If they know for a fact that's what they're carrying, they won't shoot at the hospital ships. But if they shoot at the *Teddy R* and the other four ships that clearly *aren't* carrying passengers, there's always the possibility of collateral damage." He paused. "I suppose the best course of action is to convince them that these really *are* hospital ships, get their commitment not to fire on them but instead to escort them the rest of the way to Meadowbrook, and have our five ships beat it hell for leather for the Inner Frontier."

"Will they believe the man they've been ordered to kill?" asked Jacovic.

"Not a chance. But they may believe someone like Bertha Salinas."

"The administrator?"

"She can make a better case for them to help her patients get to the hospital than I can," said Cole. "I know you've been fighting the Republic for most of your life, and there's no question that they'll destroy the *Teddy R* if they can, but they're not monsters. Once they know the situation, I guarantee they'll give the patients safe passage to Meadowbrook."

"I never thought they were monsters," replied Jacovic. "Just wrong."

"Hell, sometimes it's hard to figure out what we're even fighting about," said Cole. "Probably one of my long-dead great-uncles said something offensive to one of your long-dead great-uncles or vice versa, and both sides have been killing each other ever since."

"It's comforting to know you do not credit the Teroni Federation with one hundred percent of the blame," replied Jacovic.

"There's more than enough blame to go around," answered Cole. "And like most wars, only the innocent get killed until the final few days. Let's hope the patients aren't among them." He raised his voice. "Jack-in-the-Box, put me through to Bertha Salinas."

"Give me a few seconds," said the Mollute. "I have it now."

"What do you want?" demanded Bertha's image, and it was clear that she'd been tending to the patients, just as the doctors and nurses had.

"We find ourselves confronted by a fleet of Navy ships," said Cole. "I had hoped most of them would be stationed further into the war zone, and probably most of them are—but for whatever reason, they've left a dozen warships and fighter ships behind. The *Teddy R* has what you might call a long-standing disagreement with them, so I think they're more likely to listen to you than to me. I've going to have one of my people feed the communication codes to your computer and let you try to convince them of the gravity of your situation and the urgency of your needs."

"But—"

"Believe me, you can make a more convincing case, especially if you can transmit images of the patients," said Cole. "And we can't afford to waste any time. Will you do it?"

"Yes, Captain," said Bertha.

"I'll have one of my officers feed the codes into your computer. You should have them within twenty seconds." He broke the connection. "Jack?"

"Yes, sir?" said Jaxtaboxl.

"Feed all the com codes for Meadowbrook and the Navy into Bertha Salinas's computer. You might as well also send her any maps we have of the hospital, any lists of its personnel, anything at all that might prove useful provided she survives long enough to get there."

There was a brief silence.

"Done, sir."

"All right," said Cole. "It's up to her now, and good luck to her, because we're sure as hell not going to be any help. Hell, I wouldn't if I could."

"I don't follow you, Captain Cole," said Jacovic, frowning. "You say you wouldn't help her if you could. Excuse me, but that doesn't sound like you."

"We're here in the hope that our presence would scare off the isolated Teroni ship," answered Cole. "We didn't bargain for a small fleet of Republic ships. If I had the capability of wiping out those twelve ships, I wouldn't do it. Not unless they were firing at me, and even then I'd sooner run than fight. That's the Navy in which I served almost my whole adult life out there. I can't kill a thousand crewmen just for following orders to hunt down a mutineer. They're mostly kids like Rachel Marcos. They don't know why I took over command of the *Teddy R*, and no one on their side is going to tell them."

"You're a decent and intelligent Man, Captain Cole," said the Teroni after a moment's silence. "I can see why the Navy had no use for you."

"Sir?" said Jaxtaboxl. "She's contacted them."

"Good," said Cole. "I want everyone up there—you, Domak, even Four Eyes, and also the captains of the other four ships—to start monitoring all transmissions from the Navy ships. Especially transmissions from one Navy ship to another. Put me through to Christine."

"But she's—"

"Yeah, I know. Do it anyway."

"Yes, sir?" said Christine groggily as Cole's signal woke her.

"I hate to do this twice to you in one shift," said Cole, "but I want you to get up to the bridge as fast as you can."

"Are we under attack?" she asked, swinging her feet to the floor, suddenly alert.

"No, not yet. But we're facing a dozen Navy ships. They're doubtless using scramble codes, and I've got to know everything the Navy ships are saying to each other."

"It's a good thing I was so tired I slept in my uniform," she said, getting to her feet. "I'm on my way."

"Thanks."

The connection ended, and he turned back to Jacovic. "Theoretically anyone can work the equipment, but she's got the magic touch—and I'm getting an idea that can utilize it."

"What is it?" asked Jacovic.

"Soon," said Cole. "I want to hear what they reply to Bertha Salinas first." He instructed the table to produce a cup of coffee for him. "I just remembered why I came down here in the first place," he said with a smile.

"Humans seem addicted to that drink," noted Jacovic.

"Most of them like it for the caffeine, which is a mild stimulant. It helps keep them awake and alert. Me, I like it for the taste. We insist on using real coffee beans on this ship. Damned near everything else in the galley is artificial, mostly soya products made up to resemble real food."

"I found my food both authentic and very satisfying," noted the Teroni.

Cole smiled. "That's the advantage of being a non-human on a ship built by Men," he said. "They couldn't be sure of who else would be aboard, so they made no provision for artificial or substitute food for the non-human crew. As a result, everything we carry for you and Domak and Four Eyes and the others is natural food. Everything we carry for ourselves is phony. Except the coffee," he concluded, taking a sip.

Christine's image materialized above the table. "Sir, the Navy has just agreed to let the patients continue to Meadowbrook."

"And?"

"That's all so far, sir."

"Keep monitoring them. What they say to each other in the next couple of minutes will determine what we do."

"Yes, sir," she said as her image vanished.

"Will they keep their word, Captain?" asked Jacovic.

"Probably," said Cole. "They have nothing to fear from a bunch of hospital ships. You can be sure they'll scan the interiors to make certain we're sending them patients and not bombs." He paused. "We might as well assume they're telling the truth. There's no way we can stop them if they decide to start shooting."

"It seems reasonable to assume that if we accompany the hospital ships we'll become very easy targets," agreed Jacovic. "Since the hospital ships have been promised safe passage to Meadowbrook, shouldn't we head back to the Inner Frontier immediately?"

"We will, but as I pointed out, the concept of hot pursuit is especially elastic out here near the Frontier border. I want to make sure they don't follow us."

"How do you propose to do that, if I may ask?"

"Like I said, I've got an idea," replied Cole. "I just need to know exactly what they're up to."

Forrice entered the mess hall and joined them.

"I thought you were minding the store," said Cole.

"They're two hours away—well, an hour and forty minutes, anyway—and Domak or Christine can summon me if I'm needed. In the meantime, I figured you two were sitting here telling dirty jokes, and I thought I'd listen in."

"You have to excuse my First Officer," said Cole to Jacovic. "Someone told him Molarians have a sense of humor, and he believed it."

"All right, I'll be serious for a minute," said Forrice. "Have you got some plan, or are we just waiting until those Navy ships are close enough to blow us away? We're still approaching them, you know."

"I know."

"Well, then?"

"Keep your shirt on."

"Wilson, we're not going to stay out of range forever," said Forrice. "If you've got something in mind, it would be thoughtful to let your First Officer know what it is."

"I plan to go back to the Inner Frontier."

"Good!" said the Molarian. "Let's go!"

"Not yet."

"If you tease them enough, Wilson, they'll follow you all the way to the black hole at the Core," said Forrice. "You know that, don't you?"

"I just need to find out if they're summoning help or coming with just the twelve ships," said Cole.

"What difference does it make?" demanded Forrice. "We probably couldn't beat any single one of them."

"Just relax, Four Eyes," said Cole. "The trick isn't getting out of here in one piece. That's a given. The object of the exercise, now that they've agreed to take the patients, is to make sure we don't have to be looking over our shoulder for the next month."

"We'll know in just a second," said Cole as Christine's image reappeared.

"It took the computer almost a full minute to decode their scramble code once I found the frequency they were conferring on, sir," she said. "They have decided that if no military ships—by which it's clear they mean us and our four satellites—accompany the hospital ships, they will trust to Meadowbrook's scanners and defenses to ferret out any potential threats, and will attack the *Teddy R* with all twelve ships. They assume that we won't approach any closer, but if any of the other four do, they'll leave two ships behind, which is clearly more than they will need against such relatively small ships."

She fell silent, and finally Cole said, "That's it?"

"That's everything that was said, yes, sir."

"Nothing about summoning help from other systems?"

"No, sir," answered Christine. "They seem to think they have ample firepower without requesting more."

"Okay, that's it," said Cole decisively. "Contact the nearest of the four ships and have it dock at our shuttle bay as quickly as possible. Tell the other three to spread out and be ready to enter the wormhole that leads back to the Frontier on my command."

"That's what you were waiting for?" asked Forrice, puzzled. "But you knew they were going to attack us."

"Of course I knew. But I had to know how many ships they planned on sending. If they'd asked for more from neighboring systems, we'd have had to change the script."

"What script?"

"To the play that Commander Jacovic and I are going to perform for them," answered Cole.

"Which of the ships has docked with us?" asked Cole as he walked onto the bridge, accompanied by Forrice and Jacovic.

"The *Silent Dart*, sir," said Domak.

"Okay," said Cole. "That's the ship Jacovic will command." He turned to the Teroni. "Can you come up with a good Teroni name for it, one that isn't in use?"

"*Korabota*," replied Jacovic. "It would translate as 'Killer Snake' in Terran."

"Good. For the next few hours the *Silent Dart* will become the *Korabota*. Christine, Domak, this is very important: under no circumstance will you refer to it as anything except the *Korabota*. Four Eyes, have Briggs enter the *Silent Dart* and change whatever needs changing to *Korabota*—subspace radio ID, whatever."

"Do you want me to have Slick change the insignia on the exterior of the ship?"

Cole shook his head. "Hopefully no one's going to get close enough to see it. Christine?"

"Sir?"

"What frequencies can the Navy ships read from this distance?"

"Just about all of them, sir," she said. "Perhaps if I knew what you had in mind . . ."

"You will," answered Cole. "Have we got some frequency that's relatively difficult to read from this distance? I don't want to make this too easy for them."

"Probably Frequency number Q03W6—"

"I don't need to know the number," he interrupted her. "But give it to Mr. Briggs and tell him that I want him to adjust the subspace radio on the *Silent*— . . . on the *Korabota* to send only on that frequency."

"Yes, sir," said Christine. "What about receiving?"

"Let it receive on all frequencies."

"I'll pass the word to Mr. Briggs."

"All right," said Cole. "I think that takes care of everything that needs to be done on the *Teddy R* and the *Korabota*."

"I'll do what you ask, sir," said Christine, a puzzled frown on her face, "but I really don't see what I'm doing it *for*."

Cole smiled. "That's because you're young and idealistic and honorable, Lieutenant. Not to worry; you'll grow out of all three." He turned to Forrice and Jacovic. "You two jaded realists have doubtless figured it out, of course."

"I've figured it out, all right," said the Molarian. "But they're never going to buy it."

"Why not?" replied Cole. "I'm Number One on their Most Wanted list. I deposed a starship captain in wartime. I broke out of a military prison. I returned covertly to the Republic to sell stolen diamonds. I am a villain of titanic proportions if I say so myself."

"You have a point," admitted Forrice. "Maybe I should turn you in for the reward."

"It is a shame you don't have anyone aboard the *Theodore Roosevelt* who speaks the Teroni tongue," said Jacovic. "It would lend to the illusion."

"I agree," said Cole. "We'll just have to make do with what we've got. I know you speak Terran fluently, but it'll make more of an impression if you take a T-pack along, speak Teron, and let it translate you into that annoying monotone."

"Ah!" said Christine excitedly. "Now I see!"

"We'll have to be clear on some details," said Cole. "You can't say you're still commanding the Fifth Teroni Fleet. It's too easy for them to check its whereabouts." He paused and considered the problem. "How many fleets does the Teroni Federation have now?"

"Fourteen," replied Jacovic.

"All right," said Cole. "You've been chosen to head the newly formed Fifteenth Fleet. You're not up to strength yet, but you've got close to two hundred ships with you. You've been whipping them into shape, holding maneuvers on the Inner Frontier."

"How did we meet?"

"I contacted you with a proposition. We'll argue about it once you're aboard the *Korabota*."

"Should I go there now?" asked Jacovic.

"Wait until Lieutenant Briggs tells us that he's adjusted the radio."

"Oh my goodness!" exclaimed Christine. "I was so fascinated by what you were saying that I forgot to tell him!"

"It's all right," said Cole soothingly. "Calm down. It only cost us a minute, and the Navy ships are still an hour and a half away."

"I'm sorry, sir," she said miserably. "I just—"

"Contact Briggs now," said Cole. "Apologize later."

"Yes, sir."

"How long do we wait?" asked Jacovic as Christine was transmitting the instructions to Briggs.

"We don't want them getting too close," said Cole. "They've got to be faster than we are, and I'm sure they've got the latest in long-range weaponry." He was silent for a moment as he considered the problem. "If they haven't bought it in ten minutes, we'd better run hell for leather through the wormhole and hope we beat them out the other end. And we don't rendezvous. We split up, make them divide their forces, and meet the survivors back at Singapore Station in ten Standard days. But hopefully it won't come to that."

Briggs's image appeared a minute later and announced that the radio had been adjusted.

"Okay," said Cole. "Good luck."

Jacovic saluted—Cole assumed it was a salute; it wasn't like any he'd ever seen before, but he couldn't think of what else it might be—and headed off to the shuttle bay.

"Christine, get me the captain of the *Silent Dart*. And this is an intraship communication, not a subspace message. I don't want the Navy ships to be able to read it."

"I'll make the signal so weak that no one more than a mile away can pick it up, sir." There was a brief pause. "You're connected, sir."

"In another minute Commander Jacovic, the Third Officer of the *Teddy R*, is going to board your ship. I want you to turn over command of it to him for a period of one hour. Should you be attacked, command will automatically and instantly revert to you. Commander Jacovic will have full access to the subspace radio. I want every member of the crew, including yourself, out of holo range, so that when his messages and image are transmitted, no one else can be seen or detected. Is that clear?"

"Yes, sir," said the captain of the *Silent Dart*. "Just for an hour, you say?"

"That's right. And during that hour, no one contradicts him, no one says a word. If he calls your ship by another name, if he threatens me, if he makes claims that you know to be untrue, you are to remain silent. Is that understood?"

"Yes, sir."

"Pass the word to your crew."

"We only have a crew of six, and they all can see and hear you, sir."

"As soon as you know Jacovic is safely aboard, put as much distance as you can between our two ships and then turn over command to him. I'm ending this transmission now."

He nodded to Christine, who broke the connection.

"What do we do now, sir?" asked Domak.

"Now we wait for about ten minutes, until the *Korabota* is far enough away to justify speaking to her via subspace radio. And then we see if Commander Jacovic has spent enough time associating with Men to lie convincingly."

Cole turned and walked to the airlift.

"Let me guess," said Forrice. "You're going to have another cup of that stuff you're addicted to."

"No," said Cole. "I'm going to get rid of the last two or three cups. Even your steel-bladdered Captain has to answer the occasional call of Nature."

Cole entered the human bathroom that was next to the airlift. When he was done, he slapped cold water on his face, combed his hair (which never seemed to stay in place), had half a smokeless cigarette and threw the remainder in the trash atomizer, and finally returned to the bridge. He came to a stop, hands on hips, and studied his surroundings.

"Forgotten what the place looks like?" asked Forrice after a moment.

"Just trying to decide where to stand, in case they can pick up a visual as well as an audio," replied Cole.

"Why not your office or the mess hall, which is where you usually conduct business from?"

"The Navy used to frown on that," answered Cole. "They believed that important decisions could only be made on the bridge. And since we're expecting the Navy to intercept this transmission, we want them to know that this is important business." Finally he walked over to the sensor console. "Here, I think."

"Why not by the communications station?" asked the Molarian. "It's more impressive."

"Because we're not disabling its functions, and I don't want to pretend I don't see it lighting up like a Christmas tree when it reports that all our incoming and outgoing messages are being intercepted."

"What's a Christmas tree?"

"Ask me tomorrow," said Cole, looking at the ship's chronometer. "It's time. Christine, contact the *Korabota* on the frequency you decided upon. From this point on, nobody speaks except me."

Jacovic's image popped into existence. "Greetings, Captain Cole," he said through his T-pack.

"Hello, Commander Jacovic."

"I see the Navy ships are closing in on you."

"Don't worry," said Cole. "I've got plenty of time before I have to move."

"You are a foolish man, Captain Cole," said Jacovic. "You have ten Standard minutes at the most."

"I've got more than that," replied Cole. "But ten minutes should be enough for us to reach an agreement." *Don't blow it now*, thought Cole. *Start arguing so we can let them know what the agreement is.*

"I have already entered into a binding contract with you," said the Teroni.

"Well, 'binding' is a very elastic word," said Cole. "The *Teddy R's* the ship that's at risk, not the *Korabota*. I want more."

"We have agreed upon a price, Captain Cole. This is not the time to renegotiate it."

"Look," said Cole. "I heard that you and the *Korabota* were taking this new Fifteenth Fleet out on maneuvers. Don't forget—I'm the one who contacted you and said I could lure some Navy ships to the Frontier, get so close to them that they'd claim hot pursuit and follow me right to you, where you'd be waiting for them with your two hundred ships."

"I have only one hundred and eighty-seven ships, and some of them are not battle-ready," replied Jacovic.

"Fine," said Cole. "So you'll only have a hundred and fifty or sixty to their twelve. Big deal. Once I lure them into the wormhole, they're dead meat and you know it, and the numbers are such that you have nothing to worry about. But I'm the one who's going to be bait, who has to let them get close enough to think they've got a chance of nailing me. A million credits isn't enough. I want two million."

"First, we do not deal in credits but in New Stalin rubles, as agreed. Second, I will not allow you to extort more money from the Teroni Federation. The agreement was for one million rubles, and that is what we shall pay you. Third, if you abrogate our agreement, if you make any attempt to warn the Navy that the Fifteenth Fleet lies in wait for them, I will consider that an act of war against the Teroni Federation on your part and will respond accordingly. Am I making myself clear?"

"All right, all right," said Cole, putting an edge of annoyance into his voice. "I'm going to lead them into the wormhole now. Just make sure you let the *Teddy R* pass through unscathed—and don't forget: my money is due the instant the last of the Navy ships has been destroyed."

"It will be waiting for you, if you can actually draw the twelve ships into the wormhole," said Jacovic.

"Just keep your eyes open," said Cole, signaling to Christine to break the connection. "Pilot, take us to the wormhole, but don't reach it for fifteen minutes."

Wxakgini increased the ship's speed. "Fifteen minutes, yes, sir," he announced.

Cole then ordered his other three ships to make their way to the wormhole. "Now let's see if they bought it," he said.

The Navy continued closing on the *Teddy R* for the next seven minutes, then eight, then ten.

"We will enter the wormhole in five minutes," announced Wxakgini.

And then, just as the *Korabota* disappeared into the wormhole, Forrice, studying the sensor holoscreens over Domak's shoulder, gave a hoot of triumph.

"They're shearing off!" he said.

"*That's* a relief!" said Cole as the last of the Navy ships changed course and headed back toward Meadowbrook. "I think when we retire from the mercenary business, Commander Jacovic and I have a definite future in the theater."

"I disagree, sir," said Christine.

"Oh?"

"After today, I see you as snake-oil salesmen."

The *Teddy R* and its companion ships made it back to Singapore Station without any further problems. Cole declared a three-day shore leave for all but a rotating skeleton staff, made sure the galleys were resupplied, and, accompanied by Sharon Blacksmith and David Copperfield, he soon made his way to Duke's Place. Forrice contacted the Molarian whorehouse, found out that two of the new prostitutes had come into season, and went off to pay them a visit, promising to rejoin Cole's party within two hours.

The casino was crowded as usual, and Cole noticed a certain tension as he entered the place. He spotted Csonti sitting at a *Khalimesh* table, looked around for Val, saw her at another table, and decided everyone was surprised to see both him and the redheaded Valkyrie alive and in the same place. Clearly they anticipated a fight, but Cole paid her no attention, and wandered over to where the Platinum Duke sat in isolated splendor, surveying this portion of his empire.

"I'm glad to see you all survived," he said as Cole, Sharon, and Copperfield approached him. "Have a seat. The first drink's on the house."

"Thanks," said Cole. "I'll just have a beer."

"An Antarean brandy," said Sharon.

"And I'll have a glass of 1955 A.D. *Dom Perignon*, preferably from the north slope," added Copperfield.

"Come on, David," said the Duke wearily. "No games."

"I was quite serious," said Copperfield. "However, until you see fit to properly supply your cellar, I'll have a Cygnian cognac."

"How did it go?" asked the Duke, as the table transmitted the drink orders to the bar. "Were you able to get your two crewmen out?"

Cole nodded. "Yeah. One's back on duty, the other's recuperating in our infirmary."

"He did more than that," said Copperfield proudly. "He evacuated the entire hospital station."

"I wouldn't think the whole station would fit on your ships," commented the Duke.

"It's a long story," said Cole. "I'm sure Val has told you her side of it."

The Duke shook his head. "She hasn't even stopped by to say hello."

"Well, with her and Csonti both here, I think we can assume they won," said Cole as the drinks arrived.

"I wish Csonti would go somewhere else," said the Duke. "He's been drinking and drugging since he got back, and he's pretty disruptive even when he's sober."

"So throw him out," said Sharon.

"The only person who can throw him out is your Valkyrie, and she's working for him."

"She's not *our* Valkyrie," said Cole. "And I very much doubt that she's working for Csonti now that they're back from the Prometheus system."

Val suddenly noticed them, got up from her table, and began walking over.

"You're about to find out," observed the Duke.

Cole watched Val approach, and stood up to greet her when she reached the table.

"Please sit down and join us," said the Duke.

"Thanks, I will," replied Val.

"How did it go?" asked Cole after she sat down.

"We won."

"That much is obvious," replied Cole. "After all, you're here."

"We lost six ships," she continued. "That damned planet was better defended than we'd thought."

"How much damage did you do?"

She shrugged. "As much as we had to. Csonti didn't want to kill everyone. He just wanted to make sure they changed their minds about not paying their annual tribute."

"Correct me if I'm wrong," said Cole, "but didn't you help us stop someone from doing just that on Bannister II?"

"Yes," said Val. "And we were well paid for it. This time it was the extortionist doing the paying."

"And you don't see any difference?"

"We're supposed to be mercenaries, remember?" Val shot back. "That means our services are for hire. It's not our job to make moral judgments."

"If we don't, who will?"

"You know something?" she said. "This is the same attitude that made you a lousy pirate. *You* were the one who decided we were going to give up pirating and become mercenaries. Why don't you look the word up in your computer's dictionary?"

"I was *there*, Val. The hospital station wasn't threatening anyone, and it had no defenses. There wasn't a weapon, even a handgun, on the whole damned thing, just three hundred very sick Men and aliens, and some dedicated doctors."

"You were there?" she said, surprised. "I never saw you."

"We finished evacuating the station before you got there. You didn't know that, and you blew it to pieces."

"Not me," she said. "I landed and took over the parliament building, or whatever they call the damned thing."

"*Someone* in your fleet hit it. If we hadn't gotten there first, you'd have killed four hundred people who had no means of defending themselves. Is *that* the kind of mercenary you want to be?"

"Damn it, Cole! I told you I didn't do it!"

"And I told you the guy you work for did it, or ordered it done."

"I'm not my brother's keeper."

"Any guy who goes after a hospital sure as hell needs one," said Cole.

"You're not paying attention," said Val. "I had nothing to do with the fucking hospital station! I was fighting hand-to-hand on the planet."

"Thereby freeing someone else to blow up the hospital station."

"Someone else!" she snapped. "Not me! Were you responsible for every bomb the Navy dropped on Teroni civilians?"

"I don't think I'm getting through to you at all," replied Cole.

"I made three million Maria Theresa dollars for three days' work," said Val. "You have four hundred people who owe you their lives. How much did *you* make?"

"Not a single credit."

"What happened on Prometheus III was going to happen whether I helped Csonti or not. There's probably five thousand more people alive today *because* I helped end the action sooner. If I hadn't signed on, someone else would have. This place"—she waved a hand to indicate the whole of Singapore Station—"is lousy with people who will hire out to do just about anything."

"When we got the *Pegasus* back for you from the Hammerhead Shark, do you remember why you chose to stay on the *Teddy R* instead?" said Cole.

Val shifted uncomfortably in her chair. "Situations change," she said.

"Some things change, some don't," said Cole. "You said you were going to stay because your crew had sold you out, while mine had given up their careers and even their citizenship for me, and you wanted to find out how to inspire that kind of loyalty." He paused. "They didn't do it because I side with extortionists. They didn't do it because I ally myself with people who destroy hospitals. They didn't do it because—"

"You're Navy," she interrupted. "You were all trained one way. I wasn't. Damn it, you said we were going to be mercenaries. Well, *I'm* a mercenary. What are you?"

Cole was about to answer when there was a sudden commotion across the room.

"What the hell's going on there?" said the Duke.

Suddenly bodies were being flung in every direction, and they could hear Csonti's deep bass voice bellowing in rage.

"He's destroying my place!" exclaimed the Duke, as a pair of tables crashed to the floor under the weight of flying bodies.

"He'll calm down in a few minutes," said Val. "He gets like that when he drinks too much."

"In a few minutes?" repeated the Platinum Duke. "In a few minutes he'll have killed a dozen people and destroyed most of my tables!" He looked around the table. "Will you back me up?"

"What'll you pay me to take him?" asked Val.

Before the Duke could answer her, Cole got to his feet. "Keep your money. I'll ride shotgun for you."

"You think *you* can beat him in a fair fight?" said Val, amused.

"I don't intend to find out," replied Cole. He and the Duke walked across the casino to where Csonti was wrecking havoc. When they arrived at their destination, Cole adjusted his sonic pistol's strength down from Lethal to Stun. "That's enough," he said in even tones.

Csonti looked up from the carnage. "Who the hell are you?"

"Why don't we sit down quietly and I'll be happy to tell you?" suggested Cole.

"Because I'm enjoying myself right here!" bellowed Csonti.

"I want you out of here!" demanded the Duke. "I expect you to pay for the damage, and from this day forward, you are barred from this casino."

Csonti picked up a chair and hurled it at the Duke, who barely sidestepped it.

"That's it!" said the Duke. "You are no longer welcome on Singapore Station!"

"Who's going to put me off?" roared Csonti. "You?"

"No," said Cole, firing his screecher. "Me."

Csonti staggered backward as the force of the almost-solid sound stuck him. Blood began trickling from both ears and he seemed suddenly disoriented. He fell heavily to the floor, unconscious, a second later.

"Where's your jail?" Cole asked the Duke.

"We don't have one."

"Wonderful," muttered Cole. Then, to the assembled patrons: "Is there anyone here who serves with him? Anyone who can take him back to his ship?"

Three men at the *jabob* table indicated they were part of Csonti's crew.

"But I'll be damned if I'm going to carry him back to the ship," said one. "I don't want to be around when he wakes up."

"Me neither," said one of his companions.

"Hell, he just paid me off," said Val, walking over. "I suppose I can take him to his ship in exchange for that."

She reached Csonti's huge, muscular body, picked it up as if it was a feather, hefted it over her shoulder, and carried the unconscious warlord out of the casino.

"These five are going to need medical attention," said Sharon, indicating three Men, a Lodinite, and a Mollutei that were strewn across the floor. "I suppose I might as well have them brought to the *Teddy R*'s infirmary and see if that doctor we picked up from the Prometheus station is any good."

"Yeah," assented Cole. "No sense having him work on anyone real important, like us, until we know if we can trust him."

"I assume that was a joke?" said Sharon.

Cole nodded. "But a true one."

"Whatever that means." Sharon contacted the ship and ordered five airsleds, then went around the casino recruiting volunteers to carry the injured parties back to the *Teddy R.*

"He'll be back, you know," said Cole as he and the Duke returned to the table.

"I know," replied the Duke. "But at least he'll be sober. I hope."

Cole suddenly noticed David Copperfield crawling out from under the table.

"Thanks for protecting the floor, David," he said sardonically.

"I'm a businessman, not a fighter," replied Copperfield with as much dignity as he could muster.

"Did you get much business done down there?" asked Cole.

"I have never denied my limitations," said Copperfield. "But it is unkind of you to refer to them, Steerforth."

"I apologize, David," said Cole. "I didn't mean to offend you."

"One friend cannot offend another," replied Copperfield. "But he can *hurt* him with an unkind remark."

"I'll keep it in mind."

"I assume you took care of that ruffian?"

"I think ruffian is a bit of an understatement," said Cole. "That's the biggest warlord we've come across since we reached the Inner Frontier. And the worst-tempered."

"Where is the remarkable Olivia Twist?"

"She's carrying Csonti to his ship."

"You mean guiding an airsled?" said David.

"I meant what I said."

"Damn the man!" said the Duke. "He probably did ten thousand credits' worth of damage!"

"Not counting medical expenses," said Cole, as Sharon rejoined them.

"The sleds should be here in just another minute or two," she announced.

"That bastard is never setting foot on my station again!" said the Duke.

"You start banning every criminal who drinks and drugs too much and you're going to be a mighty lonely casino owner," observed Cole.

"I'll ban everyone who behaves like *that*!" answered the Duke.

Cole turned to Sharon. "Alert the ship's medic and tell him he's about to get a little more work."

She nodded her head. "Right. I'll have Vladimir Sokolov give him a hand, since he's been confined to the ship for another few days anyway while he's recuperating."

"Will one wounded assistant be enough?" asked Cole.

"Probably," she replied. "None of the injured parties are dying. I think we may have two or three with broken bones, but they can wait their turn to have them set."

"Even so, let's not overwhelm the poor son of a bitch his first couple of days on the job. Offer five hundred Far London pounds to any of the sled guides who'll stick around until he's tended to all the patients."

"That's a lot of money for a few hours' work," noted Sharon. "What if they all volunteer?"

"Then take the first two who offer, thank the others, and send them back here."

"Ah! Here are the sleds now," said Sharon, glancing at the casino's entrance. "I think I'll go over and make the offer right now."

"And make sure they know these five are pretty busted up and need delicate handling," said Cole as she got up and left the table, almost bumping into Jacovic, who was approaching the table.

"I heard there was a disturbance here," he said. "I thought I'd see if it involved our crew."

"Word gets out fast," remarked Cole as the Teroni sat down. "It couldn't have happened more than five minutes ago."

"I was dining at a restaurant just down the street," answered Jacovic.

"A drunken warlord named Csonti got out of hand," said the Duke. "He injured some customers, and he did at least fifteen thousand credits' damage to my furnishings."

"I thought it was ten thousand," said Cole.

"Ten, fifteen, what's the difference?" said the Duke irritably. "The man went berserk. Hell, he probably cost me more than that, just from the loss of business. A couple of those people who are being carried out on airsleds were high rollers, and I saw a few others head for the exit."

"You're all heart, Duke," said Cole. "It's nice to know you care."

"Obviously someone stopped him," noted Jacovic.

"Your Captain did," said the Duke.

"Is he the type to carry a grudge?" asked the Teroni.

"Who knows?" said Cole with a shrug. "Even if he does, it was a choice between that or letting him put another five or six into our infirmary before he ran out of energy."

"And he's been banned from Singapore Station," added the Duke. "Once he sobers up, he'll go away and bother some other casino."

Sharon returned to the table. "All taken care of," she announced. "We had three volunteers to help the new medic, so I made the offer three hundred pounds apiece. We saved a hundred pounds and got an extra helper in the bargain. I told Sokolov to go back to his cabin, but he insisted on helping."

"Fine. How are the wounded holding up?"

"I think most of them are glad to still be alive," answered Sharon.

"Or surprised, anyway. I gather Csonti's rages are not exactly a closely kept secret, and he's done worse than hospitalize bystanders on a number of occasions."

"Sweet fellow," commented Cole. Suddenly he smiled. "He'd better not take a swing at Val. He'll never know what hit him."

"You sound like you still admire her," said Jacovic.

"I admire what she can do," said Cole, sipping his beer and making a face as he realized it was now warm. "And I admire what she could become. She's like a very headstrong but very promising young pet. She just needs a little discipline and a little maturity."

"Preferably before she's killed off the whole Inner Frontier," added Sharon.

"If we had been a little slower reaching Prometheus, or she had been a little faster, she might have fired on us," said Jacovic.

Cole shook his head. "No. She's capable of a lot of dumb things, but that isn't one of them. She's not without a sense of loyalty, and we helped her out when she lost her ship."

"Speaking of the devil . . ." said Sharon, looking at the entrance, where Val had just appeared.

The redhead walked straight to their table, towering above all the other humans as usual, and sat down on the chair she had vacated after the altercation.

"How's the patient?" asked Cole.

"He's awake," said Val. "And mad as hell."

"At anyone in particular, or just at the whole damned galaxy?" asked Cole.

"He's really pissed off at you," she replied.

"He has that in common with the Republic and the Teroni Federation," said Cole. "He'll have to wait in line."

"But he's maddest of all at the Duke for banishing him from the

station in front of everyone," Val continued. "He thinks you've publicly humiliated him in front of his friends."

"He hasn't got any friends," said Cole.

"I'm not letting him back," replied the Duke adamantly.

"*That's* not the problem," said Val. "He doesn't plan to set foot on
Singapore Station ever again."

"Good," said the Duke. "Surprising, but good."

"You didn't let me finish. He doesn't plan for anyone else to ever
set foot here again either."

"Explain," demanded Cole.

"He's going to do to Singapore Station what he did to the
Prometheus hospital station." Val turned to the Duke. "He's offered
the *Red Sphinx* four million Far London pounds to join him. What will
you offer us to defend you?"

"Not one credit," said Cole before the Platinum Duke could
answer. "We don't attack our friends."

"You say the Duke is my friend," said Val. "But I exposed cheaters
here and got nothing for it."

"Bullshit," said Cole. "You got a ship for your trouble."

"He gave *you* the assignment, not me—and we had to work our
asses off for that ship," Val shot back. "If he's my friend and Csonti
isn't, then why won't he match what Csonti is offering?"

"Csonti's not anyone's friend," said Cole. "Do you really think he
gives a damn about anyone but himself?"

"Don't try to confuse the issue. I'm offering my services to the
Duke. He can afford them. If he chooses not to purchase them, then
they go to the only other bidder."

"Do you know how many people live on Singapore Station, how
many people you'll kill if you destroy it?" demanded the Duke.

"The only ones facing any danger are those who stay and fight," said Val. "I'll make sure Csonti doesn't attack for at least three days, which will give everyone who wants to leave enough time to do so. I owe Cole that much."

"You owe him a hell of a lot more than that," said Sharon sharply.

"Then have him convince the Duke to match Csonti's offer," replied Val.

"Not a chance," said Cole.

"Then we have nothing more to say," said Val, getting to her feet.

"Excuse me," said Jacovic, speaking for the first time since Val had arrived. "If any of this is because I now hold your former position aboard the *Theodore Roosevelt*, I would be happy to relinquish it to you."

"I was a Captain before I met Wilson Cole, and I'm a Captain now," she replied. "What the hell do I want to be a Third Officer for?"

And with that, she turned her back on them and walked out of the casino.

"I hope to hell the station's got some defenses built into it," said Cole. "Csonti's going to have at least thirty ships, maybe as many as forty. We've got five, and four of them don't have much firepower."

"We are not without defenses," responded the Duke. "Not as many as I wish we had at this moment, but we are not totally defenseless."

"We've got three days," said Cole. "Sharon, pass the word: all shore leaves are canceled. They should be getting used to that. Then tell Four Eyes and Mustapha Odom that I want them to inspect the station's offensive and defensive capabilities immediately. Oh—and have Briggs and Bull accompany them. They know weaponry better than any of the other crew members."

"Bull Pampas is still aboard the *Red Sphinx*," Sharon reminded him.

"Shit! I forgot," said Cole. "Contact him and explain that if he stays there he's going to find himself fighting against the *Teddy R.*"

"Anything else?" she said.

"Not right now."

"I'll contact them from the bathroom," she said, getting up. "There's too much background noise here."

"I thought," said Jacovic as Sharon began walking away, "that the Valkyrie would never take up arms against the *Theodore Roosevelt*."

"I wonder what idiot said that?" replied Cole.

A full day had passed.

Odom, Briggs, and Forrice had spent the time inspecting the station and examining such minimal blueprints as existed. Bull Pampas had shown up halfway through the day, moved his gear back onto the *Teddy R*, and joined them.

Cole had held two meetings with the captains of the four smaller ships, and had finally sent them back to prepare their vessels' weapons and defenses, and to see if they could come up with any viable strategy between them.

"We aren't getting anything accomplished," he admitted to Jacovic as the two sat alone at a table at Duke's Place. "How do you deploy four small ships that possess minimal firepower against a fleet of thirty-five to forty enemy ships?"

"You go for the head, and the body will be directionless," answered Jacovic. "That's the first thing they teach Teroni officers. If you're outnumbered, and escape is impossible or impractical, go after your opponents' leader with everything you have."

"I'm not worried about Csonti as much as I am about the *Red Sphinx*," said Cole.

"There's an alternative," said the Teroni.

"Cut and run?"

Jacovic nodded. "You're under no obligation to defend Singapore Station. All you did was break up a fight."

"They wouldn't be coming after the station if I hadn't broken it up," said Cole. "Would *you* run?"

"No, probably not," admitted Jacovic.

Cole took a swallow of his beer. "This stuff is getting flat," he complained. "Where's the Duke?"

"I haven't seen him."

"He'd better not be packing his gear into a ship," said Cole. "If *he* deserts the station, I'll be damned if we're going to stay and defend it."

Almost as if on cue the Platinum Duke walked over and sat down at the table.

"Where the hell were you?" demanded Cole.

"Sleeping," answered the Duke. "There are no days or nights here, so I sleep when I'm tired and I stay awake when I'm not."

"My beer's gone flat."

"How long have you been nursing it?"

"I don't know. Jacovic, how long have we been figuring the odds against defeating Csonti's fleet?"

"Two hours, maybe three," answered the Teroni.

"Two more beers," the Duke ordered, and the table responded with fresh beers almost instantly. "I'm sure you're being facetious. I keep telling you: the station is not without defenses."

"They're being analyzed right now," said Cole.

"Then why are you sitting here?" said the Duke. "Why aren't you out with your team?"

"Because they know a lot more about weaponry than I do," said Cole.

"But you're the Captain."

"A good Captain knows when he'd just be in the way," responded Cole.

"So, for that matter, does a good Fleet Commander," added Jacovic. "And a good business owner. I notice, for example, that you don't deal cards at the tables, although it is your money that's at stake."

"I find myself liking this Teroni better and better," said Cole. "I hope to hell we both live long enough to see him get his own warship."

"I've *had* a warship," replied Jacovic. "What I need now is a *cause*."

"I should think beating back Csonti and his damned killers is cause enough," said the Duke.

"I have nothing against Csonti," said Jacovic. "Since he will be attacking, I will of course do everything I can to defend myself and destroy him, but this is a *circumstance*, not a cause."

"Semantics," said the Duke. "It's kill or be killed. You should both be eager to destroy that son of a bitch."

"No military man is ever anxious to fight," said Cole. "We've seen war, and we've seen peace, and there's not a soldier or sailor anywhere in the galaxy who doesn't think peace is better." He paused, frowning. "Also, I'm going to have to go up against the finest warrior I've ever seen, and I'm more than a little resentful of it."

"Csonti?" asked the Duke. "I didn't know you'd seen him in action."

Cole shook his head. "I'm referring to Val. It didn't have to come to this."

"She deserted you."

Cole sighed. "It's not that simple."

"It's precisely that simple," responded the Duke.

"I convinced her to give up a very successful career as a pirate. I showed her that a military unit that was having difficulty paying its way as pirates could do very well as mercenaries. She bought into it. I can't blame her for doing what I convinced her to do."

"You never told her to fight against the *Theodore Roosevelt*," said the Duke.

"You don't understand her," said Cole. "She grew up an outlaw. In a society that rewards guts and strength, she reached the top of a profession that most women don't even enter and in which most men don't live to see thirty. There's not a member of the *Teddy R* that isn't indebted to her one way or another. We'll fight her, even kill her, if we have to, but I'm not happy about it."

"You sound like you were grooming her for great things," said Jacovic.

"She was capable of them," answered Cole. "I was just trying to smooth off the rough edges and point her in the right direction."

"And now we will have to kill her," said the Teroni.

"If we're lucky," said Cole. "She's about the least killable person I ever saw."

They fell silent for a moment. Then Cole noticed Forrice and Mustapha Odom entering the casino. He waved to them, and they made their way through the crowd.

"Have a seat," said the Duke. "The drinks are on the house. I trust you bear good tidings."

"Well, tidings, anyway," said Forrice.

"What's the bottom line?" asked Cole.

"To borrow a human expression," said the Molarian, "we're sitting ducks."

"No!" exclaimed the Duke angrily. "I've got more than one hundred and fifty thumper and burner cannons positioned around the station."

"They're all Level 2s," said Odom.

"What the hell does that mean?" demanded the Duke.

"It means the pulse cannon fire dissipates after fifteen thousand miles, and the laser is weak enough that about eighty-five percent of the ships on the Frontier can deflect it. All they have to do is park their fleet twenty thousand miles out and start firing."

"So much for weaponry," said Cole. "What about the station's defenses?"

"Its shields and deflectors can ward off anything up to Level 4," replied Odom. "But I've asked around, and Csonti's got at least nine ships with Level 4 thumpers or burners."

"How long would it take to upgrade?"

"Two weeks for defense, just a day or two for offense," answered Odom. "However, the expense to cover the whole station at one time would break him."

"But what's here now is in working order?" asked Cole.

"The cannons and shields we tested are."

"It all works," said the Duke. "I have everything tested every Standard month."

"Okay," said Cole. "Thank you, Mr. Odom." He looked at the Molarian. "Have you got anything to add, Four Eyes?"

"Just that Singapore Station can't possibly defend itself against Csonti's fleet. The only question is whether the *Teddy R* can take them all on, and that depends, to a great extent, on the nature of their weaponry."

"It's not a viable alternative," put in Jacovic.

"It might be," said Forrice. "If they don't have anything above Level 5 . . ."

"Oh, the *Theodore Roosevelt* might survive, though I doubt it," said Jacovic. "But unless Csonti is such a totally inept commander that he keeps his ships in a tight formation so we can confront them all at once, half of them can be attacking the station while the rest are holding the *Theodore Roosevelt* at bay in a firefight."

"He's right," said Cole. "The station can't defend itself or harm Csonti's fleet, and even if the *Teddy R* is powerful enough to take on all of Csonti's ships at one, which is a highly dubious proposition, we can't fight him and defend the station at the same time."

"So we're beaten before we begin?" asked the Duke.

"I didn't say that," answered Cole. "It just means we're going to have to come up with a strategy that plays to our strengths instead of one that fails to mask the station's weaknesses."

"Spare me the jargon and tell me what we're going to do," said the Duke.

Cole almost looked amused. "I'm good, but I'm not that good. If I'd come up with a strategy already, I would have told you about it."

"But they're coming in just three days!" said the Duke. "And your experts just told us that the station is virtually indefensible in this situation."

"No," said Cole. "They said it can't be defended by conventional means, and they're right. We're not giving up; we just need to come up with a different means of accomplishing our goal."

"You don't surrender just because the numbers are against you," added Jacovic. "That is where skill, intelligence, experience, and innovation come in."

"Right," said Forrice. "Since coming to the Inner Frontier the *Teddy R* has probably won more battles by avoiding direct confrontation than by engaging in it."

"Well, it sounds good, anyway," said the Duke, suddenly relaxed. "All right, gentlemen, I've had my two minutes of panic. I'll be fine now. Just tell me what I can do to help, and I'm at your service."

"I appreciate that," said Cole. "And as soon as we've hit upon a course of action, we'll let you know how you can help." He paused for a moment. "Mr. Odom?"

"Yes?"

"If we divert all the station's power into its defenses—shields, screens, deflectors, whatever the hell it's got—can we strengthen them enough to buy us some time?"

Odom shook his head. "There's no shortage of power on the station, sir," he replied. "There's simply no way to strengthen what's here, rather than replacing it." He looked at the Platinum Duke. "You shouldn't have stinted on your defenses."

"We never anticipated a major attack," answered the Duke. "We installed our shields to protect us from cosmic garbage, and out-of-control ships, and the occasional attack by a single bandit or pirate ship."

"Stupid," said Odom. "Any military dreadnought could vaporize Singapore Station in ten seconds."

"They never come this far into the Inner Frontier."

"Neither do Navy warships with battle-hardened crews, but I notice you've got one defending you. You have to anticipate the worst that can happen, multiply it by a factor of three, and then hope you're lucky."

"I think he gets the point, Mr. Odom," said Cole.

"Pity he didn't get it a few years sooner," said Odom, getting to his feet. "I'll be back at the ship when you need me."

He walked off as the Duke said, "Doesn't he mean *if* we need him?"

"I think he meant what he said," offered Forrice.

"I want you to go back to the ship too, Four Eyes," said Cole. "Run a number of simulations, and see if there's any offensive or defensive formation that will give us an advantage over a fleet of thirty-five ships. You know what kind of weaponry the *Red Sphinx* carries. Stipulate that Csonti's got at least four or five ships that are even better armed."

"I don't think any computer is smart enough to come up with a winning formation," said Forrice.

"I know, but we have to go through all of the possibilities."

"May I add something?" said Jacovic.

"Be my guest."

"If the computer actually does come up with an advantageous formation, then add the defense of Singapore Station into the equation."

"We're not going to get that far," said Forrice.

"But if God drops everything else and you do," said Cole, "then add a further stipulation that they're trying to destroy the station and we're trying to defend it."

"Will do," said the Molarian, getting up and heading to the door with his surprisingly graceful spinning gait.

"He's going to come up empty," said the Duke.

"Probably," replied Cole. "Would you rather he sat here and drank your liquor?"

"No, of course not."

"Look," said Cole. "We're not giving up and we're not running away, but we have a very limited number of options, so we're going to have to explore each of them in the next day."

"And if you don't find any?"

"We'll improvise. But I have to know what we're doing within the next fifteen hours, twenty at the outside."

"Why?" asked the Duke, curious. "Not that I don't want you to decide on a strategy. But Csonti won't be here for at least two more days."

"You've got about sixty thousand permanent residents and probably at least that many visitors and transients on an inadequately defended station that's about to come under attack," explained Cole. "If we don't come up with some plan that looks like it's got a pretty good chance of victory—or even if we do—we're almost certainly going to have to evacuate the station."

"I hadn't thought of that," admitted the Duke.

"To quote my First Officer, if they stay here they're sitting ducks."

"Yes, I suppose they need at least one Standard day to get away from here," agreed the Duke. "Seriously, do you think there's any likelihood at all of coming up with a viable plan?"

Cole shrugged. "You never know. Sometimes they come from the least likely sources."

As it turned out, the solution was right in front of him.

Cole took a brief nap in his hotel room, then returned to the *Teddy R*, where he sought out Forrice, who was sitting at the main computer console on the bridge.

"How's it going?" he asked.

"About what you'd expect," answered the Molarian. "The machine has rejected"—he looked at a number on the holoscreen—"just over four thousand formations."

"I assume it hasn't approved any?"

"If it had approved even one, I wouldn't still be sitting here," said Forrice.

"Tell it to stop."

"I might as well," said Forrice. "If it hasn't come up with an acceptable formation yet, it's not going to."

"I'm amazed that it can come up with four thousand for just five ships."

"They don't differ all that much," said Forrice, getting to his feet.

"Where are you going?" said Cole.

"Probably to the mess hall, or maybe I'll make one last trip to my favorite location on the station."

"Later," said Cole. "You're not done yet."

"But you said—"

"I said to stop trying to come up with formations. I want you to spend another hour or two seeing what the results are if we attack and disable Csonti right at the outset."

"I will if you want, but Csonti's not our biggest problem, and you know it."

"He's got the biggest ship, or so I'm told," responded Cole. "As for Val, of course she's our most formidable antagonist, but you can't program intangibles into the computer. Or can you?"

"Not really," answered the Molarian. "Once I program them in, they become tangible, they have limits, and they don't change."

"So find out what happens if we attack Csonti *before* he's within range of the station."

Forrice shrugged an alien shrug. "You're the boss."

Jacovic's image suddenly appeared on the bridge.

"Ah, there you are, Captain Cole!" he said. "I've been looking for you at your hotel and the casino."

"What's up?"

"It probably won't help, but I have found another Teroni on the station, and convinced him to fight on our side."

"What kind of ship has he got?"

"Class-QH," said Jacovic. "It's not much, but he's got a Level 3 laser cannon. He might be able to take out one or two of Csonti's smaller ships."

"We'll take all the help we can get," said Cole. "I'll talk to him later. Where is he docked?"

"Dock M, port 483," answered Jacovic.

"Hell, that's out in the next county," complained Cole. Suddenly he froze.

"Are you all right, Captain?" said Jacovic after a few seconds. "Commander Forrice, is the Captain ill?"

Forrice got up and spun over to where Cole was standing.

"Son of a bitch!" said Cole so suddenly that the Molarian inadvertently spun back, startled. "I'm an idiot! It was staring me right in the face! Hell, I even discussed it with you two and the Duke, and I still didn't see it!"

Jacovic was silent for a moment. "Of course!" he shouted at last. "It was when I mentioned the ship's location, wasn't it?"

"You got it," said Cole, trying to control his excitement.

"*I* don't have it," said Forrice. "What are you two talking about?"

"Think about it, Four Eyes! What did Jacovic just tell me about his friend's ship?"

"That it's got a Level 3 burner."

"After that."

"After that?" repeated Forrice, frowning. "Nothing."

"He told me it's in port 483 of M Dock."

"So?"

"So why wasn't it in port 1?"

"Because another ship was already there, obviously."

"Or port 200?"

Suddenly a huge smile spread across the Molarian's face. "I see!"

"We already know we have to evacuate well over one hundred thousand Men and aliens," said Cole. "How many of them have ships?"

"I'll tell you in twenty seconds," said Forrice, uttering a pair of coded commands to the computer. "It's checking with the station's traffic computer." Another five seconds. "There are 17,304 ships currently docked at Singapore Station."

"I'd say that'll improve the odds a little, wouldn't you?" asked Cole with a smile.

"They won't all have weapons, and not all the ships with weapons will fight to defend the station," said Forrice.

"I don't need them all. But remember, sixty thousand Men and aliens live here. *They've* got a vested interest in defending the place."

"It makes sense," conceded Forrice.

"Thank you, Jacovic," said Cole. "If you hadn't found this Teroni with the ship, all three of us could have overlooked this until it was too late. Are you in the casino now?"

"Yes."

"I'm coming over. I want you to hunt up the Platinum Duke. A contained environment like Singapore Station must have a holographic public address system. Tell him I want to use it as soon as I get there."

"I'll take care of it, Captain," said Jacovic, and his image vanished.

"I think you can stop playing with your computer now," said Cole to Forrice. "Come back to the station with me."

"Happy to," said the Molarian.

"I'll drop you off at your whorehouse on the way."

"The whorehouse can wait," said Forrice. "I want to be there when you address the . . . what should I call them? The populace."

"Call them the station's navy," replied Cole. "That's what I want them to become. Now let's go."

They took the airlift down to the main hatch in the shuttle bay, then rode a slidewalk a quarter mile to a monorail station. The single car picked them up and transported them the rest of the way.

"How could I have made this trip past hundreds of ships on Dock J every day and not figured it out?" said Cole. "I mean, Dock J, for God's sake! If there are five hundred ports per dock, and J is the tenth letter . . . Hell, how could I have missed them?"

"They're not warships, and they haven't declared for one side or the other," said Forrice. "We all just naturally thought of them as civilians."

"Probably most of them will choose to stay civilians," acknowledged Cole. "But with this many to start with, I've got to be able to recruit a couple of hundred, which is more than we need." He smiled again. "I think Csonti is going to have a little surprise waiting for him when he shows up."

"Preferably half a light-year or so *before* he gets here," replied the Molarian. "No sense letting him get within firing range."

"Let's recruit our forces first," said Cole, as the car dropped them off at the end of the dock. "Then we'll worry about how to deploy them."

They got on the slidewalk that took them to the center of the station, then transferred to another that brought them to the front door of the casino. They entered, and found the Platinum Duke waiting for them at his table.

"Everything's ready for you," he said. "Where do you want to speak from?"

"Any place that's convenient."

"How about my private office?"

"I thought this table was your private office," said Cole with a smile.

"This table is my *public* office," said the Duke. "Follow me."

"You might as well wait here," said Cole to Forrice. "This shouldn't take long."

The Duke led Cole to the back of the casino, waited for a door to iris and let them pass through, then walked down a short corridor to a large, elegant office at the end of it. The office door scanned the Duke's one natural retina, analyzed the molecular structure of the platinum that composed most of his body, and allowed him and his guest to pass through.

"All the Teroni told me was that you needed to address the whole station," said the Duke, trying to restrain his excitement. "You must have a plan worked out, right?"

"I have a plan *thought* out," said Cole. "What I'm doing now is working out the details."

"Can you tell me what it is?"

"We're each donating the things we're best suited to donate. Stick around and listen." He paused. "Where do I stand?"

"Anywhere you want. The holo cameras will key on your body heat and the motion sensors will follow you if you feel like walking around while you're speaking."

"It's not going to be that long a speech."

"Give me just a minute to program the cameras."

The Duke gave half a dozen commands to the computer that controlled all his office equipment including the cameras, then nodded to Cole. "It'll start when you do."

"Residents of Singapore Station, and visitors as well, I have an important message for you," said Cole. "I'm going to give you a few seconds to end your conversations and concentrate on what I'm about to say." He paused, counted to fifteen, and spoke again. "Most of you are unaware of it, but a fleet of thirty-five to forty ships, led by the warlord known as Csonti, is on its way here to destroy Singapore Station. They are not expected to reach us for at least thirty-five Standard hours. Those of you who wish to evacuate the station will have more than a full Standard day to do so. But there is an alternative, one I hope many of you will consider."

He paused again to make sure he had their attention and that they weren't all racing for their valuables and their ships.

"I am in command of a former Republic warship and four other vessels, and I plan to stay and fight. I know that as of half an hour ago there were more than seventeen thousand ships docked at Singapore Station. If one out of every seventeen ships will put itself under my command, we can meet Csonti's forty ships with an overwhelming force of one thousand. If one out of every fifty ships will put itself under my command, we will still have a fleet of more than three hundred to stand against Csonti. If you're willing to volunteer your services, we'll be taking names and contact information at Duke's Place. Any damages to your ships will be paid for by the Platinum Duke—*if* you've signed on to help me. There will be no compensation if you choose not to help defend the station."

The Duke looked like he was about to protest, then considered the alternatives and remained silent. Cole stepped closer to the camera so that every line in his face could be clearly seen.

"Some of you may wonder why you should put yourself under my command, rather than flee from the invaders or simply freelance with your own weaponry. There are two reasons. The first concerns why you should trust my military capabilities. My name is Wilson Cole, I have commanded three different starships in the Republic's Navy, and I am the first man ever to win four Medals of Courage from the Space Service. The second reason concerns why you of the Inner Frontier should trust me: I am wanted dead or alive by both the Teroni Federation and the Republic."

. He nodded to the Duke, who ended the transmission.

"I've stored it, and will play it throughout the station every hour on the hour," announced the Duke.

"Let's hope it works."

"We've got seventeen thousand ships to draw from," said the Duke. "Of course it'll work."

"It's not how many ships are docked here," replied Cole. "It's how many of their owners are willing to risk *their* necks to save *your* space station."

"I never looked at it that way," admitted the Duke, suddenly nervous. "Do you think we can draw a hundred, anyway?"

Cole shrugged. "Who knows?"

"What's the absolute minimum we need?"

"It depends on his mood," said Cole. "If he's still as mad as when he left here, probably two thousand ships won't deter him. If he's sobered up and we can muster a fleet of twenty, he may decide it's not worth losing half his fleet to destroy the station. Don't forget—you've got half a dozen arms dealers using the station as their permanent base. I guarantee each of them will have at least one ship that can match any firepower Csonti's got."

"Right!" said the Duke enthusiastically. "I hadn't thought of that!"

"Hey Wilson, Duke—you'd better come out here," said Forrice, his image suddenly appearing inside the office.

"More problems?" asked Cole.

"In a way."

"What's up?"

"The second your transmission ended, they started lining up at the casino to enlist," said Forrice. "The line's already a block long, and at the rate it's growing, it could reach half a mile within an hour."

"I guess being a decorated war hero has its advantages," said Cole.

"Not around here," answered Forrice. "It was when you announced that the Republic and the Federation both want your head that everyone stood up and cheered."

"Governments—*any* governments—are not popular out here," said the Duke. "That's why most people come to the Inner Frontier in the first place—to get away from authority and government."

"Or their navies," added Forrice with an alien hoot of laughter.

"Four Eyes," said Cole, "get Christine, Briggs, Braxite, Jacillios, Rachel, and Domak from the ship—or wherever the hell they are—and have them start processing all the volunteers." He walked to the office door. "Come on, Duke—let's have a victory drink and hope it's not premature."

They walked down the corridor and into the casino. As soon as the crowd saw Cole they began cheering, and didn't stop for another five minutes after he sat down at the Duke's table with his host and Jacovic.

"Damn!" said Cole. "If I'd have known it would bring this kind of reaction, I'd have deposed my first three captains as well as Podok."

"Don't get too cheerful just yet," said the Duke. "Only half of them are cheering you. The other half are cheering the price on your head and trying to figure out how to go about collecting it."

The response was amazing, though in retrospect it probably should have been expected.

"Where the hell are they all coming from?" asked Sharon Blacksmith as the line still stretched into the next block two hours later.

She had come over from the *Teddy R* when she heard Cole's announcement, which was not only broadcast throughout the station but had also been piped into all the thousands of docked ships. She'd fought her way through the crowd of volunteers and was now sitting at the Duke's table with Cole, Forrice, and Jacovic.

"They live here," answered Cole. "Why the hell shouldn't they line up to defend their homeland, however small and artificial it is?"

"Five'll get you ten that half of them are outlaws," she said.

"Maybe in the Republic," replied Forrice. "Out here they're citizens."

"And before long they may even be heroes," added Cole.

"How are you going to teach them military discipline in a day and a half?" asked Sharon.

"They don't have to fly in a perfect formation," said Cole. "There are going to be a thousand or more of us, and only forty of the enemy. All they really have to do is go where I tell them to go without bumping into each other."

"It wouldn't hurt to leave a small force behind, to protect the station if one of Csonti's ships gets through," suggested Jacovic.

"It's hardly likely, given the odds," replied Cole.

"True," agreed Jacovic, "but holding twenty ships back out of this vast number won't make you any less formidable, and they just might discourage—or kill—any enemy ship that approaches Singapore Station."

"He's right, you know," said Forrice.

"Yeah, I know," admitted Cole. "It sounds like the voice of experience."

"I've been in analogous situations," answered Jacovic. "No matter how overwhelming your numbers, you must always assume that the occasional Wilson Cole will find a way through them."

"I'm flattered," said Cole. "But hopefully Csonti and his lieutenants will take one look at us and suddenly remember they have urgent business elsewhere."

"If they do, they'll be back," said Sharon.

"Why should they bother?" said Cole. "We're proving right now that we can put together an overwhelming force in a couple of hours' time. Csonti's the one who's mad at us. The rest of them have no reason to want to take on a fleet of a thousand ships, and every reason not to."

"Maybe they're more afraid of Csonti than of us," offered Forrice.

Cole seemed amused. "You think Val is afraid of anyone or anything?"

"No," admitted the Molarian. "But there are thirty-five or forty other ships, and I'll bet most of *their* captains live in mortal fear of Csonti. The man is three hundred pounds of solid muscle, and I've heard stories about his temper. I think even Val would be overmatched against him."

Cole was about to answer when he was interrupted by the Duke's image, which popped into view right next to him. "Captain Cole? Can you please come to my office?"

"On my way," said Cole, getting to his feet.

"Is there a problem?" asked Forrice.

"Undoubtedly," said Cole. "But there's no threat. I gave him a code word to use if there was."

Then he was crossing the casino, going through the first door, entering the corridor, and finally standing before the Duke's office. He knew that the retina scan and other security systems wouldn't pass him, but he also knew the Duke would be waiting for him and would order the door to let him through.

The door irised, and he entered the office. The Platinum Duke sat behind his desk, and sitting on a pair of chairs were an immaculately clad man who appeared to be in late middle age, and a huge Torqual wearing his race's usual garb of furs and leather. The latter almost had to duck his head to avoid contact with the ceiling, even though he was seated.

"What's up?" asked Cole as he stepped into the room.

"Allow me to introduce you to Mr. Swenson"—the Man inclined his head—"and Tcharisn." The Torqual stared at him, unblinking.

"Okay, they're Swenson and Tcharisn," said Cole. "Now what?"

"They represent a very select yet unofficial organization, and wish to discuss the current situation with us."

"Let me take a wild guess and suggest that they represent Singapore Station's arms dealers," said Cole.

"That is correct, Captain Cole," said the Torqual. "We have come to offer our services."

"Offer or sell?" asked Cole sharply.

"I meant what I said," replied the Torqual.

"It is in all of our best interests that Singapore Station remain free and intact," added Swenson. "Our group will arm up to a dozen ships free of charge, and will donate any further stock you need at cost."

"I'll tell you what," countered Cole. "Instead of arming any ships, why don't you arm Singapore Station itself? My First Officer and my engineer can pinpoint its most vulnerable areas, and based on their considerable experience can suggest whether each area needs offensive or defensive upgrading, or perhaps both. Your services are more valuable there than on a fleet of thousand or more ships that is facing a fleet or forty or less."

"It makes sense," said Swenson.

"I agree," said the Torqual. "That is what we shall do."

"How many of you are there?" asked Cole curiously.

"Weapon dealers on Singapore Station?" replied Swenson. "There must be at least a hundred."

"I mean, how many in your group, or cartel, or whatever the hell you choose to call it?"

"There are six of us," answered Swenson, "but we are the six largest, and are not without some influence with our colleagues."

"We appreciate your patriotism," said Cole. "My First Officer is on the premises right now. I'll send him in here when I leave, and you can get to work on the problem immediately."

"It's strange to think of myself as a patriot," said Swenson, "or the defense of an independent space station in a galactic No-Man's Land as an act of patriotism."

"You live here," responded Cole. "That means Singapore Station is your homeland, and you're defending it against invaders who want to either destroy it or take it away from you. What would you call that *except* patriotism?"

"I never looked at it that way," said Swenson.

"Nor did I," added the Torqual.

"Nor, I would wager, did Charlemagne," continued Swenson.

"Charlemagne?" repeated Cole.

"I have no idea what his birth name is," answered Swenson. "He took the name of Charlemagne when he arrived on the Inner Frontier."

"Is there some reason why I should give a damn about this Charlemagne?" asked Cole.

"He equipped Csonti's flagship and a number of his other ships," answered Swenson. "He knows everything about them. And he's one of us." A quick smile. "That should come in handy very shortly, should it not?"

"Absolutely!" said the Duke enthusiastically. "Once Charlemagne tells us everything we need to know about Csonti's ships, he has an unlimited line of credit at the bar for a period of one hundred Standard days."

Cole summoned Forrice to the office, then left as the Molarian was pinpointing the exact spots that required reinforcements on a holo map the Duke's computer supplied.

Sharon Blacksmith had taken it upon herself to better organize the registration of volunteers, and things were moving a little more smoothly. Cole checked in with the *Teddy R* to see if there had been any reports of Csonti's whereabouts; the answer was negative.

"That could be a problem," he confided to Jacovic when he rejoined the Terroni in the casino. "If we don't know where Csonti and his fleet are, I can't take a thousand ships out to meet him. I mean, hell, what if I lead them in one direction and he attacks from another?"

"The only answer is to send out some ships to serve as scouts," said Jacovic.

"I know. I just don't like depending on people I don't know and that I've never worked with before."

"The alternative is to post your entire fleet around the station."

Cole shook his head. "If we're massed together when we meet him out in space, we have an enormous advantage. But if we're massed together around the station, he could wipe out fifty ships before we even know he's there. Don't forget—an awful lot of our ships are one-, two-, and three-man jobs, and they weren't built to withstand military-strength thumpers and burners."

"Then it's the scouts," said Jacovic.

"Then it's the scouts," Cole agreed.

"You already have enough to do," said the Teroni, getting to his feet. "I'll get a list of our volunteers from Colonel Blacksmith and send some out immediately."

"Fine," agreed Cole. "You've used scouts before, I'm sure."

"On occasion."

"Good. Then you'll know how to position them."

The Teroni walked over to Sharon, downloaded a number of names and contact information into his pocket computer, and left the casino in search of his lookouts.

Suddenly a pair of well-armed men approached Cole's table and sat down on each side of him.

"Hello, Captain Cole," said one of them.

"Do I know you?"

"You'd like to," said the other. "We could do you a lot of good."

"How?"

"We've fought a lot of actions just like the one you're going to fight against Csonti."

"And you're for hire?" said Cole.

"We don't come cheap, but we're worth it."

"You know what?" said Cole. "I don't doubt it for a second. But I've got over a thousand volunteers to face a fleet of thirty-five. Why should I pay you?"

"If you don't, I'll bet Csonti will," said the first one meaningfully.

"There's only two problems with that," said Cole.

"Oh?"

He nodded. "First, you don't know where he is. And second, if you join him, it'll be a thousand to thirty-six or thirty-seven instead of a thousand to thirty-five. Are you in that much of hurry to face those odds?"

The two men glared at him, but they had nothing further to say, and they soon left the table.

Cole decided that if he remained there, every would-be mercenary on the station was eventually going to seek him out, so he got up, made sure Sharon didn't need any help, and made his way back to the ship.

When he arrived he called Briggs and Christine to the bridge.

"Yes, sir?" said Briggs, reporting a moment before Christine.

"Mr. Briggs, you and Christine Mboya are the two best computer and communications experts I have on board," began Cole, as Christine joined them.

"Oh, I don't know about that, sir," said Briggs.

"Save the false modesty. You're the best, and I need your input."

"Yes, sir?" said Christine.

"You're aware of the situation," said Cole. "As soon as we know where Csonti's fleet is, we're going out to meet him, so the action will hopefully not take place anywhere near Singapore Station. The problem is, I don't want a thousand ships trailing in our wake. We haven't got time to drill them or get them to stay in a precise military formation, but I'd like to split them into groups of seventy-five to a hundred ships. We've got four captains already, and I want the rest to be under the direction of members of the *Teddy R*, who in turn will be under *my* direction. Tell Jacovic, Forrice, Domak, Jacillios, Sokolov, and Pampas that they'll each transfer to a ship that will act as the leader of a particular group."

"Yes, sir."

"If they have any questions, have them contact me personally. Also, once we're moving, I can't lose touch with them. Does our com system have the capacity to keep in constant touch with these ten group leaders?"

"I think so," said Christine.

"Yes," agreed Briggs. "We'll set up separate coded frequencies for the leaders, and we'll scramble them so Csonti can't read them." He paused, frowning. "Now, what frequencies would work best?"

The two started speaking enthusiastically in technical jargon that made no more sense to Cole than untranslated Molarian, and finally he went off to get something to eat.

Cole supervised preparations for the next day. Then, when he felt he had done everything he could, he went to his cabin, slipped out of his boots, and was asleep in seconds.

He didn't know how long he'd slept, but he was awakened by Christine's disembodied voice.

"Sir?"

He grunted and rolled onto his other side.

"Captain Cole?"

"Yeah, what is it?" he said, resigned to having to speak and hence wake up.

"We've spotted Csonti's ships, sir."

"Great!" said Cole, suddenly awake. "Are all our senior officers on board the ship?"

"No, sir. Colonel Blacksmith, Commander Forrice, and Mr. Odom are still on the station. So are Lieutenant Mueller and Mr. Chadwick."

"Get them back here within half an hour, and patch me through to Domak."

The image of the warrior-caste Polonoi appeared in front of him.

"Lieutenant, contact Colonel Blacksmith. She has a list of all those who volunteered to join us in our battle against Csonti. More to the point, she has a list of their ships. Choose the six fastest. These, plus our four smaller ships, will be our group leaders. Lieutenant Mboya has a list of the six officers who will temporarily take over command of those ships."

"I know, sir," replied Domak. "I'm one of them."

"Each group leader will be under my direct command. Nobody breaks formation and nobody fires except on my express order. Is that understood?"

"Yes, sir."

"Good. It's your job to make sure the other nine leaders understand the chain of command."

"Yes, sir."

Her image vanished, to be replaced by Forrice's.

"What's up, Wilson?" said the Molarian.

"We've spotted his fleet. We're taking off as soon as possible. Don't come back to the *Teddy R*. Christine or Domak will tell you what ship to report to."

"Did Sharon give you the count?" said Forrice. "Last time I spoke with her, which couldn't have been ten minutes ago, we have a fleet of one thousand, two hundred and thirty-seven ships."

"That many?"

"And counting."

"Good," said Cole. "Let's get ready to kick some ass."

It was the non-event Cole had hoped it would be when he assembled his fleet.

The scout ships pinpointed Csonti's location out by the Offenbach system. There were thirty-seven ships, including the *Red Sphinx*.

Csonti took one look at the massive force that was approaching him, knew he was totally overmatched, and beat a hasty retreat. Most of his ships, now leaderless, hovered nervously, not quite sure what to do next. One ship—the *Red Sphinx*—boldly held its ground.

Finally a message came in via the *Teddy R*'s subspace radio:

"*You win today, but you haven't heard the last of me.*"

"Have we a reply, sir?" asked Christine.

"Yeah, we do. Am I on?"

"Yes, sir."

"Say that again, Csonti, and we'll follow you all the way to the Core if necessary, and blow you apart."

There was a moment's silence.

"He received it, sir," said Christine. "No reply."

"All right. Now I want to address all his remaining ships."

"Including the *Red Sphinx*, sir?"

"Yeah, whether she hears it or not, she'll know what I'm going to offer. Let me know when I can speak to them."

She nodded a minute later. "All set, sir."

"Thanks." He cleared his throat. "This is Wilson Cole, the Captain of the *Theodore Roosevelt*. Your leader has deserted you and fled in disgrace. Each of his remaining ships has three options: you can stand and fight, in which case we will destroy you; you can follow Csonti, in which case you will not be harmed or pursued, but you will be marked for destruction should you ever return to this sector; or you can swear your allegiance to the *Theodore Roosevelt*, in which case you will become part of my growing fleet and all prior crimes, including this one, will be forgiven. There is no fourth alternative. I expect each of you to decide within ten Standard minutes."

"I'll lay plenty of five-hundred-to-one that no one selects Option One," said Briggs with a grin.

"They're starting to call in already, sir," said Christine.

"Let me know the score in ten minutes," replied Cole.

It only took seven minutes. Twenty-two ships opted to join Cole's fleet, and thirteen took off for parts unknown.

"What about Val?" he asked.

"The *Red Sphinx* hasn't budged. It's not firing, it's not advancing, it's not retreating, and it's not replying."

"I think that's her way of saying she's not intimidated," said Cole. "All right, order the fleet, including the new ships, back to Singapore Station."

"What about the *Red Sphinx*, sir?"

Cole shrugged. "She'll follow along when she feels like it."

Cole declared a week's shore leave at Singapore Station, while he became acquainted with the captains and executive officers of his twenty-two new ships.

Val showed up on the second day, walked into Duke's Place as if she'd never left it, but kept her distance from the crew of the *Teddy R.* Her attitude seemed to be that since she hadn't fired a single shot, she had every right to be on the station she had been paid to destroy.

Cole and Sharon rented a hotel room, which seemed enormous to them after the close confines of the ship. Forrice divided his time between the Molarian brothel and the *stort* table, Jacovic found four more Teronis and spent most of his time with them, and the other members of the crew found other ways to amuse themselves.

Perez entered the casino on the third day, and walked right over to the Platinum Duke's table, where the Duke, Cole, Sharon, and David Copperfield were sitting with their drinks.

"I've got to talk to you, sir," said Perez.

"Is it private, or can you discuss it right here?" asked Cole.

"There's nothing private about it," said Perez. "Sir, I want a position aboard the *Theodore Roosevelt.* I don't care how menial it is, but I have to get off the *Red Sphinx.*"

"What happened?"

"I told her that I would refuse any order to fire on the *Theodore Roosevelt.* She locked me in the brig until this morning, then turned me loose and told me she doesn't want me back on the ship, which suits me just fine."

"I can see her point of view," said Cole. "You disobeyed your Captain's direct orders in a military confrontation."

"I signed on to fight *for* you, not *against* you, sir," said Perez. "If you won't take me on, I'll hang around Singapore Station until I can latch on with another ship."

"That's not a problem," said Cole. "We've got more ships than I can even name right now." He sighed. "Yeah, we'll find a spot for you."

"Thank you, sir."

Perez turned and walked over to one of the gaming tables.

"He's a good man," said Cole.

"So is Commander Jacovic," said Sharon.

"I know. And we probably picked up another dozen this week," said Cole. "It seems a shame that once we whip them all into shape, we're still just mercenaries hiring out to the highest bidder. There ought to be something more useful to do with a force of damned near thirty ships."

"Hell," said the Duke, "if all you want is a purpose and a challenge, I'll pay you to go to war with Fleet Admiral Garcia."

"The odds get a little better every week," replied Cole with a smile, "but it's still a couple of hundred million to twenty-seven."

"Not twenty-eight?" asked Sharon.

"She was ready to fight against us for money," explained Cole. "Fighting for money has become our business, and I won't hold it against her, but it doesn't make her part of our fleet anymore."

"Well, *I* hold it against her," said the Duke. "She hasn't even stopped by to apologize, or mend fences, or anything. Look at her over at the tables, drinking and gambling as if we weren't even in the same building."

"I know how her mind works," said Cole. "She doesn't think she has anything to apologize for."

"You're being too soft on her."

"There's every likelihood that most or all of the *Teddy R*'s crew would be dead without her," replied Cole. "That buys her some leeway."

The Duke shook his head. "I don't understand that attitude."

"I thought I did once," said Sharon. "There was a time I thought he was infatuated with her. But he wasn't. He just sees something special in her."

"She's got a lot of admirable traits and abilities," said Cole.

"She's big and she's strong," said the Duke, clearly unimpressed. "So is Csonti."

"She's a lot more than that," replied Cole. "When I brought her on board the *Teddy R*, every member of the crew was dead-set against her. After all, I promoted her over all but two of them. But within two weeks she was the most popular person on the ship." He paused. "Captains, as my friend the Security Chief here is contantly telling me, don't leave their ships in enemy territory. I've had to on occasion, and each time I've trusted Val to watch my back. She never let me down." He looked across the room and saw a swirl of red hair towering above one of the tables. "We're going to miss her."

"So you lost her and picked up twenty-two ships," said the Duke. "I'd say you came out ahead."

"What do you think, David?" asked Cole.

"I'd rather have the Valkyrie than the ships," answered Copperfield.

Cole looked across the table at the Duke. "There's your answer."

"All right," said the Duke, "you know your personnel better than I do. But it seems to me that you're romanticizing a traitor."

"You're allowed your opinion," said Cole. "Hell, you might even be right. My judgment's not perfect." He smiled ruefully. "If it was, I'd still be fighting for your Admiral Garcia."

"Perish the thought," said the Duke.

"Wilson! *Duck!*" yelled Sharon suddenly.

Startled, Cole turned toward her as a heavy chair flew through the air and bounced off his head.

He fell to the floor, then pulled himself groggily to his feet, blood running into his left eye from a huge gash on his forehead. It took him a moment to recover his balance and focus his one clear eye, and when he did, he found himself facing Csonti.

"How the hell did you get in here?" mumbled Cole.

"You think I only have one ship?" demanded the huge man. "I told you you hadn't seen the last of me! But I'm the last thing you'll ever see!"

He swung a roundhouse right. Cole, his eye filled with blood, never saw it coming. It connected, and he crashed right through the Duke's table.

"Get up, little man!" bellowed Csonti. "Get up and meet your death!"

Cole tried to stand, fell to his knees, and tried again. Before he could get to his feet, a man had hurled himself onto Csonti's back and wrapped his arms around the huge man's throat.

Csonti grunted in surprise, staggered a few steps, then got his hand around one of the man's wrists. For a moment neither of them moved. Then there was a loud *crack!* and the man lost his grip.

It was Perez, and it was obvious that his wrist had been broken. Csonti spun around, grabbed him by the throat, and squeezed. Perez began flailing his arms. Gradually the flailing lessened, then ceased, and Csonti let the unconscious man fall to the floor.

"Stupid, stupid man!" growled Csonti, delivering a gratuitous kick to Perez's head. "As if he could stop *me!*" He turned back to Cole, who was swaying on wobbly feet and trying to keep the blood out of his eye. "Now, where were we?"

And suddenly an immaculately clad alien stepped between them.

"You leave him alone!" said David Copperfield in a shaky voice.

"Get out of my way before I squash you like an insect!" snarled Csonti.

Copperfield began trembling, but he held his ground. "He's my friend. I won't let you harm him."

"This is going to be fun!" said Csonti with a nasty grin. "Do you know what I'm going to do to you, you ugly little wart?" He took a menacing step forward. "I'm going to pull off your ears and pluck out your eyes for having the audacity to stand between Csonti and his enemy!"

He reached out a hand toward Copperfield, and suddenly a strong female hand shot out of nowhere and grabbed his wrist.

"Maybe you should try fighting against grown-ups," said Val, pushing him back. "Go hide under the table, David. I'll take it from here."

"I don't want you!" Csonti said, suddenly wary. "I want *him!*" He gestured toward Cole.

"You can't always have what you want, shithead," she said, aiming a kick at Csonti's knee. "I never liked you anyway."

He was back up in a second, favoring the leg but still formidable. He swung a blow that would have decapitated her if it had landed, but she ducked and delivered a swift chop to his Adam's apple. He leaned over, choking, and she brought her knee up into his face. There wasn't much left of his nose when he straightened up.

"You're not so much," said Val contemptuously. "Hell, Bull Pampas could take you without working up a sweat."

"Damn it, you're working for me!"

"Correction," said Val. "I work for *me.*"

Csonti pulled a dagger out of his boot and charged at her. What happened next happened so fast that no two accounts of it were quite the same, but everyone agreed that an instant later Csonti was flying head over heels, and that he uttered a terrible scream when he landed. He rolled over, blood spurting up from the artery his dagger had slashed when he landed on it.

It took him another three minutes to die. No one made any effort to help him or stanch the flow of blood. When he was clearly dead, the Duke ordered two of his robots to carry the body out to the trash atomizer behind the kitchen.

Val turned to David. "Why did you do that?" she demanded. "You're the most cowardly creature I've ever met!"

"He's my friend," replied Copperfield.

"You wouldn't have lasted five seconds."

"I know."

Cole, still semiconscious, was propped up on a chair, with Sharon tending to his wounds. A pair of bystanders half-walked, half-carried Perez to the *Teddy R*'s infirmary.

When his head cleared somewhat, Cole reached out and laid a hand on Copperfield's shoulder.

"Thank you, David," he mumbled. "I know the effort that took."

"You're not even a member of the crew," said Val, frowning in puzzlement. "And still you risked your life."

"Steerforth is an honorable man, one of the few," answered Copperfield. "What better reason is there?"

"And Perez, who wouldn't fight for a share of the millions we were being paid, attacked Csonti for free," she continued, staring at Cole. "For *you*."

Cole stared blearily up at her. "I hope you don't expect me to say I'm unworthy of it." He attempted a wry smile, but winced in pain instead.

"Actually, that's exactly what I expected you to say."

"Well, if push comes to shove, I *am* unworthy of it."

"The hell you are!" said Sharon, still tending to the gash on his forehead. "Almost every member of the *Teddy R* would have done the same thing if they'd been here."

"But *why?*" demanded Val, puzzled and clearly distressed. "I'm the only one on Singapore Station who was never in any danger from Csonti. He would have killed anyone else he faced."

"If you don't know, I can't tell you," said Sharon.

Val was silent, lost in thought, for a full minute. Finally she spoke: "Perez can have the *Red Sphinx* back. And get the Teroni his own ship. I'm coming back as Third Officer. Until I understand why David and Perez would do what they did for you, and how to get my crew to do it for me, I've got a lot more to learn from you."

"I'll decide who's my Third Officer," said Cole.

"You're right," she said. "I'm here to learn, not to give you orders. I was out of line, and I apologize."

"Say that again?"

"I said I apologize."

There was a brief silence.

"Welcome to the ranks of the adults," said Cole, just before he passed out. "Third Officer."

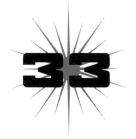

Cole had the ship's communications system upgraded so that messages from the other twenty-seven ships could get through immediately and not have to wait in line.

The most powerful of the new ships was the *Silent Dart*, and Cole put Jacovic in charge of it. Perez was given the *Red Sphinx*. David Copperfield and the Platinum Duke began pooling their contacts and came up with a couple of sweet, high-paying jobs, and the *Teddy R* and its companions were preparing to take off on the first of them.

"It's not as easy as you'd think, finding work for what is fast becoming a legitimate fleet," Copperfield was explaining to Cole as they both sat in the *Teddy R*'s mess hall. "Ninety-eight percent of the jobs simply don't require anywhere near this many ships, and the ones that do are often beyond the client's ability to pay."

"That's what we have you for, David," said Cole, who bore a fresh scar on his forehead above his left eye.

"Well, the Duke and I," replied Copperfield. "We've decided to become partners."

"In all things?" asked Cole.

"No, just as your business agents, Steerforth," answered the alien. "Though I would dearly love to become a partner in Singapore Station, especially since you decreed that it is now our official headquarters."

"I'm sure you can buy into a couple of the gambling joints," said Cole.

"I already have."

Cole smiled. "Somehow I'm not surprised." He paused. "You could have stayed back at the station, you know."

"Don't be silly," said Copperfield. "You know you'd be lost without me."

"If you say so."

Val's image popped into view. "Sir," she said, "we're ready to take off."

"Fine," said Cole. "Pass the word to the fleet and let's get this show on the road."

"Yes, sir," she said, as her holograph vanished.

"Did you hear that, David?" said Cole, smiling. "She called me 'sir.' Twice."

"Even the immortal Charles couldn't account for every miracle," replied Copperfield.

"I'm looking forward to these next two missions," said Cole as the *Teddy R* slowly moved away from the dock. "We're at full strength, everyone's healthy, we've got a legitimate fleet behind us, we're got the Commander of the Fifth Teroni Fleet on our side, we've even got the Valkyrie back."

"You sound exceptionally proud, Steerforth," said Copperfield.

"I am. For an outlaw ship that's wanted by every government in the galaxy, we've come a long way."

"Need I remind you what goeth before a fall, my old school chum?"

"Spare me your platitudes, David," said Cole. "Look at what we've already accomplished against much greater odds than we figure to face this week." He emptied his coffee cup. "We started out as one lone ship. Now we've got twenty-seven, run by some damned good officers, and we've got the firepower to stand up to just about anything we find on the Frontier. What *could* go wrong?"

If there was, as old spacehands believed, a sardonic Galactic Spirit, it must have laughed aloud at that line.

APPENDIXES

# Appendix One

# THE ORIGIN OF THE
# BIRTHRIGHT UNIVERSE

t happened in the 1970s. Carol and I were watching a truly awful movie at a local theater, and about halfway through it I muttered, "Why am I wasting my time here when I could be doing something really interesting, like, say, writing the entire history of the human race from now until its extinction?" And she whispered back, "So why don't you?" We got up immediately, walked out of the theater, and that night I outlined a novel called *Birthright: The Book of Man*, which would tell the story of the human race from its attainment of faster-than-light flight until its death eighteen thousand years from now.

It was a long book to write. I divided the future into five political eras—Republic, Democracy, Oligarchy, Monarchy, and Anarchy—and wrote twenty-six connected stories ("demonstrations," *Analog* called them, and rightly so), displaying every facet of the human race, both admirable and not so admirable. Since each is set a few centuries from the last, there are no continuing characters (unless you consider Man, with a capital *M*, the main character, in which case you could make an argument—or at least, *I* could—that it's really a character study).

I sold it to Signet, along with another novel, titled *The Soul Eater*. My editor there, Sheila Gilbert, loved the Birthright Universe and asked me if I would be willing to make a few changes to *The Soul Eater* so that it was set in that future. I agreed, and the changes actually took less than a day. She made the same request—in advance, this time—for the four-book Tales of the Galactic Midway series, the four-book Tales of the Velvet Comet series, and *Walpurgis III*. Looking back, I see that only two of the thirteen novels I wrote for Signet were *not* set there.

When I moved to Tor Books, my editor there, Beth Meacham, had a fondness for the Birthright Universe, and most of my books for her—not all, but most—were set in it: *Santiago, Ivory, Paradise, Purgatory, Inferno, A Miracle of Rare Design, A Hunger in the Soul, The Outpost*, and *The Return of Santiago*.

When Ace agreed to buy *Soothsayer, Oracle*, and *Prophet* from me, my editor, Ginjer Buchanan, assumed that of course they'd be set in the Birthright Universe—and of course they were, because as I learned a little more about my eighteen-thousand-year, two-million-world future, I felt a lot more comfortable writing about it.

In fact, I started setting short stories in the Birthright Universe. Two of my Hugo winners—"Seven Views of Olduvai Gorge" and "The 43 Antarean Dynasties"—are set there, and so are perhaps fifteen others.

When Bantam agreed to take the Widowmaker trilogy from me, it was a foregone conclusion that Janna Silverstein, who purchased the books but had moved to another company before they came out, would want them to take place in the Birthright Universe. She did indeed request it, and I did indeed agree.

I recently handed in a book to Meisha Merlin, set—where else?—in the Birthright Universe.

And when it came time to suggest a series of books to Lou Anders for the new Pyr line of science fiction, I don't think I ever considered any ideas or stories that *weren't* set in the Birthright Universe.

I've gotten so much of my career from the Birthright Universe that I wish I could remember the name of that turkey we walked out of all those years ago so I could write the producers and thank them.

# Appendix Two

# THE LAYOUT OF THE BIRTHRIGHT UNIVERSE

The most heavily populated (by both stars and inhabitants) section of the Birthright Universe is always referred to by its political identity, which evolves from Republic to Democracy to Oligarchy to Monarchy. It encompasses millions of inhabited and habitable worlds. Earth is too small and too far out of the mainstream of galactic commerce to remain Man's capital world, and within a couple of thousand years the capital has been moved lock, stock, and barrel halfway across the galaxy to Deluros VIII, a huge world with about ten times Earth's surface and near-identical atmosphere and gravity. By the middle of the Democracy, perhaps four thousand years from now, the entire planet is covered by one huge sprawling city. By the time of the Oligarchy, even Deluros VIII isn't big enough for our billions of empire-running bureaucrats, and Deluros VI, another large world, is broken up into forty-eight planetoids, each housing a major department of the government (with four planetoids given over entirely to the military).

Earth itself is way out in the boonies, on the Spiral Arm. I don't believe I've set more than parts of a couple of stories on the Arm.

At the outer edge of the galaxy is the Rim, where worlds are spread out and underpopulated. There's so little of value or military interest on the Rim that one ship, such as the *Theodore Roosevelt*, can patrol a couple of hundred worlds by itself. In later eras, the Rim will be dominated by feuding warlords, but it's so far away from the center of things that the governments, for the most part, just ignore it.

Then there are the Inner and Outer Frontiers. The Outer Frontier is that vast but sparsely populated area between the outer edge of the Republic/Democracy/Oligarchy/Monarchy and the Rim. The Inner Frontier is that somewhat smaller (but still huge) area between the inner reaches of the Republic/etc. and the black hole at the core of the galaxy.

It's on the Inner Frontier that I've chosen to set more than half of my novels. Years ago the brilliant writer R. A. Lafferty wrote, "Will there be a mythology of the future, they used to ask, after all has become science? Will high deeds be told in epic, or only in computer code?" I decided that I'd like to spend at least a part of my career trying to create those myths of the future, and it seems to me that myths, with their bigger-than-life characters and colorful settings, work best on frontiers where there aren't too many people around to chronicle them accurately, or too many authority figures around to prevent them from playing out to their inevitable conclusions. So I arbitrarily decided that the Inner Frontier was where *my* myths would take place, and I populated it with people bearing names like Catastrophe Baker, the Widowmaker, the Cyborg de Milo, the ageless Forever Kid, and the like. It not only allows me to tell my heroic (and sometimes antiheroic) myths, but lets me tell more realistic stories occurring at the very same time a few thousand light-years away in the Republic or Democracy or whatever happens to exist at that moment.

Over the years I've fleshed out the galaxy. There are the star clusters—the Albion Cluster, the Quinellus Cluster, a few others. There are the individual worlds, some important enough to appear as the title of a book, such as Walpurgis III, some reappearing throughout the time periods and stories, such as Deluros VIII, Antares III, Binder X, Keepsake, Spica II, and some others, and hundreds (maybe thousands by now) of worlds (and races, now that I think about it) mentioned once and never again.

Then there are, if not the bad guys, at least what I think of as the Disloyal Opposition. Some, like the Sett Empire, get into one war with humanity and that's the end of it. Some, like the Canphor Twins (Canphor VI and Canphor VII), have been a thorn in Man's side for the better part of ten millennia. Some, like Lodin XI, vary almost daily in their loyalties depending on the political situation.

I've been building this universe, politically and geographically, for a quarter of a century now, and with each passing book and story it feels a little more real to me. Give me another thirty years and I'll probably believe every word I've written about it.

# Appendix Three

# CHRONOLOGY OF THE BIRTHRIGHT UNIVERSE

| Year | Era | World | Story or Novel |
|------|-----|-------|----------------|
| 1885 | A.D. | | "The Hunter" (*Ivory*) |
| 1898 | A.D. | | "Himself" (*Ivory*) |
| 1982 | A.D. | | *Sideshow* |
| 1983 | A.D. | | *The Three-Legged Hootch Dancer* |
| 1985 | A.D. | | *The Wild Alien Tamer* |
| 1987 | A.D. | | *The Best Rootin' Tootin' Shootin' Gunslinger in the Whole Damned Galaxy* |
| 2057 | A.D. | | "The Politician" (*Ivory*) |
| 2988 | A.D. = 1 G.E. | | |
| 16 | G.E. | Republic | "The Curator" (*Ivory*) |
| 264 | G.E. | Republic | "The Pioneers" (*Birthright*) |
| 332 | G.E. | Republic | "The Cartographers" (*Birthright*) |
| 346 | G.E. | Republic | *Walpurgis III* |
| 367 | G.E. | Republic | *Eros Ascending* |
| 396 | G.E. | Republic | "The Miners" (*Birthright*) |
| 401 | G.E. | Republic | *Eros at Zenith* |
| 442 | G.E. | Republic | *Eros Descending* |
| 465 | G.E. | Republic | *Eros at Nadir* |
| 522 | G.E. | Republic | "All the Things You Are" |
| 588 | G.E. | Republic | "The Psychologists" (*Birthright*) |

| | | | |
|---|---|---|---|
| 616 | G.E. | Republic | *A Miracle of Rare Design* |
| 882 | G.E. | Republic | "The Potentate" (*Ivory*) |
| 962 | G.E. | Republic | "The Merchants" (*Birthright*) |
| 1150 | G.E. | Republic | "Cobbling Together a Solution" |
| 1151 | G.E. | Republic | "Nowhere in Particular" |
| 1152 | G.E. | Republic | "The God Biz" |
| 1394 | G.E. | Republic | "Keepsakes" |
| 1701 | G.E. | Republic | "The Artist" (*Ivory*) |
| 1813 | G.E. | Republic | "Dawn" (*Paradise*) |
| 1826 | G.E. | Republic | *Purgatory* |
| 1859 | G.E. | Republic | "Noon" (*Paradise*) |
| 1888 | G.E. | Republic | "Midafternoon" (*Paradise*) |
| 1902 | G.E. | Republic | "Dusk" (*Paradise*) |
| 1921 | G.E. | Republic | *Inferno* |
| 1966 | G.E. | Republic | *Starship: Mutiny* |
| 1967 | G.E. | Republic | *Starship: Pirate* |
| 1968 | G.E. | Republic | *Starship: Mercenary* |
| 1969 | G.E. | Republic | *Starship: Rebel* |
| 1970 | G.E. | Republic | *Starship: Flagship* |
| | | | |
| 2122 | G.E. | Democracy | "The 43 Antarean Dynasties" |
| 2154 | G.E. | Democracy | "The Diplomats" (*Birthright*) |
| 2239 | G.E. | Democracy | "Monuments of Flesh and Stone" |
| 2275 | G.E. | Democracy | "The Olympians" (*Birthright*) |
| 2469 | G.E. | Democracy | "The Barristers" (*Birthright*) |
| 2885 | G.E. | Democracy | "Robots Don't Cry" |
| 2911 | G.E. | Democracy | "The Medics" (*Birthright*) |
| 3004 | G.E. | Democracy | "The Policitians" (*Birthright*) |
| 3042 | G.E. | Democracy | "The Gambler" (*Ivory*) |
| 3286 | G.E. | Democracy | *Santiago* |
| 3322 | G.E. | Democracy | *A Hunger in the Soul* |

| 3324 | G.E. | Democracy | *The Soul Eater* |
|------|------|-----------|------------------|
| 3324 | G.E. | Democracy | "Nicobar Lane: The Soul Eater's Story" |
| 3407 | G.E. | Democracy | *The Return of Santiago* |
| 3427 | G.E. | Democracy | *Soothsayer* |
| 3441 | G.E. | Democracy | *Oracle* |
| 3447 | G.E. | Democracy | *Prophet* |
| 3502 | G.E. | Democracy | "Guardian Angel" |
| 3504 | G.E. | Democracy | "A Locked-Planet Mystery" |
| 3504 | G.E. | Democracy | "Honorable Enemies" |
| 3719 | G.E. | Democracy | "Hunting the Snark" |
| 4375 | G.E. | Democracy | "The Graverobber" (*Ivory*) |
| | | | |
| 4822 | G.E. | Oligarchy | "The Administrators" (*Birthright*) |
| 4839 | G.E. | Oligarchy | *The Dark Lady* |
| 5101 | G.E. | Oligarchy | *The Widowmaker* |
| 5103 | G.E. | Oligarchy | *The Widowmaker Reborn* |
| 5106 | G.E. | Oligarchy | *The Widowmaker Unleashed* |
| 5108 | G.E. | Oligarchy | *A Gathering of Widowmakers* |
| 5461 | G.E. | Oligarchy | "The Media" (*Birthright*) |
| 5492 | G.E. | Oligarchy | "The Artists" (*Birthright*) |
| 5521 | G.E. | Oligarchy | "The Warlord" (*Ivory*) |
| 5655 | G.E. | Oligarchy | "The Biochemists" (*Birthright*) |
| 5912 | G.E. | Oligarchy | "The Warlords" (*Birthright*) |
| 5993 | G.E. | Oligarchy | "The Conspirators" (*Birthright*) |
| | | | |
| 6304 | G.E. | Monarchy | *Ivory* |
| 6321 | G.E. | Monarchy | "The Rulers" (*Birthright*) |
| 6400 | G.E. | Monarchy | "The Symbiotics" (*Birthright*) |
| 6521 | G.E. | Monarchy | "Catastrophe Baker and the Cold Equations" |
| 6523 | G.E. | Monarchy | *The Outpost* |

| 6599 | G.E. | Monarchy | "The Philosophers" (*Birthright*) |
| 6746 | G.E. | Monarchy | "The Architects" (*Birthright*) |
| 6962 | G.E. | Monarchy | "The Collectors" (*Birthright*) |
| 7019 | G.E. | Monarchy | "The Rebels" (*Birthright*) |
| | | | |
| 16201 | G.E. | Anarchy | "The Archaeologists" (*Birthright*) |
| 16673 | G.E. | Anarchy | "The Priests" (*Birthright*) |
| 16888 | G.E. | Anarchy | "The Pacifists" (*Birthright*) |
| 17001 | G.E. | Anarchy | "The Destroyers" (*Birthright*) |
| | | | |
| 21703 | G.E. | | "Seven Views of Olduvai Gorge" |

## Novels not set in this future

*Adventures* (1922–1926 A.D.)
*Exploits* (1926–1931 A.D.)
*Encounters* (1931–1934 A.D.)
*Hazards* (1934–1939 A.D.)
*Stalking the Unicorn* ("Tonight")
*Stalking the Vampire* ("Tonight")
*The Branch* (2047–2051 A.D.)
*Second Contact* (2065 A.D.)
*Bully!* (1910–1912 A.D.)
*Kirinyaga* (2123–2137 A.D.)
*Lady with an Alien* (1490 A.D.)
*A Club in Montmartre* (1890–1901 A.D.)
*Dragon America: Revolution* (1779–1780 A.D.)
*The World behind the Door* (1928 A.D.)
*The Other Teddy Roosevelts* (1888–1919 A.D.)

# SINGAPORE STATION
## A Short Infrastructure History

### By Deborah Oakes

Singapore Station is known galaxy-wide for its unique diplomatic status and the vitality of its trade. Few stop to consider what a truly amazing engineering feat this aggregate station represents. When Saville Station and the Lewis Outpost decided to combine forces, forming the seed that was to grow into Singapore Station, they possessed similar power systems, standard atmospheres, and construction techniques. Even so, they placed their combined station carefully at a Lagrange point in the new system to minimize gravitational stress on the structure. For the first fifty years, only stations with standard atmospheres were added to Singapore Station. Wherever possible, power and communication systems were integrated into the Singapore Station grid. Airlocks and docking facilities were used to join neighboring stations, or detached and moved to the ever-growing fringe of Singapore Station. Some sections became so interconnected that only business addresses revealed which station a section had formerly been. In other places, unique holdovers from a station's history survive. Stresses on the total structure are balanced carefully and monitored continuously. In all Singapore Station's history, there has never been an involuntary station breech or decoupling—a remarkable feat for so complex a structure. Both personnel and cargo lift shafts connect all sections with a dedicated transportation level. The lift shafts and stations of the transportation level are among the few structures built specifically for Singapore Station, rather than being cannibalized from merging stations. Cargo handling is automated, using spherical cargo pods and a magnetic induction system. All sections and ship docking facilities are connected by monorail on the transportation level. It is a characteristic of the station that mechanized travel laterally within the standard atmosphere levels is virtually nonexistent.

When a consortium of chlorine-breathing stations first approached Singapore Station with a merger proposal, there was considerable opposition from the infrastructure engineers. Interfacing two mutually deadly atmospheric systems carried a high risk. Of necessity, power systems and structural standards of the chlorine-atmosphere stations were radically different. Chlorine is a very active element, and corrosive to many metals, so the stations used massive natural and artificial stone analogs extensively. In the end, as might be expected for Singapore Station, a compromise was reached. A new level was created, not attached to the existing two levels at standard atmosphere, but on the opposite side of the transportation level. The new level was integrated into the overall structure flexibly, at the transportation level, and remained responsible for maintaining its own dynamic stability and services. Dedicated interfaces with the transportation system were limited, and chlorine breathers could use some facilities only when suited. This became the template for adding nonstandard stations to Singapore Station. The next level to be added was a negotiation level with no atmosphere, located "beneath" the chlorine level. Facilities are limited to conference rooms, computational services, and transportation and emergency facilities. Untenanted except for negotiators during conferences, it also serves as a buffer between the chlorine level and the ammonia-atmosphere habitats.

The ammonia-breathers' habitats are a collection of interconnected cylinders and spheres with a wide variety of atmospheric pressure, gravity, and temperature. Many gleam beautifully, being coated with highly reflective materials to help maintain the low temperatures found on the moons that are home to many ammonia breathers. Some residents prefer an ammonia-methane mixture. Their habitats serve as an interface between the ammonia habitats and the final level on Singapore Station—the massive habitats of the methane breathers. Two of these enormous space stations are the newest nonstandard additions to Singapore Station. Huge flattened ovoids with massive structural ribs, these stations provide the high-pressure atmosphere required by the only known pure methane-breathing race, which developed in the atmosphere of the galaxy's gas giants.

Just as new levels have been added for chlorine, ammonia, and methane breathers, so the standard atmosphere side of Singapore Station has continued to grow outward, reaching four levels, and over five miles in diameter at spots. In some areas, lateral connections have been limited by the architecture of the original stations. Highly connected stations tend to become commercial centers. Those with limited personnel access but good cargo access became havens for traders and the occasion local manufacturer. Any sections with overall poor transportation become mainly residential or warehouse space.

Occasionally, a feature on a merged station will prove unexpectedly advantageous. For instance, the experimental farm dome was once part of a research station. Enclosed by station growth, it is now lit by artificial light and maintained as York section's own park—lined by some of the most expensive residences on Singapore Station. In another case, an enormous water tank, part of a radiation barrier on an early station, is now a favorite recreational stop on station, and serves double duty as an emergency water reserve. There are many such unique features to be found throughout the many levels of the station. Visitors wishing to see more of the facilities are encouraged to employ a local guide. Enjoy exploring Singapore Station.

Deborah Oakes is an aerospace engineer, a lifetime science fiction fan, and the secretary/treasurer of the venerable Cincinnati Fantasy Group.

# Appendix Five

# DUKE'S PLACE
# CASINO SCHEMATIC

## By Deborah Oakes

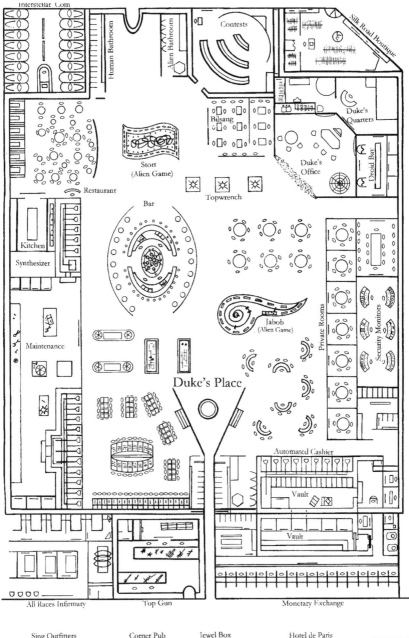

Interstellar Com

Human Bathroom

Alien Bathroom

Contests

Silk Road Boutique

Bilsang

Duke's Quarters

Duke's Office

Droid Bar

Stort
(Alien Game)

Restaurant

Topwrench

Bar

Kitchen

Synthesizer

Jabob
(Alien Game)

Maintenance

**Duke's Place**

Private Rooms

Security Monitors

Automated Cashier

Vault

Vault

All Races Infirmary

Top Gun

Monetary Exchange

Sing Outfitters

Corner Pub

Jewel Box

Hotel de Paris

# Appendix Six

# PIRATE QUEENS

## By Mike Resnick

Something interesting happened on the way to writing this appendix. I began getting tons of fan mail about *Starship: Pirate*, and almost all of it concerned Val. Although she never made an appearance until halfway through the second *Starship* book, she is clearly the most popular character in the series.

A lot of the letters asked how I came up with the unique notion of a Pirate Queen. So I guess it's time for a confession: Pirate Queens have been around for even longer than the field of science fiction. And that led me to think that maybe you'd like to know a little something about their history.

Hugo Gernsback, who created the field as a separate publishing category with *Amazing Stories* back in 1926, defined science fiction (his first term for it, which fell flat on its face, was "scientifiction") as a branch of fiction that would get young boys interested in science. Young girls were presumably too busy playing with their dolls.

But young boys didn't have any disposable income during the

Depression, so after Buck Rogers and Hawk Carse and the crew of Doc Smith's *Skylark* had made their debuts, publishers decided that maybe they ought to start running some stuff that appealed to older boys—like from fifteen to ninety.

Enter the Pirate Queens.

The most memorable of the early ones was probably Belit, who proved a perfect match for the redoubtable Conan, in Robert E. Howard's classic "Queen of the Black Coast."

Then Stanley Weinbaum came up with the Red Peri, who, like Belit, had a young Sophia Loren's looks and a fictional Tarzan's physical skills.

A. Merritt added the gorgeous Sharane, goddess, temptress, priestess, and, yes, Pirate Queen aboard *The Ship of Ishtar*.

And suddenly it was Katie-bar-the-door, and gorgeous, sword-wielding Pirate Queens were popping up all over the place, some good, some evil, all dressed for extremely warm weather. You couldn't turn around without running into one.

And then something happened, and that something was John W. Campbell Jr., the most influential editor in the history of science fiction. He took over the editorship of *Astounding* in the late 1930s, made it the most prestigious magazine in the field, and paid so much (for that time) that it was more economically feasible for an author to rewrite a story a couple of times to Campbell's specifications than to sell it fresh out of the typewriter anywhere else.

Campbell didn't allow sex or sexual innuendo in *Astounding*—and nobody could deny that gorgeous, half-naked Pirate Queens had more than a little sexual appeal for the boys and the boys-at-heart who had made them so popular.

They didn't vanish—nobody has ever made Topic Number One vanish—but they moved to the cheaper magazines, and at a quarter-cent to a half-cent a word subtlety went out the window, and most of their physical skills soon went the way of the dinosaur. Boys wanted heroes they could identify with, so the Good Guys were always males . . . but they also wanted half-naked Pirate Queens, and for the better part of the next decade Pirate Queens became villains, out to conquer the galaxy (frequently by seducing it, one hero at a time).

They became such self-parodies following the advent of Campbell's editorship and their mass migration to the cheapest pulp magazines that eventually a fine non-science-fiction writer named William Knoles wrote a very humorous piece of nostalgia for the November 1960 issue of *Playboy* titled "Girls for the Slime God," a fond look back at all the vanished Pirate Queens and their vanishing clothes. Knoles's definition pretty much says it all: "Unlike other Space Girls, Pirate Queens (the term is a generic one and includes High Priestesses and Amazon Despots) had things pretty much their own way until the last page. They playfully slaughtered passengers on space liners, jealously tortured the heroine, and forcefully seduced the hero."

Alas, that was indeed the case. In 1997 I gathered together Knoles's article, three Pirate Queen tales by Henry Kuttner, a tongue-in-cheek fictional rebuttal ("Playboy and the Slime God") by Isaac Asimov, and a couple of related items, and the anthology *Girls for the Slime God* was published by Obscura Press.

Even last year people, including your humble undersigned, were making fun of the typical 1940s Pirate Queens. In my short story "Catastrophe Baker and the Cold Equations," the Pirate Queen, who has been stowing away on the hero's ship, asks him how he managed to identify her occupation so quickly. "Well, ma'am," he replies, "in my long experience, Pirate Queens can always be identified by their exotic names, their lustful natures, their soul-destroying greed, and their proud arrogant bosoms."

Easy targets, those 1940s Pirate Queens.

But like many another young boy who looks in the mirror and wonders where all that gray hair came from and why it no longer covers the top of his head, I have a residual fondness for Pirate Queens. So I thought I'd bring one back—but not one of the arrogant-bosomed empty-headed 1940s Pirate Queens. I reached a little further back in science fiction's history for my source, back to Belit and the Red Peri and some of the Pirate Queens' close relatives, like C. L. Moore's wonderful Jirel of Joiry.

I knew she had to be good-looking, but I didn't know why she had to be five foot four, so I made her the size of a pro basketball forward. I knew that if she grew up on the Inner Frontier and captained her own pirate ship for a dozen years, she'd have to be tougher than nails—not because she was a woman, but because she kept a crew of cutthroats in line all that time. I figured she'd probably drink a little too much, have indiscriminate sex a little too often, and swear like a sailor—but those traits would never mask her competence from Wilson Cole, who is not sexually attracted to her but sees all of her untapped virtues. He's very much like the trainer of a headstrong two-year-old racehorse who is determined to bring out the best in her without breaking her spirit.

I've had a lot of fun inventing her; what surprised me was how quickly and passionately the readers took to her.

You know, maybe, just maybe, science fiction is ready for a few more [*sigh*] Pirate Queens.

# ABOUT THE AUTHOR

Locus, *the trade journal of science fiction, keeps a list of the winners of major science fiction awards on its Web page. Mike Resnick is currently fourth in the all-time standings, ahead of Isaac Asimov, Sir Arthur C. Clarke, Ray Bradbury, and Robert A. Heinlein. He is the leading award-winner among all authors, living and dead, for short science fiction.*

\* \* \* \* \* \*

Mike was born on March 5, 1942. He sold his first article in 1957, his first short story in 1959, and his first book in 1962.

He attended the University of Chicago from 1959 through 1961, won three letters on the fencing team, and met and married Carol. Their daughter, Laura, was born in 1962, and has since become a writer herself, winning two awards for her romance novels and the 1993 Campbell Award for Best New Science Fiction Writer.

Mike and Carol discovered science fiction fandom in 1962, attended their first Worldcon in 1963, and fifty science fiction books into his career, Mike still considers himself a fan and frequently contributes articles to fanzines. He and Carol appeared in five Worldcon masquerades in the 1970s in costumes that she created, and they won four of them.

Mike labored anonymously but profitably from 1964 through 1976, selling more than two hundred novels, three hundred short stories, and two thousand articles, almost all of them under pseudonyms, most of them in the "adult" field. He edited seven different tabloid newspapers and a trio of men's magazines, as well.

In 1968 Mike and Carol became serious breeders and exhibitors of collies, a pursuit they continued through 1981. During that time they bred and/or exhibited twenty-seven champion collies, and they were the country's leading breeders and exhibitors during various years along the way.

This led them to purchase the Briarwood Pet Motel in Cincinnati in 1976. It was the country's second-largest luxury boarding and grooming establishment, and they worked full-time at it for the next few years. By 1980 the kennel was being run by a staff of twenty-one, and Mike was free to return to his first love, science fiction, albeit at a far slower pace than his previous writing. They sold the kennel in 1993.

Mike's first novel in this "second career" was *The Soul Eater*, which was followed shortly by *Birthright: The Book of Man*, *Walpurgis III*, the four-book Tales of the Galactic Midway series, *The Branch*, the four-book Tales of the Velvet Comet series, and *Adventures*, all from Signet. His breakthrough novel was the international best seller *Santiago*, published by Tor in 1986. Tor has since published *Stalking the Unicorn*, *The Dark Lady*, *Ivory*, *Second Contact*, *Paradise*, *Purgatory*, *Inferno*, the Double *Bwana/Bully!*, and the collection *Will the Last Person to Leave the Planet Please Shut Off the Sun?* His most recent Tor releases were *A Miracle of Rare Design*, *A Hunger in the Soul*, *The Outpost*, and the *The Return of Santiago*.

Even at his reduced rate, Mike is too prolific for one publisher, and in the 1990s Ace published *Soothsayer*, *Oracle*, and *Prophet*; Questar published *Lucifer Jones*; Bantam brought out the *Locus* best-selling trilogy of *The Widowmaker*, *The Widowmaker Reborn*, and *The Widowmaker Unleashed*; and Del Rey published *Kirinyaga: A Fable of Utopia* and *Lara Croft, Tomb Raider: The Amulet of Power*. His current releases include *A Gathering of Widowmakers* for Meisha Merlin, *Dragon America* for Phobos, and *Lady with an Alien*, *A Club in Montmarte*, and *The World behind the Door* for Watson-Guptill.

Beginning with *Shaggy B.E.M. Stories* in 1988, Mike has also become an anthology editor (and was nominated for a Best Editor Hugo in 1994 and 1995). His list of anthologies in print and in press totals forty-eight, and includes *Alternate Presidents*, *Alternate Kennedys*, *Sherlock Holmes in Orbit*, *By Any Other Fame*, *Dinosaur Fantastic*, and *Christmas Ghosts*, plus the recent *Stars*, coedited with superstar singer Janis Ian.

Mike has always supported the "specialty press," and he has numerous books and collections out in limited editions from such diverse publishers as Phantasia Press, Axolotl Press, Misfit Press, Pulphouse Publishing, Wildside Press, Dark Regions Press, NESFA Press, WSFA Press, Obscura Press, Farthest Star, and others. He recently served a stint as the science fiction editor for BenBella Books, and in 2006 he became the executive editor of *Jim Baen's Universe*.

Mike was never interested in writing short stories early in his career, producing only seven between 1976 and 1986. Then something clicked, and he has written and sold more than 175 stories since 1986, and now spends more time on short fiction than on novels. The writing that has brought him the most acclaim thus far in his career is the Kirinyaga series, which, with sixty-seven major and minor awards and nominations to date, is the most honored series of stories in the history of science fiction.

He also began writing short nonfiction as well. He sold a four-part series, "Forgotten Treasures," to the *Magazine of Fantasy and Science Fiction*, was a regular columnist for *Speculations* ("Ask Bwana") for twelve years, currently appears in every issue of the *SFWA Bulletin* ("The

Resnick/Malzberg Dialogues"), and wrote a biweekly column for the late, lamented GalaxyOnline.com.

Carol has always been Mike's uncredited collaborator on his science fiction, but in the past few years they have sold two movie scripts—*Santiago* and *The Widowmaker*, both based on Mike's books—and Carol *is* listed as his collaborator on those.

Readers of Mike's works are aware of his fascination with Africa, and the many uses to which he has put it in his science fiction. Mike and Carol have taken numerous safaris, visiting Kenya (four times), Tanzania, Malawi, Zimbabwe, Egypt, Botswana, and Uganda. Mike edited the Library of African Adventure series for St. Martin's Press, and is currently editing *The Resnick Library of African Adventure* and, with Carol as coeditor, *The Resnick Library of Worldwide Adventure*, for Alexander Books.

Since 1989, Mike has won five Hugo Awards (for "Kirinyaga," "The Manamouki," "Seven Views of Olduvai Gorge," "The 43 Antarean Dynasties," and "Travels with My Cats") and a Nebula Award (for "Seven Views of Olduvai Gorge"), and has been nominated for thirty Hugos, eleven Nebulas, a Clarke (British), and six Seiun-sho (Japanese). He has also won a Seiun-sho, a Prix Tour Eiffel (French), two Prix Ozones (French), ten HOMer Awards, an Alexander Award, a Golden Pagoda Award, a Hayakawa SF Award (Japanese), a Locus Award, three Ignotus Awards (Spanish), a Xatafi-Cyberdark Award (Spanish), a Futura Award (Croatia), an El Melocoton Mechanico (Spanish), two Sfinks Awards (Polish), and a Fantastyka Award (Polish), and has topped the Science Fiction Chronicle Poll six times, the Scifi Weekly Hugo Straw Poll three times, and the Asimov's Readers Poll five times. In 1993 he was awarded the Skylark Award for Lifetime Achievement in Science Fiction, and both in 2001 and in 2004 he was named Fictionwise.com's Author of the Year.

His work has been translated into French, Italian, German, Spanish, Japanese, Korean, Bulgarian, Hungarian, Hebrew, Russian, Latvian, Lithuanian, Polish, Czech, Dutch, Swedish, Romanian, Finnish, Danish, Chinese, and Croatian.

He was recently the subject of Fiona Kelleghan's massive *Mike Resnick: An Annotated Bibliography and Guide to His Work*. Adrienne Gormley is currently preparing a second edition.